FINDING A STRANGER

T C Wilson

Published by Gordian Books, an imprint of Winged Publications

Editor: Cynthia Hickey
Book Design by Winged Publications

Fiction and Literature:
Christian Romantic Suspense

ISBN: 978-1-959788-28-7

DEDICATION

To my husband Randy, my children Hunter and Brendon, and my second daughter Kensley without you, there would be no need for this page.

Contents

ACKNOWLEDGEMENTS

I offer my love and gratitude to those who pushed me beyond the realm of what I ever dreamed possible.

To my mom, from reading the neverending drafts I shoved before you to keeping me on task, your endless love carried me forward.

To my "twin," your words of wisdom and guidance helped keep me centered when I veered onto other pathways.

To my fabulous "sistas," who knew when God mixed our lives together in the pot of "life," we would become besties forever. Thanks for standing beside me.

To Leigh Anne, a heartfelt thanks. Your friendship, feedback, and encouragement helped make this happen. Without you, I'm relatively sure I would be bald!

To Cynthia Hickey, the editing team, and everyone at Winged Publications, I remain eternally grateful to you for turning my dream into a reality.

And lastly, thank you, Chick Fil A. If not for you, my family may never have survived.

CHAPTER ONE

Summer in Bridgeport, Louisiana, felt hotter than the molten ash from an angry volcano. Residents born and raised in this tropical moisture realized it could quickly spawn a devastating hurricane or render a soft, comforting slow rain. Yet, the locals conditioned to deal with the sweltering daily temperatures from birth moved effortlessly about their regular business.

Leah Reynolds found herself struggling to adjust to the barrage of heat from the moment she arrived in Bridgeport. She had the whole small-town stigma under control, being the only child of a modest family from South Carolina. She knew the experiences of growing up in a one-red-light town and could even relate to the unrelenting humidity on any given day, but Louisiana was another entity in itself. Adapting was proving to be painful.

Adjustment to the temperature was not the only thing she struggled to master. Loneliness often swallowed up her days. Her job consumed much of her time, a positive thing when trying to make a name for yourself in the business world. Men seemed to propel themselves into the limelight in the blink of an eye. On the other hand, women often needed to claw their way up the ladder of success, competing with not only their male counterparts but also time itself. Leah vowed she would traverse the path to success before her life turned to marriage and childbearing.

Her hopes of gaining a few female sisterly allies during the journey remained a high priority. Women committed to standing with women, providing a support system for each other, regardless of occupation, and offering assurance that none would fail in their mission. It had been a motto she adopted and pledged her allegiance to in college.

Graduating at the top of her class with a master's degree in Mergers and Acquisitions presented limitless opportunities for a 24-year-old wholesome "Carolina" girl. Corporations in every region of the country touted endless possibilities for triumph; however, Leah found most were empty promises. Entry-level positions, modest salaries, and extended work hours were the only guarantees, making success an arduous task for a female. Every company courted the top students, yet, she discovered that not all job descriptions offered complete transparency of their expectations, making it challenging to choose the ideal path fresh out of college.

Her first few months of employment at Watts Enterprises had Leah contemplating whether she'd made a huge mistake accepting a job at the small town's primary business. The overwhelming tug on her heart by the stagnant area's need for revitalization turned out to be more than she could resist. Heart over head ruled her first choice of employment after graduation.

Perhaps the lessons I learn on this smaller platform will render a wealth of knowledge usable in more extensive corporate settings to come,

Shaking her head, reminding herself of the commitment made to this company and its employees, propelled her onward up the sidewalk into Watts Enterprises

The yellowing walls of the dreary factory closed in on her today as she passed the mundane offices. A nagging feeling that told her the day was going to get much worse crawled up her spine and into the recesses of her mind. Her summoning to John Watts's office this early in the morning could not be good. Lord knows for what this time. Leah continued to look forward to the upcoming day that would start her two-week vacation. Unfortunately, it would require her to navigate through the week first.

It seemed she wasn't the only one experiencing a frantic morning. While passing their stereotypical cafeteria, a disgruntled woman was having a loud conversation with herself that Leah couldn't help overhearing. The woman appeared to be a modern-day version of Marilyn Monroe. In her mid-thirties, her hair was a natural blonde with sun-kissed streaks framing her face. She continued through the haphazardly placed array of tables to a coffee bar scowling along the way. Sensing her displeasure, Leah could sympathize with a "bad Monday morning mood." She, too, had one a few moments ago. Forcing herself back into happiness, Leah vowed nothing would spoil her disposition. A week from today, she had a reservation with a lounge chair, glowing warm sun, and a good book in a tropical location known only to her. The effects of moderating the upcoming merger between her company and Holcomb Industries had taken their toll. A lack of sleep, accompanied by binges of eating late into the evening, forced Leah into a lifestyle that she would be happy to leave behind after the merger.

Leah, ever the moderator and well-wisher, found it impossible to depart from the cafeteria without discovering the lady's plight. Strolling casually over to the coffee bar, she began filling a cup as a ruse to initiate conversation. The Watts Industries badge pinned to the woman's lapel further justified Leah's obligation to help cheer her.

"Good Monday morning. They come around way too rapidly, don't they?" Displaying a genuine smile, unsure whether the conversation would drift toward warmth or anger, Leah hesitated while awaiting a response.

Turning to face Leah, the woman scowled, "Yes, they

do. Every Monday, there seem to be more unrealistic expectations for managers. Accompany that with staff members who have no concept of 'don't call me on the weekend' and lousy coffee makes me miserable and angry before I ever begin. This merger is killing me." Her blonde hair was accentuated by a red face now flaming with embarrassment.

"Please, tell me you did not hear the unpleasant conversation I had with myself earlier," she huffed, blowing a wisp of hair from her eyes.

Nodding at the woman's ID badge, Leah extended her hand. "Well, Rhonda, don't feel as though you have a monopoly on the unsatisfied employee department." In appreciation of her struggles, Leah laughed and gently shook her hand. "Leah Reynolds, Mergers and Acquisitions. I'm afraid I am the one partly responsible for your merger woes. I know everyone feels bogged down with demands during the acquisition process, myself included, but hang in there. Things will change very soon."

"Can I have a little of your optimism in a cup, please, instead of this lousy coffee?" Rhonda managed a smile as the redness in her cheeks began to fade.

"The day will be what you make of it. So make it your best!" Leah repeated the words for both their benefits. "As a disclaimer, though, I must tell you this optimistic attitude stems from a vacation I have planned for next week."

Rhonda burst into laughter.

"I figured there had to be a catch." Composing herself, the attractive blonde continued, "I don't know what brought you into the cafeteria today, Ms. Reynolds, but it is a pleasure to meet you. Your joyous optimism will be welcome around me anytime. God knows I can use it. Maybe we can have lunch one day soon. I've only been here for a few months; it would be nice to have some company. My work in the Design Department keeps me pretty isolated. Just give me a call when you have free time, and oh, enjoy your vacation. I'm jealous."

"Thank you, Rhonda. I will do my best to cleanse my body and mind with two weeks of glorious beach time. It was nice to meet you. We will get together when I return tan and rested."

Rhonda exited the cafeteria with a wave acknowledging her approval. Leah topped off her cup of coffee, added a hint of cream, and reached to grab a lid. Out of the corner of her eye, she detected a man staring in her direction. Standing in the shadows of the unopened drapes holding the morning sun at bay, the man focused on Leah and her actions. Experiencing a strange sense of uneasiness, she turned, blinking to gain a better view across the room. The lack of sufficient lighting in the corner made it impossible to recognize the man or distinguish any familiar features. With the merger taking place in a few weeks, different people entered the buildings often, which never really bothered her. But his presence sent echoes of restlessness coursing through her body. This gentleman certainly seemed intent on observing her.

Why me?

Leah convinced herself she had not consumed enough coffee. Leah threw the man a smile and made her way toward the door. Fighting the urge to turn around, she continued walking but could not shake the odd vibe of being not only watched but studied. Instantly, she thought, *I do need a vacation!*

Having lost track of how much time she'd spent in the cafeteria, Leah quickened her steps and moved on to the beckoning call of the most demanding boss in the world. Rounding the corner to John Watts's office, Leah could hear the nervousness in his voice, which sounded like little more than ranting and screaming to the majority of people who encountered him.

"Where is Leah? She knows not to leave the office

when I have to make a conference call. I want all the merger paperwork on my desk pronto. Someone find her now!" John Watts slammed his fist on the desk, conveying the importance of meeting his requests promptly.

Picking up a spreadsheet from the secretary's desk, Leah smiled, walking into the office. Once there, she couldn't help but notice Mr. Watts had copies of everything he needed right in front of him. To say he was uneasy about the call was an understatement. Diplomacy was not one of John Watts's better character traits. A man of large stature, his deep booming voice tended to portray him over the phone as somewhat of an ogre with an "it's my way or the highway" mentality during their conference calls. She recognized all too well her role before the conversation ever started. Only Leah knew his bark was much worse than his bite; she just had to convince the people on the other end of the phone.

"Leah, what are you thinking, leaving the office fifteen minutes before the merger call? You know I want you here to handle things. You're the only one who can talk sense to these people and keep everyone on a level plane."

Leah's insides warmed. It was rare that Mr. Watts delivered a compliment, and to her, that statement was as close to one as she would ever get. "Everything will be fine, Mr. Watts. Things are in order; the paperwork you need is just to your left."

"Why did you put it on my left? You know I'm right-handed." Then grumbling even louder, he snatched up the papers.

Once again, John Watts assumed everyone was a mind reader. In his opinion, he was never wrong. While picking up the phone to begin a three-hour negotiation journey with Holcomb Industries, his quiet mumbles reminded Leah of his faith in her to remain the catalyst for the success of this and all other calls. John exhaled deeply, relaxing with relief.

Finally, after a long, tough telephone conversation, things somehow ended on a positive note. The merger would be complete within six weeks, offering both parties a win/win situation. Holcomb Industries would gain stock interests in Watts Enterprises while the factory earned substantial revenue to invest in much-needed equipment and the town's revitalization.

As Leah gathered her things, John Watts looked hesitantly at her, stating sheepishly. "You do realize I'm going to need you to fly to Charlotte now to fulfill all those fancy promises you made on the phone? Before your vacation, of course. It shouldn't take more than two days, and you'll be back in plenty of time to begin your break next week."

Stunned, Leah swallowed hard to control her seething fury. She locked eyes with her boss, "Mr. Watts, you are aware there is way too much that requires our attention. How do you expect me to have time to finalize things in both Charlotte and here in two days?"

In the back of her mind, she'd known something would come up; it always did.

John glanced away, nonchalantly muttering, "Aw, Leah, you have expert organizational skills. Hell, you're the Yoda of organization. I have faith in you. You fly out tomorrow; Carol has made all the arrangements. See you on Friday when you return." With that, he picked up the phone to terrorize someone else with his demanding demeanor.

Leah's intuition was correct again. Her vacation and time off requests seemed to provide an immediate breeding ground for a cesspool of problems. According to everyone at the factory, the place should close when she went away because it never ran up to its full capacity during her absence. Her fellow employees described her in one word: indispensable. The only person who can deal with Mr. Watts.

Humbled by their compliments, she believed nobody

could be that important. Besides, she had only been with the company for a short time.

Leah contemplated her future on her way home from work to pack for a trip she so terribly didn't want to take.

Maybe I won't go; perhaps I will call Mr. Watts and tell him I refuse to go on this trip,

It all sounded good in her head, but it would never happen. Needing her job, Leah was unwilling to jeopardize it by making a useless and confrontational argument. She would be on that plane tomorrow and would make the best of it.

Dragging her body up five flights of stairs to her apartment only added to her distress. Her night would consist of packing and reviewing endless mounds of paperwork for the meeting with Evan Holcomb. Thank God she managed to bring most of the correspondence home last week. The small piles lay scattered around the room, covering every inch of free space available in the small apartment. Leah had been revising the necessary documents little by little each night for weeks. Tonight would require minimal revisions and more familiarization with the pending changes for Watts Enterprises.

Inserting her key into the door lock, Leah frowned as she noticed a slip in the deadbolt. The door swung slowly inward, but not before she wriggled the key to force the bolt to slide open. She'd never experienced a problem with the lock before. Why now? The weather had been unseasonably hot; perhaps the deadbolt was no longer properly aligned due to heat-induced swelling of the wooden door. Confused, she made a mental note to have the building superintendent check it while she was in

Charlotte.

Chunking her briefcase and purse on the kitchen table, all she could manage was a smile as she watched the case slide into her breakfast plates sending them crashing to the floor. Chalk it up to having another rung snatched from her ladder of happiness. The crap she fed Rhonda this morning was biting her in the backside. Her day had officially gone from bad to worse.

As she began sweeping the endless bits of broken dishes into a dustpan, Leah glanced over to her desk and the paper-saturated room, dreading the time she must spend tonight on business. Food and wine made for a much more enjoyable evening, but she decided both must wait. Trashing the pieces of pottery and grabbing a bottle of water, Leah sluggishly walked over to the stacks of paperwork. Struggling to comprehend why this merger required so many duplicate forms, she issued herself a mental pep talk.

The work will not complete itself.

Placing her hand on the closet stack of files, Leah felt a strange sensation tingle down her back. Her sixth sense, if you could call it that, told her there was a change in the arrangement of the documents. Always the perfectionist, Leah had devised a system to ensure nothing ever got lost.

Nevertheless, the piles somehow looked shifted and shuffled from where she'd last placed them. Breathing deeply, Leah struggled to remember the exact order the papers were in the previous evening. Although she was unable to convince herself of their precise location, a nagging feeling remained, reinforcing her suspicions.

Telling herself she must be going crazy from the day's events, Leah opted for fresh air and a hot bath before returning to the mounds of work. When she separated the curtains to open the window, she caught a glimpse of a shadow in the courtyard adjacent to her apartment, moving skillfully along the fenceline. She dismissed the image as one of her neighbors out for a walk. Leah stretched for the lock while noticing their stealthy movements. They focused on the light beaming from her window. It was as though the person were looking directly into her building.

But why would someone be staring into her apartment?

Her brain racing with uneasiness forced her to jerk the flowy curtains closed. A random thought popped into her mind, w*as this the same man from the cafeteria earlier in the day?* The height was relatively the same. No, it couldn't be him, Leah decided. The hot bath was a must now, just without the open window to be on the safe side, and that glass of wine was no longer an option but a necessity. Plus, packing remained for a meeting with a man she only knew by his deep assertive voice awaited her. Evan Holcomb tended to be quite the negotiator on the phone; time would tell if he had that same power in person.

CHAPTER TWO

Leah drudged through the airport, lethargically making her way to a flight she did not want to take. She turned her focus to a man ahead of her, embarking on the same plane. Her eyes popped open, remedying her of the sleep-filled trance that had engulfed her only moments earlier. Standing in the entryway was a living, breathing Adonis. Admittedly, the best-looking male she'd seen in some time. A six-foot-tall statuesque man with piercing blue eyes that could sear into your soul, sucking out your most private thoughts.

One day, I will make time to get involved in a real relationship.

Leah laughed at the thought. While grabbing one last look at this gift of nature, she caught him staring in her direction. Snapping her head around, looking straight ahead, and acting unfazed, Leah found herself toppling headfirst over the last small step into the plane. An air-bound carryon, skirt over her head, and heel malfunction had Leah scrambling to stand when she felt a tight grip on her elbow and heard a voice that oozed southern sex appeal.

"Can I help you miss?" The words billowed through the air like musical notes.

Of course, it would be him. Why couldn't the chubby, round older man in front of her help?

Gazing up slowly, Leah found herself looking into

those sea-blue eyes. She was mesmerized by a smile so bright it could usher a ship into port on the darkest night. The handsome stranger tugged her arm ever so gently.

Mortified, red-faced, tugging on her skirt, Leah began to scramble up and face the embarrassment that an uncomfortable situation inevitably caused. “I think I’m fine,” Leah whispered.

“Well, it could have been worse if the gentleman in front of you hadn’t provided his backside for support on your way down.” His boyish grin and playful words attempting to lighten the mood only made him more attractive. “You sure you’re okay?”

“I’m fine… I appreciate your help Mr…?”

“No worries, miss, I’m Brent Scott. Have a great flight. Get the flight attendant to bring you some ice for the bruise,” he said, pointing to Leah’s knee. His soft words played musical love notes in her ears.

“I will. Thank you again.” Leah muttered, turning away, irritated with herself for acting so stupid.

Her humiliation complete, she wandered to her seat, attempting to recover from the embarrassment she’d just experienced. A bright smile, cheerful eyes, and a warm voice greeted her as she dropped exasperated into her seat. “May I be of assistance?” the cheery flight attendant asked.

“Can I please have an ice pack for my knee, a strong cup of coffee, and a new unscathed ego as soon as you are free?” Leah groaned.

Laughing, the attendant softly whispered, “I’m sorry I couldn’t get to you quicker. It was not all that bad, really; people hardly noticed.” Her bright eyes tried to reassure Leah.

“Sure, they didn’t. Good thing I was wearing underwear today,” Leah expressed, rubbing her forehead in continued disgrace. “That could have gone much worse in so many ways.” Her face still burned as thoughts of her recent mishap raced through her head.

The flight attendant smiled, obviously familiar with the humiliation involved in such a situation. “Don’t worry; flight attendants see crazy things go on all the time. These things happen to us too. We are not immune. It’s over, and by the way, my name is Amber. I’ll be right back with that ice.”

Drawing a deep breath and closing her eyes, Leah tried to recompose her emotions. After repeating the mantra, “all is well,” several times, her eyes fluttered open. It seemed deep breathing didn’t resolve her anxiety when she encountered Mr. Brent Scott sitting four rows from her. All the red ruddiness of shame crept back into her face. Quickly turning to look out the plane window, hoping he wouldn’t notice their proximity, her thoughts ran rampant.

A face like his can make a girl's day go better, well, most of the time.

Pulled back to reality by Amber's kind words, “Here’s your ice, a strong coffee, and a two-hour flight to invent that new ego you want. Good thing Mr. Nice Guy was there to help.” Amber tilted her head in Brent’s direction.

“Yes, he was nice enough to pick me up off the floor so the remaining passengers could board.” Leah bowed her head in shame. “I would have to sprawl in the middle of the entryway and have the hottest guy on the plane see me. Call me lucky! This trip is really starting with a bang.” She muttered sarcastically.

“You think he’s hot?” Amber’s eyebrows raised in question. “I think he’s average. I’ve seen much better.” Then, moving on quickly with a wink, Amber couldn’t help but stifle a laugh.

Brent Scott had one objective in life; to do his job and

do it well every day. However, today's event made his day much more enjoyable. What cosmic force had placed this woman four rows over from him, compelling his mind to linger on thoughts of her? A woman rarely captured his attention in this way. Unlike most of the women he passed daily, nothing about her screamed racy or fake. Her tall frame, long chocolate brown hair, and contrasting sapphire blue eyes reflected an all-American girl. One who wore blue jeans, and baseball caps, loved sports, and looked damn good doing it. It was those mystical eyes that he noticed immediately, saying so much with their brilliant glow without uttering a word

Smiling, he could only think, *I am so lucky she couldn't maneuver the steps of an airplane.* He intentionally did not ask her name. Getting her name would only encourage him to know more about her or offer a dinner invitation. A luxurious distraction he could not afford right now. Too many things could happen in his job. Things that require his undivided attention. So for today, satisfaction would need to be derived from gaining a glimpse of the gorgeous brunette he would love to meet again, under different circumstances and different timing.

Unfortunately, today was not that day.

After a smooth landing, Leah began to gather her things. She could not arrive at the hotel fast enough. Another day that a hot bath, a good glass of wine, and a hearty dinner would improve everything. Tomorrow's schedule held a full slate of meetings at Holcomb Industries from dawn to dusk. Who knew what issues required her attention in Charlotte? Having never spoken with anyone except Evan Holcomb on the phone, Leah was unsure what to expect. Confidence and self-assurance were the keys to her success; however, everyone knew playing coy political games ensured the happiness of all involved and was a necessary evil. Leah would need to be at her best. After all, it was in the best interest of both companies to make this merger happen quickly. Too many people, the town, and its inhabitants were counting on success.

Bending to secure her briefcase, Leah found herself dwarfed by a shadow from behind. She straightened, poised defensively for an encounter as she turned to meet the owner of the enormous silhouette. Her heart fluttered so hard; she was sure he'd notice. The shadow belonged to none other than Brent Scott.

His sex appeal oozed into her space. "You have a great afternoon, okay? And remember, to watch out for that last step."

All Leah could do was nod, smile, and choke out a weak, "thank you."

Watching him leave the plane, she sighed. How could she negotiate a massive corporate merger and not carry on an intelligent conversation with this guy? She gathered the remainder of her personal belongings, lost in thought.

Thank the Lord; I will never see him again. He probably thinks I am the dumbest person in the world. Besides, there's way too much work to handle.

A sandy beach was calling her name; she mustn't forget.

CHAPTER THREE

Arriving at the hotel and finding the lobby packed with an endless array of NASCAR fans pushed Leah further into despair. NASCAR races were the summer equivalent to college football. The sport obviously provided substantial revenue to the southern town's economy based on the hotel's vast number of people. Maneuvering her way through the crowded space toward the front desk, Leah was unable to miss the hotel guests displaying their undying loyalty and chattering loudly. The fans seemed to control every inch of the place. Huffing in frustration, she would be ready to kill Carol when she arrived back at Watts Enterprises. Leah prayed Carol had an excellent reason for choosing this hotel. Scanning her surroundings in disbelief, a familiar face came into focus; it was Amber, her flight attendant.

As Amber approached, Leah issued a small wave smiling and saying,

"Welcome to the wonderful world of NASCAR!"

Amber's dissatisfaction was written all over her face. "I despise NASCAR. It's way too loud for me, but I guess you also have the good fortune of having a reservation here." Amber spouted sarcastically.

Amber continued leaving Leah no time to answer, her face adorned with a frown, "I can't imagine why the airline would make reservations here for the layover. Every hotel in the city must be full. Unfortunately, it appears we will have to make the best of it. By the way, how's the knee? Better, I hope."

"Okay, I think. A little stiff, but I'll survive. I'm still working on that new ego," Leah snickered. "It's nothing a nice glass of white wine and a good conversation can't fix. I realize we just met, but are you up for having dinner once we get settled in our rooms? I think we both may need a break from NASCAR hell."

Stepping forward between the sporting diehards, Amber gleefully uttered, "That sounds wonderful. My layovers normally consist of a boring book and cold food; having dinner with someone will be a welcome change. Meet you in the lobby in an hour?"

"See you then." Leah began weaving her way through the crowd, happy to depart the overcrowded, loud atrium.

Leah looked forward to having dinner with someone. It wasn't the long hot bath she had dreamed of, but much better. Good conversation and tasty food surpassed eating alone again. Amber was a stunning twenty-something of average height with soft features and a small turned-up nose. Her friendly personality radiated sunshine and positivity. Her posturing and soothing voice echoed sentiments of, tell me your troubles, and I will tell you life is not nearly as awful as you think. Her upbeat attitude was a plus when it came to being a flight attendant.

Airline travel had become one of the most harrowing necessities of the day and severely tested one's patience. There was never enough room between seats, someone's child was always crying, and everyone had their reasons why they had the right to complain. Of course, it was forever someone else's fault when problems arose. Amber certainly had the looks and the calming nature to keep everyone happy. Leah had witnessed her in action during her flight. She could change someone's attitude in 0.2 seconds. Instantly the glass would become half full and the world a better place. Yes, having a friend like Amber would undoubtedly enrich your life.

A short walk from the hotel sat a small restaurant claiming to make the "best pasta on earth." As the women approached the quaint family-operated business, both smiled.

"Can you think of a better way to end a terrible day than pasta?" Leah quipped.

The vision of Amber licking her lips signaled her agreement with the idea. After locating a table and opening a bottle of Merlot, Amber sighed with relief while Leah laughed uncontrollably.

Picking up the half-empty glass, Amber rolled her eyes at Leah, "Please don't tell me you are someone who becomes tipsy on two sips of wine?"

"No, I am just rethinking what an idiot I made of myself in front of that guy today. Tripping up the last plane step, getting a bird's eye view of the man's bottom in front of me and showing my derriere wasn't in the plan when my alarm clock went off this morning."

"It was pretty funny to see that gentleman's eyes when you grabbed his right butt cheek on the way down," Amber giggled.

"I'm not even sure why I am still thinking about him. I will never see Mr. Scott again. I'm sure of it. He spoke to me twice, and I couldn't even utter more than two syllables in response. No guy of that caliber would be interested in someone who can't walk a straight line. Only in my dreams will I ever see him again," Leah sighed quietly, biting her bottom lip.

"You never know; stranger things have happened. I have an idea that man is more than what you see on the surface. Our airline does claim to help people make their dreams come true," Amber chuckled. "If you fly this line often, you may just run into both of us again. I travel from Louisiana to Charlotte quite often." Amber relaxed back into the chair.

"It would be nice to know someone in charge next time I fly, just in case I need a backup. Who knows what could happen? I can only promise it won't be boring."

They laughed until their sides ached.

Ending their delicious meal on a high note and feeling much better about the day's mishaps, the women agreed to exchange telephone numbers. Before departing the NASCAR inner sanctum for their rooms, they vowed to talk soon. Leah could not escape the feeling she had just formed a lifelong friendship.

The wake-up call came way too early for Leah's taste, especially after consuming two bottles of wine with the previous night's dinner. Clutching her head and wandering to the shower, she knew multiple cups of hot coffee were a must. Then, after strategically placing concealer in all the right places, curling a few strands of hair, and dressing in her "go-to" black suit, she was ready to see what made Holcomb Industries so successful.

Her background search of Evan Holcomb revealed he had built the business from the ground up while becoming the youngest CEO of industrialized equipment manufacturing in the southeast. At 30, he held the title of Charlotte's most eligible bachelor. He was the oldest of four children, always playing the role of a father figure his siblings never had. He, too, had an integrated interest in acquisitions and showed interest in Watts Enterprises over a year ago. However, it wasn't until just recently that Leah realized Evan Holcomb's only interest was to bring Watts Enterprises into the twentieth century. Unlike other prosperous companies whose main goal was to drain the factory's surplus and leave the town stranded without its primary employer.

Driving to Holcomb Industries, Leah recalled John Watts and Evan Holcomb's complete disdain for each other in the beginning. Old school mentality and tech-savvy ideas did not mesh during their initial negotiations; however, after Leah's tempered moderation, each side could see the benefits of the merge. Besides, Evan Holcomb stood to make a vast amount of money if Watts Enterprises succeeded. Never having met Evan Holcomb in person, she could hardly wait to see the face behind the confident-sounding voice. In less than thirty minutes, her wait will be over.

CHAPTER FOUR

As Brent Scott made his way out of the terminal, his gaze lifted to see the gorgeous woman from the plane wrestling to pull her baggage from the turnstile, utterly oblivious of the many male admirers around her. His failure to ask her name now conjured the nickname of "Miss Blue-Eyed Wonder" in his head.

What a wonder she was.

The hair, voice, eyes, smile. Everything about her had him mesmerized. Yet, the woman had barely said two words to him. Either out of lack of interest or from pure embarrassment over the entire ordeal. Reading women had always been a tricky situation for him. Past mistakes made him leery of even trying anymore, but somehow, this woman had him rethink that choice.

Clearing his head, he began the trek to the airport security office. Another flight down with no incidents; most days being an Air Marshal was a pretty dull job. Occasional squabbles over seat space or echoing music from someone's headphones were always problems, but his presence was a precaution more often than not. Since 9/11, air traffic patrol remained a necessity on the off chance something may happen. He prayed it never would. During his military career, his experience in tight situations engrained a "sixth sense" for the peculiar, making him a valuable asset and ready for the unknown if needed.

Brent's buddy Cooper was laughing intently at the

airport monitors when he entered the office. Cooper was a 20-year veteran of airport security. A gleeful round man with balding hair and a personality that was probably better suited for stand-up comedy. Cooper's stories of airport passenger mishaps were the things of Saturday Night Live monologs. There always seemed to be people texting and stumbling into fountains. Or passengers were climbing onto baggage carriers impatiently grabbing luggage. If Cooper ever chose the comedy circuit over security, Brent knew he would be a rich man.

"What's up, Coop?"

"Same ole, same ole." Cooper nodded, lifting his chin. "People never cease to amaze me; they have no idea how comical their actions can be at times. How was the flight?"

"Interesting today. Since you enjoy passenger comedy, you should have been with me in Louisiana a few hours ago. A young woman missed the last step boarding, plunging to the floor. Not before she made a panicked grab for the elderly gentlemen's buttocks in front of her. The most exciting incident in weeks." Brent grinned as he recalled the image.

"You're kidding. No injuries, I hope. Please tell me the woman was not attractive." Cooper's eyes alight with curiosity.

"Wish I could Coop, but she is the most beautiful woman I have seen in a while, and no, not serious ones."

"You did get her number, right?" Cooper knew the answer to that question before Brent ever responded.

"Nope. I helped the lady up and moved on. Pretty dumb on my part, now that I look back on it. I don't think she was interested anyway. Besides, my work doesn't allow me to get involved. Too much travel, you know that." Brent was unsure if he was trying to convince Cooper of that fact or himself.

"One day Brent, you have to let go. Don't make work

your entire life." Shaking his head in frustration, Cooper returned to scanning the security monitors.

Maybe Cooper was right. What harm could a simple dinner cause? People have to eat.

Making a promise to himself, Brent vowed that she would not slip away so easily if he ever saw "Miss Blue-Eyed Wonder" again.

After a lengthy exhale, Brent settled back against the rickety desk chair and rubbed his

forehead. He despised doing paperwork.

Being the guardian angel for dozens of people each day is not a responsibility one can take lightly. Brent liked people; most people had good hearts and caring natures. Fortune had smiled on him, delivering only one vodka-induced encounter over the past several years. Observing people was his pastime, and more often than not, he tended to be an excellent judge of character.

Airport security was a demanding and time-consuming job. It produced the usual baggage screenings, limitations for carrying on items, and random background checks. Still, he could quickly spot a wayward spouse with his mistress, a teenage runaway, or an elderly couple on their second honeymoon. It was the hard stuff, the hidden stuff, that would never show itself. His training and military experience prepared him for that lone wolf passenger. If and when one did show, he'd be ready. Ready to protect those who couldn't defend themselves and, in all probability, had no idea they were ever in real danger.

With a quick flip of the pen, Brent finished his flight report, chunked the paper into Steve's inbox with the other 50 statements, and headed toward the door.

"Cooper, keep things under control. I'll see you in the morning."

Taking one last jab at Brent with a cat-like grin, Cooper spouted, "If I see your beauty on the monitors for any reason, I'll make sure I get her number. Not for you, though, but for me. We know I am irresistible!"

"Yeah, Coop, you do that! I'm sure your animal magnetism will win her over immediately."

It was time for Brent to move on to the other items on his list, hailing a cab to the hotel and getting some rest. He knew his evening would consist of dry, bland food from the room service menu and eventually nodding off to the sounds of the television. Unfortunately, it was his nightly routine.

A sudden flash caught Brent's attention as he hailed the cab. Those keen senses went on high alert. The curbside pick-up area was about to get a lot more exciting. To the untrained eye, everything appeared normal; however, it was very much the opposite. Brent detected the soon-to-be criminal's measured calculations as the young male approached a group of elderly ladies. Eyeing the women's purses ripe for plunder atop their baggage, the teenager scanned the section for an escape route. Babbling endlessly about the day's events completely consumed the ladies' attention, leaving them unaware. The crowded sidewalk left just enough room for the youngster to make his quick grab-and-go successful. Envisioning the crime before it happened had Brent moving toward the jabbering group in slow motion. Attempting to keep his presence a surprise, he weaved across the concrete. A little voice roared in his head,

Please don't do it, kid. I'm exhausted.

Being barely an arm's length from the group did not rescue the purses from the lightning-fast snatch of their new owner.

Glancing up just in time to see Brent heading straight

for him, the teenager started his escape to the sound of screaming voices. People were scattering as the women continued to shriek.

"Stop, you'll never make it," yelled Brent. So much for trying to be the inconspicuous airline security agent.

The young thief locked eyes with Brent and began running. Jumping over bags, doing his best to reach the bandit before he lost him in the parking lot, Brent picked up the pace while the ladies continued to scream, "Someone robbed me. Do something. Call the police."

Suddenly, the doors opened from within the airport, and the coolest five-year-old kid Brent had ever seen walked out. Barreling onto the sidewalk, pulling a superhero suitcase behind him, the child stopped dead to rights in the path of the bandit. As the lean 17-year-old robber turned to gauge Brent's approach, he slammed right into a blue Batman bag, instantly falling flat onto the concrete. Purses flew in one direction while the thief lay sprawled in the other. The superhero bag carrier was calmly staring at the assailant with a look that said, "*you just kicked batman.*"

"Looks like you are the superhero today. You just stopped a bandit," Brent declared, noticing a smug look on the little hero's face.

Sporting a broad grin, the little boy turned to his mother, "Hey, Mom, did you hear that? I just stopped a bad guy. I told you I needed to bring my cape too."

In a matter of seconds, a large crowd began to gather around. Police officers picked up the assailant while another officer returned the stolen purses to their rightful owners. The elderly ladies surrounded Brent, thanking him for stopping the criminal, while planting kisses on his cheek and offering him a reward. Fending off the rush of well-meant kisses, Brent quickly informed the ladies that he was not a hero; the real hero was about three feet tall and would probably love to have the attention. Pointing the women in the new hero's direction, Brent slowly backed out of the picture, unscathed. A cold beer and a bite to eat were the next things on his agenda as he hailed a cab and headed for the hotel.

After a hot shower and several hours of television, sleep evaded Brent. His muscles ached, exhaustion tugged at his entire body. Everything told him it was time to get some rest; however, his brain would not cooperate. Instead, Brent's mind kept wandering to thoughts of his favorite passenger from today's flight. It was crazy; he'd only seen her for a couple of hours and barely interacted with her other than offering his assistance. Brent knew the tripping episode embarrassed her to the core.

Interestingly enough, he couldn't dismiss that Amber seemed to click with the woman right away. Seeing them laughing together during the flight had made Brent feel better. Amber was a unique person that had a way of making someone feel at ease. Unsure of their topic of conversation, Brent knew they had an array of issues on which to focus their attention. The day's events certainly left a smile on more than one person's face, especially the elderly gentleman who provided his backside for support. Yet, thoughts of her beautiful face plagued him as he finally drifted off to sleep.

The loud, constant ringing of his cell phone finally woke Brent from a deep sleep. Trying to shake the sleepy daze from his head, he looked down at the number and wondered why Steve would be calling him so early. His return flight would not depart until 2:00 in the afternoon.

Steve Alexander, head of security for the airlines, was a man who focused on his job 24/7. An individual who could function on two hours of sleep a day and thrived on chaos. His profession had taken him all over the world. Steve had an innate ability to make friends quickly, allowing him to establish contacts in every branch of government, armed forces, and any other corporation he encountered. Anytime you needed help, Steve knew someone, somewhere, who could provide that help. If Steve felt the need to call this early, something was amiss.

"Okay, Steve, you happy I'm up now? My return is at 2:00; why the early wake-up call?" Brent muttered.

"Heard about your action at the airport yesterday; the word on the street is you were outmaneuvered by a five-year-old. The kid is the hero of the day." Steve chuckled.

"Okay, funny. So tell me the real reason you called. I know it wasn't for this nonsense." Brent said, getting slightly irritated that his blissful slumber had been interrupted for jokes.

"No." Steve's voice took on a serious pitch. "I called to tell you to get your butt to the airport ASAP. There is an alert regarding a possible problem in Charlotte; we have a briefing in one hour, and don't consider this another prep exercise. As much as I hate to say it, this is probably real. My information comes from a very reliable source, and this one worries me. I'll see you at the meeting in one hour."

Brent needed coffee. Was his brain processing the conversation accurately? A legitimate threat made against the airlines or its passengers? These things did not happen, especially in Charlotte, of all places. That sixth sense of his jumped into overdrive again.

CHAPTER FIVE

Walking into Holcomb Industries was like walking into a time warp.

For every old dingy hallway at Watts Enterprises, Holcomb Industries boasted clean, crisp contemporary styles with the latest technology at a person's fingertips. The employees touted a fresh, edgy street style of clothing that screamed, this is not your typical corporate office. The vibe given off by their smiles quickly made Leah realize they were happy to work for Evan Holcomb. She could see where all the ideas Evan Holcomb presented during conference calls would be put to excellent use in her factory, and the possibilities on the horizon for Watts Enterprises excited her. Leah knew, however, she'd have to find a way to keep Mr. Watts from having a heart attack once the changes started.

As she walked toward the elevators, Leah was amazed at Holcomb Industries' initial impression on her. She knew the corporate building was less than a year old; even if it were ten years old, the structure would still carry the persona of a scene out of Star Wars that meets Architectural Digest. Evan Holcomb's office was on the 14th floor of the twenty-story high-rise. It was strange a CEO would not want to be in the penthouse suite of the building, especially a CEO who'd achieved substantial success in a considerably short amount of time. Most people in Evan Holcomb's position would be all about the money and fame accompanying such success. Leah would have to make a mental note to ask him why the 14th floor. Right now, she was ready to meet the infamous CEO. All those conference calls and planning sessions had undoubtedly provided the background voice prompting her imagination to run rampant.

When the elevator arrived at its destination, the doors opened slowly to reveal a spacious waiting area. Contemporary furnishings provided the backdrop for a bodyguard disguised as a receptionist. This lady's face radiated self-assurance. Leah approached the woman mustering her most confident smile,

"Hello, I am Leah Reynolds from Watts Enterprises; I have an 8:00 with Mr. Holcomb."

Okay, this is the defining moment; she will either like me or hate me,

"THE Leah Reynolds from all of the conference calls with Watts Enterprises?" asked the receptionist with an eyebrow raised.

"That's me, the one and only. Is that a good thing?" Leah waited hesitantly for a reply.

"Honey, you are a welcome sight in this office anytime. Anyone who can convince Evan Holcomb to change his mind about something, especially business, is my idol. I'm so happy to meet you. My name is Joan. "

"It's nice to meet you, Joan." Leah breathed a sigh of relief. She wanted this woman on her side.

"If you need anything while you are here, honey, let me know. When I tell someone to do something, it gets done. Must be my winning personality," Joan snickered. "Go right in. Mr. Holcomb is expecting you." With that, she turned to continue the task at hand.

Leah grabbed the doorknob and counted to ten, preparing for whatever would meet her on the other side of the door. How bad could it be? Evan Holcomb had been assertive during their calls but always seemed reasonable.

So much for preparing. Time to meet the infamous voice in person.

Leah turned the door handle and moved forward while dozens of possible scenarios raced through her mind.

Instantly the most sensual masculine smell engulfed her senses. Her eyes scanned the room for the owner of this mysterious elixir. The stately figure standing in front of the windows eyeing the Charlotte skyline captured Leah's attention. As Evan Holcomb turned to greet his guest, Leah found herself paralyzed. His chiseled jawline. Those impressive stunning looks. He was almost spellbinding; he was so attractive.

Dressed in a navy suit creating the image of quite the professional stood a man Leah had dreamed of in her college days. The guy you prayed would one day be your co-worker or boss. Evan Holcomb maintained an all-business facade with features as dark as the suit he wore. Spellbound, Leah continued to examine the man before her. His thick black hair, mysterious eyes, and "just try me" smile assaulted her entire body in all the right ways. When he spoke, she immediately knew he could hold his own with anyone in any setting.

"Ms. Reynolds, it is a pleasure to meet you. Finally, after months of telephone conversations, putting a face with the name is truly a pleasure." Leah caught a hint of satisfaction and surprise in his tone.

"Well, I might say the same about you, Mr. Holcomb. You are not at all what I expected. In a positive way, of course." Her professional inflection masqueraded as confidence.

Indeed, Holcomb was much more like a cross between her dream boss and the savior she met on the airplane.

"Your success, unrelenting eye for business, and, might I say, above-average IQ have created you quite a reputation in the industry, Mr. Holcomb. You seem to be the perfect package wrapped in an all-male persona."

Did I really make that statement? Breathe.

Leah reminded herself the situation was controllable; they always were. Even when faced with a man who'd stepped right out of the pages of a magazine.

"Ah, come now, Ms. Reynolds, after all our interaction, you know flattery will get you nowhere but thank you for the compliment. You are not at all what I expected either." He said, smiling.

"Should I ask…what did you expect?" Leah questioned cautiously, torn between wanting to know and not.

"Well, let me put this delicately; something between my secretary Joan and a young upstart who could never hold her own in person, only on the phone. Forgive me if that sounds harsh, but I hope it helps that I am again pleasantly surprised."

Walking over to the expansive mahogany desk, Evan Holcomb's every move commanded authority and power. He was a man who knew his way around business… and women, if Leah's perceptions were correct.

"On to business, we have a lot of work to do. Are you ready for this merger?" Evan asked, searching her eyes, attempting to analyze her character quickly.

"As ready as I think we can be. I know there is still a lot of work to be done, but I am excited about the changes ahead for Watts Enterprises."

"Can we do one thing first?" Evan asked, smiling.

"And what is that, Mr. Holcomb?" Was it time for him to get demanding? Leah certainly hoped not.

"Please, call me Evan. We're going to spend a lot of time together, and the Mr. Holcomb thing is going to get old."

"I can do that if you call me Leah and answer one question."

"Sounds fair. What's your question?" His eyebrows

raised in curiosity.

"I can understand why your office location is not on the main directory list in the lobby, but why are you not up in the penthouse suite? You are the CEO, and the view is much better from there. Why did you pick the 14th floor, of all things?"

Evan released a soft chuckle. "Of all the questions you could ask, you picked that one! You just reinforced why you are so successful at what you do, Leah. Your attention to detail is astounding. Of course, not many people would care or ask that question; maybe I will give you the answer one day, but for now, let's get down to business. We still have a lot of work to do."

While they talked about the details of the new equipment installation and technology updates, Leah perceived that this man had an unrivaled passion for his work. Not only were the hardcore details essential, but so were the effects these changes would have on the staff. Evan seemed especially concerned about not overwhelming the employees, training each one at their own pace. His primary goals were to make them feel comfortable and willing to take on new responsibilities for the company's greater good.

Could it be this rock-solid, successful man has a softer side?

Maybe he did have a love for people in addition to his passion for growth and progress. Most company mergers consisted of weeding out all the senior staff while replacing them with younger "tech-savvy" employees. Evan Holcomb appeared to be more concerned with providing stability to all involved than he was about rushing changes.

Leah was beginning to realize that they were similar. Both were striving to make a difference for the enrichment of the town. This whole process may not be as bad as she'd once thought. She could bear the burden of being stuck in long meetings with her new business partner.

After six very long hours of reviewing reports, they were both blurry-eyed and ready for a break. Joan had provided an array of delicious sandwiches for lunch. Leah repeatedly tried to focus, but the sight of the food prompted her brain to scream, "I'm starving" over and over. Her eyes drifted to the tray that held goodies for even the pickiest eater; rye bread, wheat bread, pumpernickel, cheese, no cheese, vegetarian. You name your pleasure, and Joan had provided the item. While those sandwiches remained untouched on a table, it was the low grumble of Leah's stomach that caused Evan to glance at his watch.

"A little hungry, are we?" He said with a curious smile.

Her face turned crimson red, "I guess you could say that. It's been a long morning."

"Well then, never let people say I forced you into starvation with my workaholic attitude. There seems to be quite a variety of sandwiches over there; let's grab something and stop that lion's roar I'm hearing. Besides, I have to leave in about an hour for an event."

"Do you have some important corporate business?" Leah asked cautiously, knowing it was none of her business where he was going.

"My younger brother is receiving an award tonight. He's a talented football player who has worked hard to reach this point. Regrettably, the business has forced me to miss too many crucial moments in my siblings' lives. I am all they have for a father figure, and I intend to continue to fill that role until they no longer need me.

Evan's sentences carried a heavy tone. "You see, my parents were killed in a whitewater rafting accident several years ago."

Leah's body tensed from the somber turn in their conversation.

"I'm so sorry about your parents. I had no idea. It's commendable of you to take on the role of parent and sibling. Your brother is lucky to have you. Do you have just one sibling?"

"Actually, I have three, one brother and two sisters. My brother is the youngest; he is 18. My sisters are 20 and 22. I guess my parents enjoyed having their children close together in age after me. They always said the smaller the age difference, the stronger the bond. Less fighting and more love." Evan joked.

"Wow. How did that work out for your family?" Leah being an only child, never had the luxury of a sister or brother for support, and right now, feelings of envy surrounded her. However, she made a vow long ago always to remain encircled by close friends who would fill the void of those unborn siblings.

Evan eased back into the oversized leather chair, crossing his ankles. "It seemed to suit the family. Timmy was the baby, so the girls mothered him when they weren't forcing him to be their live mannequin for dress-up! Both of my sisters were interested in fashion from an early age. Kate is still attending college in New York, finishing her degree, and Pam is doing an internship in the fashion district for Kimberly Vega. Have you heard of her?"

"Who hasn't? I may live in a small town in Louisiana, but I still have somewhat of a fashion sense. She is only the hottest designer to the stars. Your sister is very fortunate, in more ways than one."

Leah took a bite of her sandwich when she realized what she had just done.

Lord. This man probably thought I was flirting with him.

Leah had made a vow to always think before speaking. She often found herself brutally honest in social settings, never wishing to play the mindless games that often accompanied the "impression" phase. She continued to nibble her lunch, hoping Evan would forget what she knew he just heard.

After a few more bites, Leah gathered her things and said, "I need to get going so you won't be late for your dinner. I think we have the vast majority of the work finished. We were extremely productive today! I'll fly back to Bridgeport in the morning and start the employee training schedules."

"Sounds like an excellent place to start. I will be visiting Watts Industries next week. So if anyone experiences a learning curve or is slow to catch on, we'll have plenty of time to adapt once the equipment software is updated."

Leah groaned slightly. "Um, there is one problem. I am leaving to go on vacation next week. A much-needed vacation, I might add." Leah cautiously awaited Evan's answer. Fearful, the look on his face said it all: she quickly interjected: "I guess I might be able to postpone until we are further into the implementation."

His face brightened. "That would be wonderful. I don't want to deprive you of a vacation; however, I do not see it happening now. So, hang in there to the end, and I promise you will have the vacation of a lifetime on me. Is it a deal?" Evan awaited her reply.

"I am not sure I have a choice. The success of this project is way too important to me and the town. I think you have a deal, Mr. Holcomb."

"Hey, what did we say? It's Evan."

"Sorry… Evan, I will see you in a few days. Have a great week." Leah turned and walked out without looking back.

Evan smiled as a thought crossed his mind.

Had Ms. Leah Reynolds made a flirtatious remark to

him?

Hmmm, time would tell. Evan stared blankly at the door for several minutes after Leah left. His trips to small-town Louisiana just became a lot more interesting.

CHAPTER SIX

Brent entered the airport meeting room, noticing all the major players were in place. Airport Security, Charlotte SWAT, Homeland Defense, Steve Alexander, and Cooper. Brent sensed the tension from around the room. What would cause this kind of uproar in Charlotte? Brent had been working air traffic in the area for years and never imagined anything like this might be possible. Sure, they'd conducted their annual drills for a disaster scenario, but this threat was real.

Steve's tense facial expressions spoke volumes to the group.

"People, we have a problem. I've received an encrypted message from an anonymous source threatening to take down one of our planes. There were no references to a particular destination or flight numbers, no specific names, and no time frame. Nothing definitive, but in my opinion, we have to take this seriously." Steve's fingers kneaded the back of his neck as he continued.

"It was forwarded directly to me, which means they're not an amateur. They're aware of my position and ability to make things happen. I can only guess it has something to do with a Charlotte-based plane. Cooper, it's going to be critical that you stay on your toes and pay close attention to those monitors for suspicious activity. No more comedy hour antics. Everything becomes essential, starting today. Report anything unusual, whether you deem it credible or not."

"Brent, you will be our eye in the sky. Every flight, look at anything that might offer us a clue. This type of thing doesn't happen overnight. Whoever this is will have to fly the route taking note of personnel, hiding locations, baggage loading, etc."

I don't need to remind you, but your anonymity will be critical. No one can know who you are or what you are doing until we have more information. Everyone is a suspect."

Brent interjected. "I don't understand. Why here? Why now? Are there any critical meetings, dignitaries, or events that would provoke this type of warning?"

"No, that's what makes it all so crazy. It is not like we are the busiest airport in the U.S. We can't even claim to have the highest thoroughfare. It makes no sense to me, but we better keep our eyes and ears open. We have no idea how many people this threat might endanger. I guess that's all for now. If anyone sees or hears anything unusual, contact me right away." Brent and Cooper remained still and expressionless as Steve left the room.

"Coop, you seen anything in the past few months that would give you any indication something like this was coming?"

"No, nothing. You know me, Brent; I watch those monitors like a hawk. I admit that I like the 'comedy central' actions of passengers, but I also take my job seriously when it counts, and I have not seen a thing out of the ordinary. So, what gives?"

Brent struggled to make sense of the whole thing. "I don't know, Coop, but Steve feels this is legitimate, so keep your eyes open." If he ever needed to keep his mind on his job, now was the time.

Brent found himself hustling to board his next flight just in the nick of time. As he placed his bag in the overhead compartment, something seemed odd. His muscular body stiffened, causing his toned arms to flex against the button-down shirt sleeves. He couldn't put his finger on it yet, but something was not right with the passenger sitting ahead of him. Nothing about his appearance bellowed "out of the ordinary."

The male in his late thirties of average height sat still. Nothing made him stand out, except for the way he appeared to be watching everyone else. Even the most observant people were not this wary of others around them. Brent was glad he was a few rows behind him. From this vantage point, he had a clear view of his every move. If the man in question left his seat, Brent would know. Of course, it could be nothing, but now that he was on high alert, the slightest abnormal actions made him suspicious. As he sat down and buckled his seat belt, he heard a familiar voice.

"Excuse me, may I get by? My seat is right there." The young woman pointed.

Well, I'll be damned. What were the chances?

It had to be a million-to-one odds that she would be sitting directly across the aisle from him, much less on the same flight. Brent shook his head in disbelief.

Just as she eased into her seat, Leah gazed across the aisle. Her jaw dropped in shock. Flashing that bright, perfect smile with his arms crossed sat Brent Scott. Amber's previous comment ran through her mind, "You never know. You might bump into him again, and if you fly this airline, you may run into both of us." Her lungs felt depleted of air. A nervous gasp escaped her. Where was Amber when she needed her? Not on this flight. Leah attempted to project the calmest smile she could muster without her lips quivering. Instead, she found herself looking directly into those dreamy blue eyes.

"Well, I see you made it to your seat without incident this time. I'm glad your friend is not here. I bet his life hasn't been the same since," teased Brent.

"I'm sure he's fine," Leah fidgeted with the collar of her blouse. "Besides, I was praying I wouldn't see anyone familiar on my return." Of course, that wasn't entirely true; deep down, she hoped by some tiny miracle that Mr. Scott would be around somewhere.

"Does that include me?" Brent unbuckled his seatbelt. "If so, I'm sorry to disappoint you. However, I can see if someone will exchange seats with me if you like."

"No, no, that won't be necessary. I didn't mean that the way it sounded. I'm trying to forget I bared my all to strangers; sorry if that sounded rude. Let's start over. Hi, I'm Leah Reynolds." She reached her hand across the aisle for a friendly handshake. Stunned by the sense of warmth their touch sent into her body, Leah quickly withdrew her hand. "I never properly thanked you for helping me the other day. Thank you," she whispered.

"Very nice to meet you, Ms. Reynolds. You're most welcome. How's the knee?" He repositioned his armrest and settled into his seat.

"Much better, thanks to you and my wonderful flight attendant. Amber was a Godsend."

"Yes, she's a nice person. She has a heart of gold and the attitude to match. One look into those lovely eyes, and your troubles seem to melt away." Leah detected a particular fondness in his tone. She wondered if the two were more than just passengers on the same plane. If so, Amber was a fortunate woman.

"Are you flying straight through to Baton Rouge?" Leah asked quizzically, trying not to seem too eager to discover his plans.

"No, my stop is Atlanta. Do you live in Baton Rouge?" He kept his voice low, staring straight ahead.

"No, just a few hours away in a tiny town called

Bridgeport. Ever heard of it?" Leah waited, hoping to hear the word, 'yes.'

"Excuse me for a moment. I'll be back." Unbuckling his seatbelt again, Brent headed straight for an attractive young stewardess.

Hurt and disappointed, Leah sat staring at the couple. What in the world ever made her think a guy like Brent would have any interest in her? First, the comment Amber had made, and now the chat session with miss tall, blonde, and voluptuous. She had no right to be upset. He was polite to her, nothing more. He'd picked her up off the floor, but what else could he do? Step over her and keep going? It would be an understatement to say that Brent's rugged good looks supply him with countless female opportunities. Sitting in silence, Leah focused her attention elsewhere.

Brent was aware a select few of the flight attendants knew the current threat, and Claire was one of them. Claire, a senior attendant capable of flying a plane as well as any pilot on staff, would be his main point of contact.

He casually strolled toward the plane's tail section and the flight attendant bay. Claire smiled and made her way across the area to Brent. They clutched each other, hugging for several minutes.

"Hey, good looking! We may have a problem. The gentleman in the restroom seems to be taking quite a long time. He's been in there for at least 15 minutes, maybe more." She whispered in Brent's ear.

"Why don't we find out what the problem is?" Brent urged her forward, nudging her shoulder.

Claire moved to the door and tapped lightly.

"Excuse me, sir, are you okay in there?" No answer.

Claire pressed her ear against the door. "Sir, can you answer me? Are you okay?" They waited for a response. Claire reached for the master key from her pocket when the door parted slightly, and out walked a peculiarly pale individual. Claire stepped to the side, allowing him room to pass.

"Are you ill? Do you have motion sickness? I have something that might be able to help with that."

Clutching his stomach, the chalk-white man only nodded. "If you'll come with me, we will have you better in no time." Wandering behind Claire, the gentleman seemed uneasy. As he passed by, Brent noted anything that may help him identify the man in the future if needed.

Brent arrived back at his seat just as the "secure seatbelts" sign illuminated, ready to focus his attention on Leah as she fastened her seatbelt and glanced away.

"I'm sorry about that. What were you saying?" Brent asked, attempting to pick up where their conversation had left off.

"It's fine. You have more urgent matters to take care of right now. It wasn't important at all." Leah muttered, turning to gaze once again out the window.

Brent could tell when a woman was giving him the cold shoulder, and this one was succeeding. Was it his imagination? He thought things were going well between them. On the other hand, maybe it was wishful thinking on his part.

Arriving at the Atlanta airport, Brent grabbed his bag from the compartment and looked at Leah. "Can I carry your bag for you and escort you off the plane, madam? After all, that first step is tricky!"

While Brent awaited an answer, he became fixated on his bathroom buddy, quickly departing the plane. Brent knew there was nothing credible to charge him with, and he had not broken the law. Letting him go was the only option. He released a slow exasperated groan. Hearing Leah's soft voice brought his attention back to her.

"No thanks. I think I can manage. I have a very short layover and will be boarding again soon. Wonderful to see you again, Mr. Scott. Safe travels to your next destination." Leah quickly turned to exit the plane and move on to the next concourse.

Brent got the distinct impression she was far from interested in him. Her words carried a short, superior air. Thinking he'd misjudged her from the beginning, Brent gathered his baggage. Still, there was a gnawing awareness in his gut. He knew Leah's eyes didn't convey callousness and conceit. Instead, much like Amber's, Leah's eyes echoed the sentiment of caring about people. Feeling the day's events taking a toll on him, Brent vowed to address this topic later. Right now, he had a job to do.

Leah walked down the concourse, trying to decide if she wanted to cry or scream out loud. Crying would be ridiculous and childish. Maybe screaming would be better. At least she could carry on a conversation with Mr. Scott if you counted three to four sentences as a legitimate conversation. Much better than the two syllables she'd uttered in their first meeting. Somehow, she'd reassured herself if she saw Brent again, it would go much better. Unfortunately, it was not better; it was worse. Her rhythmic pace turned to a slow stomp in frustration.

Replaying the scenes in her mind, the vivid images of him hugging the flight attendant and abruptly ending their conversation spoke volumes. For one, it was not only rude, but it made Leah wonder. If Mr. Scott was involved with Amber, why would he be so "friendly" with the attendant? Leah made a mental note to talk with Amber about Brent

Scott not being all he portrayed.

Shrugging her shoulders to try to clear Brent Scott from her head, Leah continued on her way. Footsteps moving in all directions echoed in her ears. People were chattering as they bumped into each other, hurrying to their various flights.

Suddenly, Leah couldn't dismiss an eerie energy wrapping around her like a cocoon. Was someone following her? A quick clasp of the gold cross dangling from her neck gave her a boost of courage. She turned around only to view dozens of people going about their business. Her first thought was that, of course, people were following her. Hartsfield's one of the busiest airports in the U.S. Still, as she turned for another glance, the nagging suspicion remained.

She remembered her mother's words, "Always access your surroundings and have an exit plan should something go wrong." Since college, Leah had remained ready for the unexpected. Speeding up her pace ensured Leah boarded her plane in record time. Exhaustion and a longing to be home occupied Leah's thoughts for the journey back to Bridgeport. Rest. She needed rest. Tomorrow would be jam-packed with meetings and preparations for the software training.

.

CHAPTER SEVEN

As Leah walked into the factory early the following morning, she heard someone call her name. She turned around, still antsy after her phantom stalker experience in the airport, to see Rhonda trudging up the sidewalk.

"Good morning. How are you this Monday morning?" Rhonda said sarcastically as she slowly moved toward Leah.

Grunting, Leah muttered, "My body didn't get the memo that today is Monday. Someday I'm going to experience the pleasure of having an entire weekend to myself. Why don't we stop by the cafeteria and grab some coffee? If I can, I need to muster some motivation to get through the day."

"Okay. I'm buying." Rhonda smiled.

"Umm, Rhonda, the coffee is free. How about you buy me lunch?"

Rhonda laughed, "Look at that, your brain is working much better than you think. At least you remember that the coffee is free. Lunch works for me; it will be my treat. I'll meet you around noon."

Nodding in agreement, Leah made her way to Mr. Watts's office. Sensing Carol was trying her best not to make eye contact, Leah called her name. Carol looked up in time to catch sight of a plastic bag flying in her direction. "I brought you a little souvenir from Charlotte. I hope you like it. And, by the way, the hotel was indescribable. Let me know how you like your surprise." Leah rolled her eyes.

Carefully opening the bag, unsure of its contents, Carol let out a slight squeal of excitement. Carol Smith was a reserved middle-aged woman who found herself a widow after ten years of married bliss, with no desire to remarry. Whenever Carol spoke of remarrying, she would express the same sentiment every time, "Who wants to give up the ability to do what you want, when you want, with whomever you want." Her ordinary wardrobe, conservative hairstyle, and minimal makeup screamed small-town America. John Watts's administrative assistant and right hand for over twenty years had joined Watts Enterprises after graduating from high school. She counted herself lucky to have secured a stable job making good money with only a high school education. Carol knew everything about anything, whether it related to the factory or the town. If you needed something, all you had to do was ask Carol.

Leah loved Carol. She was like a mother when she first arrived in Bridgeport. Carol helped Leah find a place to live, ensured essential utilities and phone service contacts were made, stocked the apartment with groceries, and kept a watchful eye on her as a mother duckling would her young as they grew closer and closer. Leah suspected Carol would do anything for her and believed that feeling was mutual. Leah could not wait to listen to Carol's comments on her "surprise" gift. Hopefully, the shirt would make the kind of impact Leah intended.

When Leah walked into John Watts's office, a tantalizing display of sweet rolls and fruit covered the table. Stunned, Leah realized he never had food delivered for meetings. Was it bribery or an apology, one of which would be determined very soon? No matter the reason, she remained ever so grateful to catch a glimpse of a steaming pot of coffee.

"Leah, Leah. I'm so happy to have you back. I trust

your travel went well." Mr. Watts cheerfully stated as he pulled the chair out for her at the conference table. "Please, fix yourself something to eat and some coffee. I ordered all this just for you as a token of my appreciation."

Speechless, Leah moved toward the chair. Mr. Watts didn't plan things just for her. There was an ulterior motive to this gesture; she was certain of it. It wasn't that Mr. Watts disliked Leah. Quite the opposite. She and Carol were the only two people he showed his true feelings to, and he was as close to them as he was capable of being with anyone other than his family.

"I received a call from Evan Holcomb yesterday, Leah. He was quite complimentary of you. He informed me that the software implementation would occur next week due to your fantastic organizational skills and planning. Remarkably, if this is the case, we will be ahead of schedule for the equipment installation. The faster we upgrade the factory, the faster we'll be able to increase production." John straightened his tie proudly.

"Mr. Holcomb also informed me he will handle most of the merger and installations on-site at Watts Enterprises because of you. Carol has made arrangements for his accommodations next week." John Watts could barely contain his enthusiasm, scattering papers from one end of his desk to the other.

"When this project is complete, the factory will need to hire about 200 additional employees." Leah noted that John now projected a considerable change of opinion for a man who had fought the merge at every turn.

"Charlie Ashby from the Bridgeport News will be coming to interview everyone next week and do a feature article on the companies. This merger is big news for Bridgeport. It's not every day that the local economy gets a boost of this magnitude. We owe it all to your insight and Evan Holcomb's willingness to expand his operations further south." Gasping for a short breath, John Watts continued his barrage of excitement.

"So tell me about Evan Holcomb. Was he what you expected? After all, people do not always have a voice that matches their physical appearance. Was he difficult to work with in person? Spill it, Leah, tell me everything. I need to understand what to expect next week when Holcomb arrives."

John Watts sat down at the conference table with eyes wide like a small child at story time, awaiting her feedback.

Should she tell John that Evan Holcomb was an incredibly handsome man who appeared to have a heart of gold, loved his siblings, had an uncanny sense for business…? And by the way, did she say handsome? Leah provided the update John hoped for regarding plans to finalize employee training schedules before next week's software start-up.

"I am quite impressed he's doing what he can to make the employees comfortable with this transition. There are dozens of people here who have worked for us for over twenty years. I have no idea what it will entail to run the equipment via software modules. Evan Holcomb's concern for the ability to learn at their own pace reassures me that we made the right decision, Leah. We both recognized that the company was on its last leg. If something didn't happen soon, the factory and the town would have closed down completely. Yes, indeed, I'm looking forward to meeting Mr. Holcomb in person." John Watts was almost teary-eyed. Leah always felt he was a softie, even if he didn't show it very often.

"I agree," said Leah, not wanting to dispel any of his enthusiasm. "I think we made a critical decision at a pivotal time, but let's not think about what could have happened. Instead, let's think about what will happen along with the endless possibilities for the factory." Leah pushed away from the table. "Are we done here? I need to be heading downstairs for a meeting." Leah found herself needing a break. She was still trying to gain a hold on another Monday morning.

Mr. Watts straightened, his hand motions waving her along, "Of course, you go do your thing. Work your organizational magic in preparation for next week. I have plenty to do here. Just continue to forward me updates."

"That I can do, Mr. Watts, and with the merger progressing much faster than we anticipated, you should be happy to learn I put my vacation on hold until this project is complete, and everyone is happy." That wasn't quite as painful as she anticipated. Leah wondered if meeting Evan Holcomb played a role in her newfound willingness to cancel her vacation.

"Whew, I'm so glad to hear you say that. It keeps me from looking like the bad guy later in the week when I was going to ask you to cancel it." Mr. Watts grinned. Once again, he got his way without asking for it.

As she opened the door to leave the office, Leah found herself toe to toe with Carol. Smiling from ear to ear, Carol spun in circles displaying her new neon yellow NASCAR shirt. Leah thought bringing the shirt back as a souvenir would drive home the point that Carol made reservations at the worst hotel possible. However, after seeing her face, it abruptly dawned on Leah that Carol was a NASCAR fan.

"How did you find out I love NASCAR? You are so thoughtful to bring me a shirt. I love it!" Carol ran her fingers over her new prize.

"I'm so glad you like it; anything for you, Carol. Unfortunately, I'm late for a meeting. I'll check in with you later." Leah walked out the door, trying to clear her mind of Carol in that ridiculous shirt.

When Leah arrived at Rhonda's office, she appeared to have everyone corralled in a staff meeting. Animated hand signs and gestures gave way to a very descriptive pep talk about all the great things the upcoming merger would mean for them and the factory. Rhonda cared very deeply about her staff, even though she confessed she threatened to kill them daily. Leah was puzzled about why they'd never met each other, but she was grateful for the change.

Over lunch, the two discussed various details regarding the upcoming training. Rhonda and Leah agreed every employee would receive individualized attention. The software modules would load on Monday, and training classes would begin on Tuesday. Evan Holcomb planned to have his best software engineers on hand to conduct the classes. He also intended to offer specialized attention to those who seemed to be struggling with the changes. Leah knew the women would consider his individualized attention a necessity if they caught a glimpse of him.

"You know, he really should be commended for being so involved in this entire venture. How often do you see the CEO take such a vested interest in the everyday details? Maybe he leads a dull life, and this is his form of excitement. The nerdy type, right?" Rhonda's words reinforced her desire to learn more about Evan Holcomb; after all, he was a male.

Leah knew Rhonda was digging for more information. "I highly doubt he leads a dull life, Rhonda. He's one of the most eligible bachelors in Charlotte." It was not her place to inform Rhonda; he was also the family patriarch.

Rhonda's brows arched. "He's a bachelor, huh? Tell

me he doesn't look like one of those guys on a Hallmark card?" she questioned.

"Wish I could," teased Leah, "but that's just not the case. He's Hallmark card material."

"Well, now, I detect a case of amnesia coming on already. It will be tough to retain any of my training information. I think I'm going to be a candidate for individualized attention!" Rhonda giggled as she twirled a gold curl through her fingers.

"Yeah, you and every other female in this place. I may have to get Mr. Watts to convince Evan to stay in Charlotte and handle his duties from there." The moment the words left her mouth, Leah felt a sense of disappointment.

"Ok, back to the business at hand," Leah shuffled her notes.

Rhonda's eyes flashed with hints of a preplanned eminent assault on Evan Holcomb's senses. Trouble, no doubt, was on the horizon.

The remainder of the week flew by. Leah found her daily schedule full of preparation activities and last-minute details for the coming week, but her nights were very dull, much to her dismay. A late dinner, some television viewing, and idle random thoughts of Brent Scott filled her head. Their last meeting had ended awkwardly, yet she continued to wonder about him. Did his character indeed reflect a ladies' man only concerned about the next conquest? The shrill of a phone ringing pulled her thoughts back to her apartment.

Who could be calling this late in the evening?

"Hello?" Leah hesitantly waited for a response.

"Hey there, stranger, how in the world are you? I'm in LA. I hope I didn't wake you?" Amber's voice on the other end was a welcome distraction from her previous thoughts.

Leah quickly calculated the time difference in her head. "No, of course not. I'm in a huddle with a group of men! What's going on in LA?" She heard the gasp escape Amber's lips.

"You are doing what? Did you say you were with a group of men? We must have a bad connection." Amber's voice was barely audible.

Leah was laughing so hard that she found it difficult to speak. "I'm watching a football game, silly! I love the sport."

"Well, okay then, now I feel better. I knew I couldn't be that bad a judge of character! I do have a question for you. Today's shopping excursions carried me into Victoria's Secret, where I spotted a nice pair of cheetah undies I thought you might like for your next bear-it- all event. You interested?" Now it was Amber's turn to laugh.

"Oh, how nice, but I think I'll pass on those. I don't plan to have an issue like that again, but if I do, what I have will work just fine."

"Wait, did you say you were watching football? You like football?" Amber choked back a roar of laughter. "I know someone else who spends their time watching grown men fight over a silly ball. Isn't it anticlimactic watching old games when you already know who wins?"

"I know it sounds crazy but watching the game seems to calm me down when I can't sleep." Unfortunately, sleep seemed to evade Leah now more than ever.

"Wow, I wish I enjoyed it that much. I need to introduce you to the other fanatic I know one day. Anyway, I have another question for you."

"Sure, what is it?" Leah prayed nothing was wrong.

"How close do you live to Baton Rouge? I have a

flight arriving there on Monday and thought we could have dinner. If it's not convenient, we can do it another time. I thought I would take a chance and see if you're free."

"Bridgeport is about an hour or so from Baton Rouge. Actually, Monday would be perfect. I have to pick someone up at the airport in the afternoon anyway. Would you mind if I brought them along to dinner?" asked Leah.

"I say the more, the merrier. I'll call you when we land. See you on Monday, and Leah, I may have you a present!" Laughter filled the air as Amber hung up the phone.

Leah would kill her if she brought those things to dinner with Evan Holcomb. Leah liked Amber. They could laugh and have a good time together. Dinner would be fun.

CHAPTER EIGHT

For Brent, the past week had been a blur. Staying in Atlanta and going through photos for a possible match to his motion-sick passenger was time-consuming. To date, there had been no matches. Brent and Steve discussed the incident on the airplane in great detail, and it appeared they were both in agreement. Steve also felt the guy's actions were suspicious, but Brent had nothing to go by but an uneasy feeling. The reality was he couldn't identify him from their files.

Maybe it was just someone who was uncomfortable on an airplane and embarrassed that he was sick.

As the search to discover the individual's name who had contacted Steve continued, all available personnel checked for leads. Unfortunately, they'd been unable to find anything credible. Brent spent untold hours looking through photos, but only one image stayed on his mind, Leah Reynolds. He would never understand why he could not get this woman out of his head. Brent glanced down at the keyboard inquisitively. A wealth of information was sitting right in front of him. Why not use it?

Typing her name into the database seemed like a betrayal of sorts. Like he was somehow stalking her. She'd dismissed him the other day as a problem child. So, what could it hurt to do a little research? There were no plans to see her anytime soon. At least this way, he would know a bit more about her.

Brent pressed the keys slowly, still unsure if he'd made the right decision, as he entered her name into the computer system. Her address and place of employment popped into view. His search continued to provide interesting information. It seemed Watts Enterprises was Bridgeport's largest employer. It was just about the only employer. The national economy issues had hit Bridgeport hard, and just like dozens of other small towns, they were having a hard time rebounding. John Watts, the company's CEO, and his wife Martha were the town's most prominent cheerleaders. Consistently participating in charity events to help get the community back on its feet, they were very generous donors to the numerous assistance programs available to town residents.

The posted news article detailed how their two sons tragically passed away several years ago in a tropical storm. The two boys were swept away in the raging waters. Their bodies remained missing to this day. Since the tragedy, Mr. and Mrs. Watts had done all they could, monetarily or by volunteering their time for those in need.

A tinge of guilt for his spy tactics crawled down Brent's back as the name Leah Reynolds, Mergers/Production Analyst, filled his screen. He discovered that she graduated at the top of her class and was a hot commodity coming out of college. Every major company in the U.S. wanted her to work for them. But the question remained, why would she go to work for a floundering company like Watts Enterprises for what was more than likely a very minimal salary? Brent strained to understand, raking his hands through his dark hair in confusion. Now he was highly intrigued. He may have to make a trip to Bridgeport at some point, but for now, he was due to fly back to Charlotte tomorrow. His hunt to find out more about Leah would have to wait until another time. There were more pressing matters to focus his attention on. His head knew this was the case; however, his heart did not want to cooperate.

Brent arrived back in Charlotte wondering if Cooper might be able to locate the suspicious man from his previous flight. This guy was not a phantom; he boarded the plane just like everyone else. There had to be something on the security footage.

Hurrying toward the security office to talk with Cooper, Brent began to replay the sickly passenger's facial features in his mind. Then, just as he passed the baggage claim area, there stood his shady friend as big as life.

You have to be kidding me.

He never thought he could be this lucky again in a million years. The man focused on retrieving his bags and never saw Brent coming.

"Hello, do you remember me?" Brent moved closer. Startled, he abruptly looked up to see Brent standing beside him.

"I'm not sure. Have we met somewhere?" The man asked quizzically.

"Yes, we have, but I'm not surprised you wouldn't remember. You were not feeling very well when I saw you on a flight to Atlanta about a week ago. I had the flight attendant check on you in the restroom. Remember?" As Brent awaited an answer, he could tell the guy was rethinking the flight in question.

Suddenly, a look of recognition sparked in the man's eyes, "Oh yes, now I remember. Thank you so much for checking on me. I've never been a good flyer. It happens to me every time. I get the worst case of motion sickness a person could imagine. I can go deep-sea fishing every day, but somehow I cannot survive a short airplane ride. Unfortunately, my work requires quite a bit of flying. Just my luck, huh!"

As he chuckled, Brent couldn't decide if he was telling the truth or very good at making up an off-the-cuff story.

"My name is Brent, and yours is?" Brent cautiously eyed the man for his reply. He patiently waited for him to provide his name.

"Troy Marshall. Nice to meet you, Brent," he said calmly, extending his hand. Troy repeated, "Thank you again for your concern the other day." Retrieving his bags from the carousel, the man added, "Maybe I'll see you again sometime. As I said, I fly a lot with my job at Holcomb Industries. Have a good one." He began moving down the corridor toward the exit and never looked back.

Brent made a mental note to research Holcomb Industries and his new friend, Troy, as he continued his trek to the security office. It also couldn't hurt to have Cooper pull the security tapes for reassurance.

Opening the door to the security office, Brent heard Steve Alexander call his name. Brent looked to Cooper for help. Some nonverbal communication from Coop before he walked in blind to a situation would be helpful, but he was again talking about Cooper. So, it was not a shock when Cooper didn't even notice him walk by the monitors.

"Hey Brent, I'm glad you're back. Did you find out any more information about our mystery passenger?" Steve Alexander was unusually calm and relaxed behind his desk, considering their current situation.

"Well, funny, you should ask. I spent an entire week in Atlanta looking at composite photos one after the other and never saw his face anywhere. Then what happens while I'm walking through the airport today? There he stands!"

"What!? You're joking with me, right?" Steve's facial expression conveyed his true feelings. Bullshit!

"I know what you're thinking; it's too good to be true. I swear, there stood our guy at the baggage claim waiting on his bags. As a concerned citizen, I felt it was my duty to check on his well-being. When I asked whether he remembered me and if he was feeling better, the story he gave me seemed real. He was so dang calm. Steve, if this guy had something to hide, my gut tells me he would have been a little more secretive during our conversation. Instead, he went into detail about how he's not a very good flyer and has terrible bouts of motion sickness. He introduced himself and said he hoped to see me again. Weird, right? His name is Troy Marshall; he works at a place called Holcomb Industries. Have you ever heard of the company?"

"Yes, I have. Holcomb Industries is a successful and upcoming organization. Evan Holcomb is the CEO of the company and one of Charlotte's 'who's who' among the society set. He's single and quite intelligent, so they say. I've never seen any unflattering press against Holcomb, but I don't regularly read the society column. Do you think that there is a connection to our passenger other than the fact he works for him?" Steve twirled a pencil between his fingers in no hurry for a response. His complete confidence in Brent's abilities was on display.

"You know, I tried to figure Troy Marshall out during our conversation and couldn't get a good read on him. I intend to find out more about him and Holcomb Industries, especially their CEO. I'll have Cooper check the surveillance tapes for me again. We may get lucky and find something out of the ordinary. Unless you have anything else, I'm heading out." Brent wanted to leave. His thoughts were consuming him.

"Yeah, yeah, no problem, Brent. Go. I'm working with someone in the Washington Office to search for clues from the encrypted message we received. It's been over a week, and we're no closer to finding out who made these threats or why. We have to close this case as soon as possible, or I have a terrible feeling people are going to get hurt." Steve began sifting through the avalanche of paperwork filling his desk.

"I got you, boss. I promise I'll research Holcomb Industries tonight and fill you in tomorrow." Walking out Steve's office door, Brent prayed he did not get called back in. Brent wanted to check on Watts Enterprises and maybe review flight schedules to Bridgeport, just in case. He stopped by to see Cooper about the security footage, intentionally cutting their conversation short on his way out. Exhausted, Brent just wanted to get comfortable somewhere.

Later in the evening, after a few hours of downtime, Brent began his research. Evan Holcomb was just what Steve described. One of Charlottes' most eligible bachelors who attended numerous fundraisers and galas. Holcomb was very "hands-on" with his company. A college graduate with an eye for business from a very early age. The company started by Evan and a good friend straight out of college was a hit. They surrounded themselves with intelligent, skilled people in every specialty to ensure the company's success. Holcomb Industries employed some of the brightest minds in the tech world. It was this technologically advanced type of equipment production that proved so profitable for them. Troy Marshall played a significant role in the software advancements they had made. All of the software modules had been developed and patented by him in conjunction with Evan Holcomb. Holcomb Industries consisted of several affiliates, which were all companies and factories acquired through various mergers.

Brent noticed one common thread between all of the affiliates. Before the mergers occurred, each company or factory was on the brink of economic destruction in a small town. After the merger, the cities and businesses began to flourish within a few short years. Not only did Holcomb Industries profit from the union, but so did the entire town. Holcomb Industries was almost like a fairy godmother that would come to their rescue. Clearly, the press could not say enough positive things about the company.

Blurry-eyed, Brent couldn't stop his research. Every article he read posed a new question. Was it a sheer coincidence that all the businesses needed redemption or were in prime locations strategically placed across the U.S.? How did Evan Holcomb know that the companies needed saving? Why was Troy Marshall flying back and forth to Charlotte from each affiliate as often as it appeared? Brent made a note to map out all the affiliate locations for possible connections.

Brent succumbed to his inner thoughts and keyed the word Bridgeport into his computer, feeling a rush of selfishness. Knowing his focus should be on discovering more about their current threat, Leah's face remained in his head. He did not plan on going to Bridgeport this soon, wondering what it would accomplish, anyway. Yet, his selfish motives spurred the need to fly there as quickly as possible. Frustrated, he had to accept that Leah may not even care after their last conversation. There were questions to be answered: was she married, previously married, hurt deeply by someone, seeing someone, wasn't interested in dating at all, engrossed in her work? He had to know if there was a chance that he should pursue this woman. He determined there were way too many questions to answer without an onsite visit to the small town of Bridgeport.

The computer's bright background highlighted his latest search: Flight 238 – one way – Baton Rouge, LA – departs Charlotte, NC – 6:01 a.m.

CHAPTER NINE

Leah walked into Watts Enterprises with enormous confidence for a Monday morning. All of the employee training schedules were complete. She and Rhonda had worked hard to ensure that every employee felt empowered regarding their new training. It was imperative to her that there be sufficient buy-in to the improvements at the factory. Every person had to feel they were an integral part of the success of Watts Enterprises. She believed if everyone worked together, failure would be impossible.

Entering John Watts's office, the first thing Leah noticed was Carol. Her swollen red eyes focused intently on the items she continuously shuffled around in circles on her desk. First, the stapler, then paper clips, and then the telephone. Each one returned to its original position for no apparent reason. Mondays were generally not Carol's favorite day; however, Leah had never seen her like this. Carol was an intelligent lady and could handle any situation thrown at her. So what in the world could cause this much distress?

"Good morning, Carol. How are you this morning?" Leah asked cautiously.

"Terrible. I'm just terrible. Did Mr. Watts call you over the weekend to tell you about this gala he is planning in Charlotte?" Carol's tear-ridden eyes searched Leah's face.

"What gala?" asked Leah stunned.

"Oh Lord, you sure answered my question. I knew it. I don't understand why I must tag along anyway. I despise those types of things. I'm more of a down-home kind of girl, so why would he need me there? I can make all of the arrangements from here. Why, oh why, do I have to go?" Carol wailed.

"Carol, calm down and tell me exactly what's going on. What gala? I'm afraid I'm clueless. What are you talking about?" Leah waited for Carol to deliver her emotion-filled details.

"Well, it appears Mr. Watts and Mr. Holcomb have decided that after the press coverage is released this week, it would be a great publicity option to schedule a gala in Charlotte. It would introduce the newest members of Holcomb Industries to representatives from the other U.S. affiliates. Mr. Watts has hand-selected the individuals who need to attend the gala, and I am one of them. Why me, Leah? Most people would be ecstatic about going to this thing. I'm not!" Carol fanned her watery eyes.

"Please, don't get so upset. I can help you with the details if you want me to. It shouldn't be too difficult. I'm sure Mr. Holcomb will have people in Charlotte handling some of the planning. It'll be fine, I promise."

Carol glanced over at Leah with a sad look. "Oh no, ma'am, you cannot help me. You will be much too busy. Evan Holcomb has specifically asked Mr. Watts to keep your schedule clear, Leah. Mr. Holcomb has an inclination he will be relying heavily on you during the merger, so I hear. Besides, I'm not worried about organizing flight schedules and trivial things. I do that stuff all the time. I do not want to go, but Mr. Watts said he must have me there for nothing else but moral support. He tried to entice me by telling me that you never know who you will meet there. He forgets that I'm not in search of another husband, but that doesn't stop him from trying to be a matchmaker for me."

Leah's mind wandered while Carol vented her frustration.

Evan Holcomb specifically requested my schedule remain clear. How interesting.

She was unsure how she should perceive Carol's tidbit of information but would not linger on it now. "Carol, don't worry, we will get through this, and I'll be right by your side. It's what friends do. Right now, we have more important things to handle. Tell Mr. Watts that software training will begin at 8:00 a.m. for Phase I. Frontline employees train first, followed by all remaining departments. Cross-training will occur later in the week. Isn't it exciting, Carol?" Leah bubbled with anticipation.

Carol gave Leah a look that could make Mt. Everest freeze over again. Regrettably, the pep talk did not work on Carol. Leah's gut told her it was time to quickly move on to another topic. "Will you remind Mr. Watts that I am picking Evan Holcomb up at the airport in Baton Rouge later today? I'll be sure to call him if any problems occur."

Turning to walk out of the office, Leah looked at Carol and smiled, "Hey Carol, don't be an old fuddy-duddy. You could meet the man of your dreams in Charlotte!" Leah jumped to the right to outmaneuver a stapler flying across the room in her direction. Leah thrust her hand over her mouth, stifling her chuckles on her way out the door.

CHAPTER TEN

During the drive to Baton Rouge, Leah had difficulty forgetting what Carol said about Evan's request to keep a clear schedule. A talented group of individuals planned to assist Evan with training. Other than the necessary introductions to the staff, Leah couldn't imagine how she would help. She planned to stay in the background unless a problem occurred; however, keeping her schedule completely open was another story. Of course, she really did not want to complain. Evan was indeed eye candy, a perfect gentleman, and had proved he was easy to work with during her time in Charlotte. What girl would complain about working with the ideal man? Things, no doubt, will be interesting.

Leah merged onto the airport off-ramp in record time. She was so focused on all the menial tasks at hand during her drive that she almost forgot about Amber coming to town tonight. She was looking forward to seeing Amber, even if it was for only a few hours. Leah sensed from their first meeting that getting to know Amber might be good. Their personalities seemed to mesh instantly. Their ability to talk about anything proved her point. Leah would have to admit that she may have enjoyed their visit tonight more if it were only the girls; nevertheless, they would have a notable guest this evening. Amber's personality would ensure dinner was a pleasurable experience. Leah could count on it.

Entering the airport lobby from the parking garage, Leah discovered there was no way to overlook the handsome executive standing in the middle of the crowd. Evan Holcomb carried an aura about him. One glance, and you recognized the man had an eye for business. His tight straight frame commanded respect while in his presence. One could easily perceive if he stumbled upon misfortune, Evan Holcomb could handle himself.

A few feet behind Evan, Leah caught sight of someone pushing through the crowd attempting to catch up with him. Her first thought was that there would be another dinner guest. Not what she was expecting, but it wasn't all bad. Amber did say the more, the merrier. Leah only hoped she meant it. Smiling, Leah waved.

Nodding back with a quick wave, Evan made his way through the busy concourse toward Leah.

The sheer sight of Evan approaching her forced Leah to take a quick deep breath. This man was quite attractive from head to toe, all six foot three of him. How lucky could she be to work with him daily? The thought of Rhonda being outrageously jealous when they returned to Bridgeport made Leah laugh.

Issuing her best smile as Evan walked nearer, Leah beamed. “Hi there, how was your flight?”

“Hello. The flight was fine. Thank you for picking me up today. I could have rented a car if it was an inconvenience for you.” Evan remained all business.

“It was not a problem at all. After all, I’m sure you’re aware my schedule is clear for the remainder of the week.” Leah jested, remembering his request.

“Yes, I’m fully aware your schedule is clear. Tell me,

what type of demanding person would do something like that?"

"Hum, probably a person who knows the value of an indispensable co-worker when he sees it." They both laughed as Evan led the way toward the doors.

"Evan," called Leah. "Don't you think we should wait for the guy with you? He looked as though he fell behind you in the crowd. I wouldn't want him to think we'd left him."

Evan stared at Leah strangely. "What guy are you referring to? I flew in by myself. My team came in on an earlier flight to get set up in Bridgeport."

Evan and Leah turned around simultaneously while each checked the airport for different reasons. Leah was confident the guy had been following Evan through the airport. She thought they were together, and now there was no sign of him.

Evan scratched his head. "I don't see anyone, but I will check with Joan when we reach the hotel just to be sure."

Leah could not have mistaken the man following Evan. They were practically in step with each other. It wasn't until she turned to tell Evan that the man slowed his pace.

"Well, I must have been incorrect. The airport is awfully crowded today. Shall we grab your bags and get the car? If it's okay with you, we'll have dinner in Baton Rouge before heading back to Bridgeport."

"I don't have a problem with that. The cuisine in Baton Rouge is delicious. Ready to go?" Evan grabbed his bags from the conveyer belt and headed to the car.

Just as they settled into Leah's Audi, her phone rang. It had to be Amber, thought Leah. She would need to tell Evan about their extra dinner guest.

"Are you going to answer that?" Looking at her and the phone skeptically, Evan asked.

Leah glanced over at Evan. "I have something I need to tell you. Hopefully, it is okay. I have invited someone to dine with us if you don't mind."

He muttered, "Sure. Just tell me where we are eating. I'm starving."

"I think you will like her. I met her on my way to Charlotte the other week. Her name is Amber. She's a flight attendant who was very kind to me during the trip.

"I'm sure I will enjoy her company if she is anything like you." His eyes held a devilish glow.

Leah felt her face starting to burn uncontrollably. Mr. Evan Holcomb had just paid her a compliment, and she liked it. She could only form one coherent thought as she focused on the traffic nightmare that engulfed them.

Amber better not embarrass me tonight.

The tall, attractive brunette stood on the curb as they pulled up to Lebeaues, a local hot spot for Cajun food. "Would that be your friend Amber standing out front?" Evan nodded in Amber's direction.

"Why yes, how did you know? Have the two of you met before?" Leah questioned.

Evan expelled a deep hmm. "Unfortunately, no, we have not. All I can say is I'll be the envy of everyone in the restaurant."

Cajun fiddle music flooded the restaurant creating a happy, carefree mood. Once seated, Leah began making all the appropriate introductions when, out of the blue, Amber proclaimed, "So, did Leah tell you how we met Evan?"

It's official. I'm going to die of embarrassment; here and now

Evan stiffened, drawing his shoulders tight, before he

stated, "Only that you were on a flight together, and you were gracious and attentive. However, I've learned that making incorrect assessments can be quite problematic, especially when dealing with women. Would you care to enlighten me on the details?"

Issuing a warm, brilliant smile, Amber continued her story. "Well, shall we say, she left a mutual acquaintance quite enamored with her?" Amber couldn't help but giggle at such an open-ended statement. Not knowing where this conversation would lead, Leah changed the topic quickly.

"Amber, I'm not sure that's the case. I only know the trip allowed me to make a wonderful new friend." Leah and Amber exchanged glances and simultaneously gushed, " Awwwww," hugging each other.

"Do I need to leave, so you two can be alone?" Evan laughed.

"I'm sorry. I didn't mean to turn this into a girl's night," Amber muttered, glancing at Evan.

"Tell me, Evan, I know you are very busy with Holcomb Industries, but what do you do in your spare time to enjoy life? Being the CEO of such a large conglomerate must be stressful."

"Well, to put it honestly, managing the business is both stressful and relaxing. I enjoy challenging situations, and I'm a sore loser. Maybe that's why I've been so successful. I play to win." Evan turned directly toward Leah. "I also have three younger siblings who keep me grounded. They are self-sufficient. I still maintain a watchful eye most of the time. To sum it up, I guess you might say I'm pretty content with life in most areas."

Leah interjected quickly, trying to direct the conversation away from Evan's personal life, "Of course, Amber has one of the best jobs in the world. She's always jet-setting around the country, visiting a different location every other day. Who wouldn't love a job like that? She's not at all like us, Evan. We stay tied to our offices on most days. Even though we love our jobs, it would be nice to take a scheduled vacation now and then." Leah said, winking.

She hoped Evan caught her reference to the vacation she'd postponed at his request.

"Well, my jet-setting days are not what they seem, Leah, and they are not that glamorous. I'd love to put down roots somewhere once in a while and have someone special to come home to." Amber whispered.

Leah saw a solemn expression sweep over Amber's face. Well, that just blew her theory that Amber and Brent Scott were an item or were even dating, for that matter. If so, Amber would not make that statement. Leah suddenly felt a rush of butterflies. That alleviated Leah's need to talk to Amber about Brent's actions on the plane.

So is he seeing the blonde flight attendant?

Leah struggled to figure out why in the world she would even care. Somehow, she did, more than she would like to admit.

"Guess you and me, Amber, are in the 'work is our life' category. What about you? Is that your motto, too, Evan?" Leah awaited his answer.

Evan gazed at Leah with a mischievous smile. "I guess it is; however, recently, I feel things may be changing." The air filled with silence as the two women glanced down at their plates.

"Well, ladies, I hate to break this up, but Leah, we have a long drive back to Bridgeport. It is going to be a long week. Maybe we should get going." Evan eased his seat away from the table, rising.

As the three exited the restaurant to hail a cab for

Amber, Evan spotted a black sedan with tinted windows approaching way too fast. Leah and Amber were only a step to his side, still engrossed in their conversation, when he sensed the car heading straight for them. In a flash, Evan shoved the women out of the way of the sedan and lunged to the open sidewalk. As the vehicle rode the curb for several feet, he struggled to see the blurry outline of the individual driving. By all appearances, it was a male of average height. Speeding away, the driver never turned to glance back.

The other restaurant patrons began racing to their aid as Evan helped Leah and Amber to their feet. Stunned, both women gaped at each other, confused by their close call.

"Are you both all right?" Evan visually scanned the two for injuries.

Leah stared blankly at Amber. Amber exclaimed, "Tell me you are not wearing the same items you wore on the plane. If you are, burn them when you get home! They are bad luck! I knew I should have gone back to Victoria's Secret." Amber winked at Leah, noting their private joke, as Evan rubbed his chin, confused. The women stopped laughing when they overheard someone in the crowd say it was probably a drunk driver and they would call the police.

After ensuring Amber was alright, Evan and Leah started their drive back to Bridgeport. Evan was overtly quiet during the ride. Swallowing the fact that the incident involved a drunk driver was a little hard for him. It was almost as if the car was intentionally trying to hit them. However, he remained undecided about which one or if it was intended for all of them.

Leah studied Evan. "I'll give you a penny for your

thoughts."

Evan's question rolled off his tongue with a "tell me more" attitude. "I really should be asking you about the bad luck burn 'them' comment. Do you care to elaborate on that?"

Leah began to giggle. "No, I don't think so. It's an inside joke between girlfriends." Adding to her humor, Leah was wearing the same type of undies.

During the drive through the quiet streets of Bridgeport to Evan's hotel, the conversation remained very light as he seemed focused on other matters. However, she could tell something was bothering him by the look on his face. It was an unforgettable night. Leah only hoped that the police would find the driver of the black sedan and arrest him before his alcohol-induced driving hurt someone.

Evan eyed Leah as the car pulled to a stop in front of the hotel. "This has, without a doubt, been a busy night. Thanks again for picking me up at the airport. I will catch a ride with the rest of the team in the morning. I want to tour Watts Enterprises and meet the staff early tomorrow morning. Drive home safely, and Leah, I'm looking forward to seeing you tomorrow."

As Evan exited the car, Leah couldn't help but think there was more to his statement than just the literal meaning. Evan Holcomb was turning out to be quite a full-time job. Reading his open-ended comments was becoming more complicated than organizing the merger. They were just business associates and too much alike. Tomorrow was another day. There would be plenty of time for analysis then.

Evan was waiting for Leah in John Watts's office the following day. As Leah approached Carol's desk, all she could see was Carol pointing toward the office. Grinning like a kid, Carol waved a piece of paper over her face to cool herself off. Lord, this was going to be much worse than she anticipated. If Miss I-never-want-another-husband couldn't function around Evan, what in the world would the other female employees do when they saw him? It must be both a curse and a blessing to be so handsome. Leah only knew of one other individual with the same type of good looks, and he was not interested in her. Maybe she should make the most of her time with Evan. After all, it did appear as if Evan was more than interested in her. It wasn't a secret that women much more attractive than Leah would love to be Evan Holcomb's companion. It must be their work connection and dedication to business that made Evan feel like they were compatible. She would need to rethink this later; duty awaited her.

Ignoring Carol, she entered John's office. Aware of Leah's arrival, John Watts rapidly exclaimed, "Well, you know, Evan, this whole merger would not have happened if not for Leah. She has believed in this project from the beginning. I could never have done this without her. She is invaluable." Leah stopped, frozen in place, and stared at John.

He would never tell her those things in person, even if he did feel that way about her. But, again, it was a pride thing.

"What's going on? Did I hear someone talking about me?"

"You most certainly did. John was paying you an amazing compliment, which I find difficult to argue. I, too, feel that you're invaluable in more ways than one." Evan nodded with a sly grin.

Unsure how to respond to Evan's comment, Leah began.

"Both of you remember Charlie Ashby will be here for interviews and pictures on Thursday, right? The late-week meeting should provide ample time to write the story and schedule a release date for the Bridgeport and Charlotte papers. The article should reflect the promising employment outlook for the residents of Bridgeport. It will breathe a little life back into the town and stop some of the masses from seeking employment elsewhere. Providing the public with a projected completion date will give them a sense of something to look forward to. Of course, we will only print the information you're both comfortable using." Leah could see both men smiling.

"What? Is something funny?" questioned Leah.

"I told you that you were invaluable!" barked Mr. Watts

Leah, never comfortable with compliments, just shook her head. "Ok, enough."

Carol knocked on the door, pushing to keep the group on schedule. Tours and staff members were waiting to meet the new wizard of technology. As the three exited the office, Carol slipped up quietly behind Leah, whispering in her ear ever so softly, "My heart be still!" Carol was clasping her chest and snickering. Shaking her finger at Carol, Leah moved down the hall to deal with the other swooning women that would appear.

The following two days went off without a hitch. Leah was ecstatic. Employee training was a huge success, particularly with the females who received personal instruction from Evan. Rhonda continued to threaten Leah with bodily harm if they did not discuss Mr. Holcomb soon. Staff members were learning their new roles and responsibilities much quicker than anticipated. Things were going great for both companies; Leah could not be happier.

CHAPTER ELEVEN

Thursday's press meeting was upon them before they knew it. Leah was somewhat unfamiliar with Charlie Ashby, having never met her. Good thing she'd performed some light research beforehand. She discovered Ms. Ashby was an accomplished journalist touting numerous commendations from a young age.

Leah, Evan, and Mr. Watts were awaiting Charlie Ashby's arrival on a day clouded with uncertainties. Breaking an uncomfortable silence that hung in the room between them, Evan interjected, "So what do either of you know about Charlie Ashby, except for the fact that she is a local reporter? This press release will reach hundreds of people. Is Ms. Ashby capable of handling such a critical task?"

Leah knew the burden of providing information regarding Ms. Ashby's background rested with her, not John.

"Well, I know Ms. Ashby achieved great success after college. Before moving to Bridgeport, she lived in New York and worked side-by-side with the police department for several years. Working in a large city like New York provided her with a knowledge base that makes her more than qualified to write our story. Besides, she's all we have in Bridgeport." Leah laughed.

"Then I guess Ms. Ashby is the woman for the job," agreed Evan.

Unexpectedly, John's phone rang. Leah noticed a blank, pale expression creep onto his face as he placed the phone down on his desk.

"Mr. Watts, is everything ok?"

Unresponsive to her question, he continued to stare into space.

"Are you all right, John?" Evan pressed for an answer.

"That was a strange and alarming phone call. I'm trying to determine if it was a prank." Confused, he stared at them.

"What? What did the caller say? Is Martha ok?" Leah's concern was evident, as was Evan's.

"The man said if we did not cancel the merger, everyone involved would pay the ultimate price, and the outcome would not be pretty. Who would do that? Why would they say such things? I'm not sure how you interpret the word 'ultimate,' but I take it to mean death." John Watts sat still and erect in a state of shock.

Gaping at each other, Leah and Evan started to rethink the restaurant incident they'd passed off as a drunk driver. Leah felt that Evan's gut had told him it was no accident or drunk driver. Instead, her mind drifted back to the man she spotted in the airport following Evan. He had assured her that the technical staff members had traveled together earlier in the day. There was no other employee on the flight with Evan.

Leah retorted. "It must be a joke. One of the employees could be playing a not-so-funny prank because of the long hours everyone is putting in. People are tired. Besides, we haven't even released the details to the public yet. Who could know about the merger? Our staff agreed to sign a non-disclosure waiver until the announcement. They are well aware of what this merger means to them. What about your people, Evan? Would one of your associates be upset about the project? Maybe one of the affiliated companies is unhappy about additional factories joining Holcomb Industries?"

"Joan and the staff here with me are the only people in my organization aware of the merger. The affiliates have no idea what's happening. Do you have a disgruntled employee you fired or someone who would want to do this?" Evan waited for John to respond. Instead, he sat staring at the phone as if in a dream. Leah shook her head in disbelief.

"This has to be one of my competitors trying to intimidate you into releasing information early in hopes of possibly making a counteroffer. Unfortunately, this kind of stuff happens all the time." Evan's relaxed assurances appeared to work.

John Watts immediately turned to Evan. Leah watched relief wash over her boss.

"Yes, that has to be it. Do you think that's what is happening? You said this happens all the time? We are little fish jumping into a big pond. We've never had to deal with this type of publicity before. Now that you mention it, I can see how it might happen. Holcomb Industries is known worldwide. Yeah, that's what it is. Whew, I'm feeling much better now." A sense of calm shone in his eyes.

Walking into the trio's meeting did not provide Charlie Ashby with a sense of welcomeness as she gazed around the room. "What did I walk into? The planning of a funeral or a friendly merger that will make you all richer?" Her tense form echoed her uncertainty. She had no way of knowing how correct she could be if the caller had his way.

When no one's expression changed, Charlie's anxiety mounted. "I'm a little early. Would you prefer for me to come back in a few minutes?"

"No, no, you're fine. We were talking about how tired we all are. Keeping a secret of this magnitude can be quite a daunting task. We're ready to have the details out in the open. Count us as appreciative and excited that you're here. I'm Leah Reynolds. This is John Watts and Evan Holcomb, CEO of Holcomb Industries."

"It's a pleasure to meet all of you. There's quite a powerful group of people in this room. It is especially a pleasure to meet you, Mr. Watts. I'm very impressed by how much you do for Bridgeport's community and charity organizations. We are very fortunate to have you here." Charlie's sincerity prompted a smile from John.

While Charlie Ashby made her introductions, Leah took note of her petite body, and her round face held a constant look of curiosity. Framed by curly red hair, Charlie's features formed a Nancy Drew sort of expression. She spoke confidently, which made Leah believe she could handle any assignment. Leah felt reasonably sure the press release was in skilled hands.

"I have some ideas about the content for the release I'd like to obtain your approval on before we get started. First, let's offer a short background paragraph on both CEOs. Nothing personal, of course. Basic information about the company startups and then continue with our main focus of an estimated merger completion date, how it will benefit all parties involved, and maybe a few pictures of the two of you shaking hands. Just your basic promo stuff. Sound good?"

Both gentlemen nodded in agreement. As Charlie was about to elaborate further on her ideas, Evan interjected. "I also think Miss Reynolds should be in the photos and mentioned in the article. She's an integral part of this merger and deserves credit for her role."

"I don't have to be included. It's more important the two of you are featured and get the real credit. I just helped facilitate a few things during the process. Honestly, I'm not a fan of having my picture taken. Photographs are something I've disliked since childhood." Leah waved away any thought of inclusion.

"Well, enough said. Your modesty and the title of being integral to the merger make it a no-brainer. There will be no arguing, Leah. If these gentlemen consider your input that vital, there's no way the story will run without you."

Charlie snapped several different photos, gathered all the data she needed, and promised a rough draft to everyone by tomorrow for approval. As Leah was escorting her to the door, Charlie addressed the uneasiness of their first few minutes.

"I'm sorry if I interrupted an important meeting by arriving early. It was not my intention to add more stress to a situation." Leah noted the sincerity in Charlie's voice.

"Believe me. It was not a problem. We were glad to see you. The sooner this merger is out in the open, the better."

"I look forward to seeing the rough draft tomorrow. Thank you again for coming. Please call me if you need anything." Leah hurriedly walked away, leaving Charlie to make her own assessments of the situation.

Walking back to her car, Charlie sensed something was out of sorts with the high-powered trio she had just met. Her previous experience working with the New York police department taught her several things. First and foremost, follow your gut. Second, something else was happening, but small-town journalism had spoiled her, making her apathetic. At the moment, she did not care what that was. Third, the press release would run Sunday.

CHAPTER TWELVE

Brent awoke on Sunday and prayed the day would provide something relevant to their investigation. Unfortunately, his research on Troy Marshall led him to a dead end. Everything backed up Troy's story. He was the Director of Software and Product Development with Holcomb Industries. His position required him to fly quite a bit from one affiliate to another. There must be something he was missing. Maybe a tie-in to Troy Marshall wasn't correct, but his instincts told him some correlation existed between the airline threat and Holcomb Industries. He just needed to figure out what it was.

Irritated, Brent opened the Sunday paper. The image before him prompted a moment of astonishment. Pictured, front and center of the business section, stood Leah Reynolds wedged between John Watts and Evan Holcomb, Charlotte's most eligible bachelor. His first impression brought an unwanted idea that Leah and Holcomb were a couple. Through further investigation, Brent discovered Leah's employer, Watts Enterprises, and Holcomb Industries were forming a merger. Holcomb Industries would provide much-needed equipment and software upgrades for the floundering business in exchange for a share in the factory. Watts Enterprises would become one of ten affiliates in the Holcomb Industries conglomerate. No wonder Holcomb was so wealthy; he already owned nine of the most profitable companies in the U.S. There was no doubt in Brent's mind that number ten would soon become as successful as the others under Evan Holcomb's watchful eye.

The article overflowed with accolades regarding how valuable Leah Reynolds was in executing the entire project. However, a sense of jealousy overcame Brent's body. No wonder she didn't give him the time of day on the plane. Working so closely with Evan Holcomb every day answered his question about why she showed no interest in someone like Brent. Holcomb was worth millions and appeared to be a hot commodity among the females.

Just because they work together doesn't automatically categorize them as a couple.

Brent stared at the picture for several more minutes, unable to read anything on Leah's face that remotely indicated they were a couple. To him, her expression said, "I hate photos!" On the other hand, Evan Holcomb's stance offered quite a different story. He appeared very happy standing beside Leah, arm entwined around hers, leaning ever so close. Yes, Evan's expression said something entirely different than Leah's. Brent quickly decided he did not care for the printed image before him.

During his earlier research, he'd discovered a common thread in Holcomb Industries' acquisitions; Holcomb Industries now owned a portion of another factory located in a valuable section of the country. Sadly, all the businesses had deteriorated for years before Holcomb stepped in and provided much-needed relief.

Could it be that Evan Holcomb had a soft spot for helping small towns and failing companies?

Reports showed that most of Holcomb Industries' competitors supported a dog-eat-dog mentality, swallowing up the smaller ones for profit. It seemed Evan Holcomb always gave as much back to the businesses as he got out. Brent wondered,

Could Evan be a different kind of businessman?

This situation just provided Brent with the perfect excuse to go to Bridgeport. Circumstances would force him to remain out of sight; however, they would not prevent him from watching from afar.

Brent formulated a plan. He would arrange to run into Evan Holcomb but stay out of Leah's sight. If caught, what excuse would he give her for being there? One thing was for sure; if he came up with a reasonable explanation, a conversation with Leah Reynolds was in his future. He'd make sure of it.

He set his plan in motion and dialed Steve Alexander's number knowing the answer would be "yes" before he asked. Several rings later, a sarcastic voice answered

"I saw it first thing this morning. It took you considerably longer to call me than I thought it would."

"Steve, your magical abilities never cease to astound me. So you agree with me? A trip to Louisiana to verify a possible correlation between the companies and the airline threat you received is a good idea?"

"It's a damn good idea. It seems a little strange that one man, an awfully young man, could own nine of the most successful companies in the United States. Also, oddly enough, they are all strategically placed in prime locations across the country. Time's running out, Brent. Another threat will come soon. Anyone willing to injure or kill innocent people to make a point should be considered nothing short of barbaric. Whoever this is won't allow much more time to elapse before issuing another warning, especially if he doesn't see a momentum change in his direction. Book the next flight available and find me some answers."

Brent hung up the phone, praying that answers would come soon for the good of everyone involved.

CHAPTER THIRTEEN

Brent was on a plane headed to Baton Rouge the next morning, where a rental car would be waiting for his drive to Bridgeport. As he placed his bag in the overhead compartment, he heard a familiar voice.

"Hello, stranger!" Turning, he saw Amber's eyes gleaming with joy.

"Well, hello, bright eyes. What are you doing on this flight? I thought they assigned you to the east/west flights for a few months."

Amber beamed, "Normally I am, but for some reason, I got a call today requesting a replacement for this flight, so here I am. The question is, what are you doing here? You're usually on flights from Charlotte to Atlanta." Scratching her head, Amber questioned, "Did you receive a call too? If you did, I'm getting off this plane pronto. Something strange always happens when we fly together, and you know it. Remember the last time we were on the same plane? A beautiful woman accosted a man while she attempted to retain her dignity. The poor girl was traumatized. I did hear you made quite an impression on her, though!" Amber tossed over her shoulder, walking away. She continued down the aisle, smiling, as Brent called her name.

Brent's mind lingered on what Amber had just told him. He did make an impression, and from Amber's tone, it was a good one. Why didn't he sense that when he talked to

Leah the other week? She had walked away without a care. He could only assume the impression wasn't good based on her actions. He would be talking to Amber before their flight ended.

Brent rubbed his forehead, puzzled, trying to figure out how Amber knew so much about Leah. Their time together was rather short. Brent noticed very little interaction between them that day.

This situation is becoming more interesting by the minute.

As the seatbelt signs cleared, Brent promptly pressed his call button, beckoning Amber's return.

Oh, this is going to be fun.

He would need to use all of his charms to discover the meaning of her earlier comments. Brent detected Amber was aware Leah made an impression on him. He saw it in her eyes that day.

"Yes, sir, how may I help you?" Amber asked, smirking as she strolled up to Brent's seat.

"Okay, tell the truth. What did you mean by 'an impression'?" Brent's determination would not wain. He required answers. Answers only Amber could give.

"Why I'm not sure what you mean, sir. Leah only said you were so kind to help her in quite an embarrassing situation." Her lips were curling into a devious smile.

"Oh, that was all. I thought Leah might have said something else. Besides, how did you have so much time to discuss anything during the flight?"

"Who said we talked about all this during the flight? I most certainly never did. It might have been discussed over dinner that evening with her." Her words carried a bit of secrecy.

Brent tried to process what he'd just heard before Amber walked away giggling. He decided Amber was delighted with both his confusion and her well-kept secret.

The detective in him could not remain dormant. Brent

started adding up the facts. One, Amber and Leah went to dinner. Two, during their dinner, Leah expressed her gratitude for his help. Three, Leah had vaguely mentioned Amber was sympathetic to her dilemma and had helped tremendously. Finally, the women just met.

Why would they randomly discuss him, and why would they go to dinner?

The plane descended to the airport landing strip. As the passengers prepared for their exit, Amber tugged abruptly on Brent's arm and whispered in his ear,

"She might have said you were quite handsome. Which leads me to ask, "Why dear brother, are you on a flight so close to Bridgeport?" Brent locked eyes with Amber. It was now his turn to smile and walk away.

CHAPTER FOURTEEN

The journey to Bridgeport provided Brent time to think.

HOT!

Leah expressed to his sister that he was extremely hot. However, an important question came to mind. Did Amber tell Leah that Brent was her brother?

Company protocol strictly prohibited the disclosure of an Air Marshal and their family members' names. If a hazardous situation arose, it might be dangerous for both of them. Brent's sister's safety was essential to him. There would be no need to tell Leah he and Amber were siblings.

Hoping his "hotness" remained on Leah's mind and kept her away from Evan Holcomb, Brent turned into the small motel parking lot. The drab single-story inn beckoned memories of motels from California's sunset strip, offering a simplistic atmosphere for Brent. He eased the car into the nearest parking space when he sensed movement on his left. Troy Marshall exited the vehicle parked next to him. Swiftly turned to face the opposite direction, Brent attempted to conceal his identity.

Suddenly, Brent realized just how tiny Bridgeport must be. He never imagined his main suspect would be so close in proximity this soon.

Did Troy Marshall recognize him?

Brent trudged up to the check-in office, sporting a New Orleans Saints trucker's hat and oversized jacket. He grabbed the room key from the clerk and headed for the door. He prayed the new attire concealed his identity from bystanders

Safe in his room, he grabbed the thin newspaper from the nightstand, searching for any information about the merger. Sure enough, Charlie Ashby's press release covered the center page, including the picture with Leah, Holcomb, and Watts. In addition, the article conveyed how profitable the merger would be for both the town and its citizens. Lastly, Ashby's report referenced a town hall meeting scheduled for tomorrow night. All Bridgeport residents were encouraged to attend to learn more firsthand from the CEOs themselves.

Brent devised a plan to blend in with the locals while attending the meeting. He knew if he stayed hidden within the group, there was no way Leah would see him. The opportunity was too valuable to pass up. Being in the same room with Marshall, Holcomb, Watts, and Leah would be a gift from heaven. He could observe everyone at the same time. The plan was in motion. Now he needed to remain unseen and occupied until tomorrow night.

Leah was so busy arranging the town hall meeting that she'd scarcely seen Evan Holcomb the past few days. However, everything in her body tensed when they happened to pass in the hallway. She sensed Evan's direct eye contact said what his lips did not.

You call this clearing your schedule for me?

They both understood, all too well, the entire project's success hinged on the public's perception of how the merger would affect them and their town. Without the town's support, all the planning, technology, and new equipment wouldn't matter. Residents needed to believe in their cause to ensure its success. So, for now, she could tell he was calmly waiting his turn.

One thing lingered on Leah's mind: the threatening phone call John Watts received.

Who would do something like that? Why would they want to hurt the very people trying to make things better for everyone?

It undoubtedly was baffling. Had there been a connection between the drunk driver, the airport incident, and now this? Not to be forgotten was the strange man in the cafeteria. Leah wasn't generally a worrier, but she'd have to admit, she was a little concerned. The mysterious events started as the merger approached its final stages.

Was there someone out there willing to hurt people if the companies merged?

Consumed in thought, Leah missed seeing Evan turning the corner toward her. A quick jolt and two masculine arms encircled her waist, steadying her. She jerked her head upright to Evan's startled smile.

"Well, had I known this would be how we would meet again, I would have sacrificed my time with you much earlier in the week instead of just the past few days!"

Her face burned with embarrassment.

"I'm so sorry I didn't see you coming around the corner. I guess I was deep in thought about the meeting tomorrow night." Her face returned to its normal flawless ivory complexion.

"Well, I'm not sorry. I couldn't think of a better place to be right now." He laughed as she struggled to control herself and wiggle free.

Evan reluctantly released her and backed away. "Are the details of the meeting covered?" His professional demeanor had returned.

Breathing deep, Leah squeezed the words from her

lungs. "Everything appears to be in place. Charlie Ashby will be attending to cover the story and field questions from residents. Are you ready to answer questions about the merger? I can't imagine any negativity, but one never knows. There always seems to be someone in the group who likes to cause a little controversy."

"I'm ready for just about anything. You learn to expect the unexpected in this business. Some people target you just for being successful. It's hard for people to understand in today's society why anyone would want to help another company, especially a competitor. So, I've made it my mission to help people better themselves whenever possible. Life is too short. Something I learned quickly when my parents passed away unexpectedly."

Leah felt a tug on her heart. Evan Holcomb was indeed a remarkable man. He'd raised his siblings from a young age yet still found time to better the world for others. She stared blankly at him.

"Hello, earth to Leah. Too bad I don't have that effect on all women."

She blinked, abruptly responding to his statement. "Oh, but you do. Do you not read the publicity about you in the papers?"

"I try not to make it my business to read what other people say about me." Evan turned with a wink. "By the way, I only care what certain people think about me."

Leah clutched her head. *Boy, am I in trouble.*

CHAPTER FIFTEEN

Bridgeport's city council building offered the perfect venue for the hall meeting. The lush tree-lined parkway delivered all the small-town aura intended. One of the few areas the city managed to allocate funding to maintain was the small park, basketball courts, and the city council building. It remained the hub of the town, continuously bringing people together for picnics, small concerts, and the like on any given day.

Leah expected the residents to attend, but she never anticipated such interest from the outlying areas. The project would establish the town as a thriving, growing community once again. Its possibilities seemed to resonate with the residents as it produced a buzz of excitement in the air.

Happier than she'd been in a long time, Leah wanted to cry, but that would never do. Charlie Ashby warned her that photographs were a must, and Leah hated pictures. However, if things went well, she would be more than happy to accommodate Charlie's request.

Besides, why wouldn't things go well?

Both Mr. Watts and Evan's attendance guaranteed the success of the meeting. She was making final arrangements on the stage when Carol and Rhonda rushed her.

"Leah Reynolds, if we didn't know you better, we'd swear you are avoiding us," Rhonda said, observing Leah's blank expression. "We think you're keeping Mr. Tall, Dark, and Handsome all to yourself. That's a problem. Friends share details, and we want them." Carol eagerly nodded her head in agreement.

"Ladies, you both know how busy I am. There are no details to give you. We're simply co-workers trying to ensure the merger is a success."

Carol erupted in laughter. "Told you she would say that, Rhonda! We've seen the way he looks at you. He wants a merger, alright, but it's not a company merger; it's a people merger. I know that look."

Leah wanted to kill them for bringing the subject up. "Ok, ok. Quiet those imaginations of yours, you two; we have a town meeting to get through. Away with both of you," Leah moaned while she shoved them from the stage. Grinning from ear to ear, Carol and Rhonda pointed over Leah's left shoulder.

Evan strolled up casually behind her, mouthing in a husky whisper, "What was all that? A little friendly encouragement from your co-workers?"

Leah steadied herself. His earthy tone stirred emotions inside her. She quickly suppressed the feelings.

"You could call it that. Are you ready for this? I never expected the outlying communities to take such an interest. It appears this will be a grand success."

Evan reached for her hand and held it ever so gently, gazing into her eyes with complete sincerity and appreciation, "You do know this would not have happened without you. You're the reason all this is transpiring. John and I initially despised each other, but because you are such an excellent moderator, we began to respect each other and realized this merger was possible. I can't thank you enough for believing in this and me."

Could she and Evan ever be more than colleagues?

Leah knew she was treading on shaky ground. She and Evan were like the male/female replica of each other. Only time would tell if their relationship could travel down a different path.

"You're welcome. Now, let's go. Your audience awaits." Notes of happiness echoed throughout her words. Leah placed her arm through Evan's and escorted him to center stage.

As people filed into the building, Brent Scott observed their progression from his car. All in all, everyone appeared legitimate. Residents entered the building sporting a cheerful, optimistic attitude.

Brent spotted Troy Marshall and his colleagues entering the building several minutes later. He raised an eyebrow as his senses went on alert.

Why was Evan Holcomb not with the group?

Before he could entertain the thought, Evan Holcomb emerged from the parking lot. He arrived with his staff. No limo. No flashy bodyguards. Nothing unusual. At first glance, Evan Holcomb carried an attractive, wealthy bachelor air about him. Perhaps Holcomb was a guy that cared about people and desired to rebuild the town's economy. Yet, Brent knew all too well looks could be quite deceiving.

Training his thoughts back on the business at hand, Brent noticed Troy Marshall emerge from a side door alone. Troy scanned the parking lot, rushed to a car, snatched a bag from the trunk, and strolled back into the building. Red flags exploded like emergency flares in Brent's mind.

He had to get inside for a closer look. And it had to be now. Brent locked the car and hurried through the hall's main door. The last attendees were arriving, offering Brent perfect cover in the standing-room-only crowd. He found himself positioned between two enormous columns that provided him with an excellent view of the platform. The situation worked in his favor while delivering a visual blockade for Leah.

As Bridgeport's mayor touted his guests' accolades, Brent scanned the stage for Leah. She was seated center stage, flanked by Watts and Holcomb. Her wholesome beauty radiated like a warm stream of sunshine. Her long dark strands of hair emphasized high cheekbones. Her bright blue eyes glowed with anticipation.

The queasiness in the pit of Brent's stomach at the sight of her was a rare experience for him. A sensation he'd only felt one other time in his life. Yet, the thrill of excitement encompassed him after their first few brief conversations.

Willing himself to turn his attention back to the meeting, he scrutinized the seating arrangements. On Leah's left was John Watts. To her right sat Evan Holcomb, appearing just as dashing as the Charlotte press made him out to be in their numerous society columns. Evan's frequent shoulder pats and mannerisms toward Leah signaled that he was perfectly content to be seated so closely. Brent struggled to dismiss the tinge of jealousy that surrounded him.

John Watts stood first to address the crowd. Watts was a proud man with a broad toothy grin. His rich voice swirled around the room, reminding residents of the endless possibilities for new job openings and town growth. The Bridgeport community displayed their love for John and Martha Watts with a rousing round of applause.

Evan Holcomb approached the microphone next to multiple whistles of approval. He launched into a speech made for a moment such as this.

"Our merger will place Bridgeport in the top twenty manufacturing towns. You and your families will be able to start new lives. Watts Industries and Holcomb Enterprises will never have anything but your best interests in mind."

He mesmerized people with his confident smile and attitude. His promises for the profound changes coming soon to their sleepy little town energized the crowd.

Closing his speech, Evan paused, "There is one person in this room who also deserves your appreciation and support. She's the anchor that holds us steady in a sea of changes. This entire project was made possible by Ms. Leah Reynolds. Please help me thank her for the hard work." Evan turned to face Leah, clapping.

Stunned, Leah stood and waved with an appreciation for the town's support, obviously uncomfortable in the limelight. Then, as Leah skimmed the crowd for familiar faces, she locked eyes with Brent Scott.

She saw Brent quickly duck back behind the columns into the crowd. Leah searched the room face by face when she recognized another face. It was the same man who followed Evan at the airport. His cold, empty eyes peered into her soul. Leah sank to her knees and looked at Evan for support.

Noting Leah's distress, Evan followed her eyes into the crowd, surveying the group.

Just as he stood to reach for Leah, a loud explosion rocked the rear of the building. Leah watched as Evan struggled to regain his senses. He jumped from the stage, appearing to be in pursuit of a man who disappeared out the side door.

"John, take care of Leah," he yelled as he bolted.

In shock, Leah fell to the ground as people screamed and rushed to the exits. Suddenly, strong arms scooped her up and whisked her into a side room clear of the traffic. Her body was trembling uncontrollably.

"Are you hurt? Answer me, are you hurt?" Brent kept repeating himself.

Leah shook her head, her eyes wide with fear. Finally, she choked out two words.

"What happened?"

Brent toiled with an answer, "Well, once again, I'm helping you in an unpleasant situation. We really have to stop meeting like this." His caring smile eased her confusion for a moment or two.

"Um, thank you. And yes, you're right, but what are you doing in Bridgeport? Do you have family close by?" Leah awaited his answer when out of nowhere, Evan appeared. Concern etched on his face. He grabbed her out of Brent's grasp and gave her a hug that would make anyone question his intentions.

"Leah, are you injured?"

"I'm fine. You can let go now." Leah began to straighten her clothing and smooth her hair.

Mortified once again, she strained to figure out how the two men she could not get out of her thoughts were standing in the same room next to her during such a dire situation. She proceeded with caution.

"Evan, this is an acquaintance of mine, Brent Scott. Brent, this is Evan Holcomb." Leah ran her hand over her forehead, still in disbelief.

Lord, wait until I talk to Amber.

Sure, what the other was thinking without vocalizing it, both men eyed each other and shook hands.

"I'm sorry we couldn't meet under better circumstances," Evan's firm grip relaxed as he released Brent's hand, trying to establish a territorial boundary.

"Likewise," Brent looked at Leah, sensing her uneasiness.

"I have a little experience with explosives, and this was a warning," Brent advised. "This incident was intended to scare the hell out of everyone. If the perpetrator wanted injuries, the blast would have occurred center stage, not in the back."

Leah glanced hesitantly at Evan. She knew the strained expression on their faces gave way to the fact they recognized a great deal more than they were saying.

"Do you have any idea why someone would want to do this, Mr. Holcomb? The crowd appeared to be highly in favor of the merger. Who would stage this type of stunt here, and why now?" Brent's relentless stare commanded an answer.

"I have no clue. Competitors do crazy things to discourage mergers; however, I've never seen any of them go to this extreme. I did catch a glimpse of a strange fellow. He stood a head taller than most of the crowd. I'd say around six feet or more. He wore jet-black clothing from head to toe and a wide-brim baseball cap. No one could withstand the oppressive heat in Bridgeport for long in that outfit. It struck me as odd that he casually headed out of the center at almost the same time the explosion occurred. I chased after him, but when I reached the outside of the building, the chaos made it impossible to spot him again. Nevertheless, I'm certain he was involved."

"I saw him too, Evan," Leah whispered, still shaken to her core.

"We locked eyes for a split second. Everything in me says the guy wanted to ensure I realized he was in attendance tonight.

He was peering at me with those black eyes of his, implying trouble by their cold callousness. I've seen him before at the airport. It was the man I thought you were traveling with from the airport. Are you sure he's not affiliated with Holcomb Industries?" Leah's wide eyes begged for assurance.

Leah was familiar with almost everyone in Bridgeport; this guy was not a resident. She supposed he could live in one of the outlying areas, but that was improbable. If so, he wouldn't have been following Evan in the airport.

So that makes two people who are not Bridgeport residents in attendance.

Brent Scott needed to explain why he was there, and Leah couldn't wait to hear the answer. Should she be excited that he may have tracked her down?

No, that was kind of creepy. What if Brent was some crazy stalker?

Leah knew there was no way. Brent Scott remained way too ruggedly handsome to be a stalker. He probably had a bevy of female admirers; there would be no need for him to stalk someone, especially her. However, confusing questions rolled through her mind a mile a minute. One thing was for sure; she would need to address her shyness and insecurity toward Brent. They were going to have a legitimate conversation. Soon.

"Was there an issue at the airport with someone?" Brent's ears perked up when he heard the word airport.

"There was no issue. Leah was a little confused regarding some of my staff. It was simply a misunderstanding." Evan's authoritative voice held unspoken meanings.

She nodded in agreement and instantly understood his implication: we will discuss this later. Unfortunately, Brent Scott seemed capable of reading between the lines. She would need to be careful.

"Leah, have you checked on John? Where is he? Is he ok?" Evan's concern for John touched Leah.

"Oh, Lord, no, I haven't. I pray John and Martha weren't hurt. I'll be right back. Brent, please don't leave; I want to talk with you before you go."

Leah began to walk away when she looked back at Brent,

"You are waiting, right?" Her eyes questioned his presence in Bridgeport.

"Of course, I'll wait. See you in a few minutes." Brent smiled at Leah as she hurried to check on the Wattses.

Acutely aware of Brent's soft tone, Evan muttered,

"Thank you for taking care of Leah until I could get back over to her."

"Not a problem. I'm glad I was here. You took a chance racing after that guy." Brent's tone carried an air of suspicion. "Now that Leah's busy elsewhere, let's talk frankly. What do you know about our mystery man or the explosion? Is there something you're not saying that might help solve this crime?" Brent asked.

"I can say that I've never had anyone, competitor or otherwise, go to this extreme to make a statement. We really cannot be sure about the identity of the specified target or targets. All we know for certain is that someone wishes to make a point. The hidden meaning of that point is yet to be determined. I guess that's about all I can tell you, Mr. Scott." His words stressed the idea Leah's welfare was extremely important to him.

Considering Evan's statements, Brent began, "I guess I'm just a little worried for all involved. Until the local authorities find out more about why this happened, I'd like to ensure Leah is not in harm's way."

Aware Leah headed toward them, Brent finished. "It was very nice to meet you, Mr. Holcomb. Maybe we will see each other again soon."

With his jaw visibly clinched, Evan replied, "Nice meeting you also, Mr. Scott. I look *FORWARD* to seeing you again.".

Leah's words carried a cheerful tone of thankfulness. "John and Martha are fine. John would like a moment with you, Evan, before he and Martha leave. Also, Charlie Ashby wants to meet with us tomorrow morning. The reporter in her will not let this go, small-town crime or not." Leah shifted her focus to Brent.

"Brent, would you mind giving me a ride home? We need to catch up a little since I haven't seen you in a while." Her face flushed with a pink glow.

"I'd be happy to give you a ride, Ms. Reynolds. I will

see you out front in five minutes." Brent could not control his grin on the way to retrieve the car.

Leah moved to Evan's side. "Things seem to be under control here; I'm going to head out. I am so happy that you are all right. I'll see you first thing in the morning. Try to get some rest." She touched his arm lightly.

"Leah, don't be out late. We have a lot to discuss. Charlie Ashby will have a barrage of questions for us tomorrow. Are you sure you're going to be safe? I couldn't bear it if anything happened to you." His concern reverberated through her body. She was well aware he meant what he said and that scared her.

"I will be just fine. It seems Brent has assisted me twice now. He's a great protector. Besides, I think the worst is over." She tossed him a reassuring smile and headed toward the exit.

Leah switched her attention to the next obstacle.

Amber will never believe me, not in a million years.

Her love life, barren for so long, now had possibilities, and that made her happy. *Explosion or not, life is good.*

CHAPTER SIXTEEN

Leah walked out of the town hall to a frenzy of fire trucks and police cars surrounding the area. Response teams and medical personnel swarmed the scene, ensuring everyone's safety. Stunned, Leah couldn't move a muscle. As the chaos swirled around her, she knew this hadn't been a coincidence. All the mysterious circumstances intertwined together too tightly. The first tingle of alarm resonated in Leah's gut.

Rhonda and Carol!

The police had assured her there were no injuries, but she wanted to check on her friends just the same. She desperately needed to talk with Evan and John about so many things. But it would have to wait until the morning.

Dismissing the evening's earlier events, Leah forced her mind to silence any anxiety that being around Brent stirred up. She no longer had the luxury of giving in to her nerves and all the stammering and silliness they brought on. Too many questions required answers. Bolstered by her resolve, Leah felt a sudden surge of empowerment.

Until she noticed Brent was waiting in the car.

Leah opened the door, sat down, and fastened her seat belt before looking at Brent. The extra few seconds allowed her to take a couple of deep breaths.

"Thank you for agreeing to give me a ride home. I'm not sure why you're in Bridgeport, but I'm delighted you're here. Once again, you have become my savior. Are you like some Good Samaritan who travels from place to place assisting damsels in distress?" Leah laughed at the truth in her statement.

"I'm not sure about the Good Samaritan part, but I do travel a lot. You, however, would be my favorite damsel if that were indeed my job. It seems you get into some rather precarious situations." He chuckled.

"So, tell me, what are you doing in Bridgeport and at the town hall meeting of all places? You said you travel a great deal, but traveling to Bridgeport? That's pretty far off the beaten path."

"Well, my job entails traveling all over the country, occasionally requiring visits to small towns. I was passing through and saw the article in the paper about the meeting and your photo. I was interested in the details, so I decided to attend the meeting and hope for a chance to say hello. I wasn't sure that you would remember me. Our last encounter was quite short and, let's say, strained. You dismissed me before we could talk more." Brent said, smiling.

"I never meant for it to appear as if I dismissed you. You seemed a little busy at the time, and I didn't want to take you away from your other interests."

Uh oh. Was that too bold?

Leah recognized the statement perhaps showed a streak of possible jealousy toward Brent's interaction with the flight attendant.

"No. Frankly, my interest walked off the plane without looking back. I was hoping to take you to dinner before your next flight. However, you gave me the impression you wanted no part of any additional conversation. I was deeply hurt." A wicked smile crossed his lips as he placed a hand over his wounded heart.

Leah rolled her eyes. "Really! I am sorry. I guess I misunderstood. Dinner would have been a welcome change from sitting in the airport for a two-hour layover. So if you're staying in Bridgeport for a few more days, how would you like to have dinner while you're here? It's the least I can do to thank you for rescuing me not once but twice."

Leah had never been this forward in her life. She squelched the nerves. Brent's visit to her tiny town placed him front and center, and she'd make the most of it.

"It would be my pleasure to have dinner with you, Ms. Reynolds. Name the time and the place, and I'll be there. I can delay my departure for a day or two. For now, you probably should tell me your address before we find ourselves driving in circles for the rest of the night." He snickered.

A strange feeling of despair enveloped Leah as Brent pulled into the driveway. She didn't want to leave Brent so quickly. The car ride home wasn't long enough for her, even though she knew they would have dinner tomorrow night.

What in the world has come over me?

"Brent, I have a question. If you're not busy tomorrow afternoon, why don't you come by the factory? I could give you a quick tour, explain some of the merger changes, and we could leave for dinner from there." Stammering, she continued, "Only if you're free, of course."

"Spending the afternoon with you or sitting in a hotel until dinner; my vote will always be for you. Besides, I find the tour idea intriguing. I'd love to see the inner workings of Watts Enterprises." His eyes twinkled with anticipation.

"How's two o'clock? I'll have a guest pass waiting for you at the front desk."

"Two o'clock it is. And Leah, you don't need to thank me for helping you. I count myself lucky. It isn't every day I get to be the hero for a beautiful woman." Pausing to catch one last glimpse of her, Brent said softly. "Goodnight, Leah. I'll see you tomorrow."

"Tomorrow."

The word rolled off her tongue, forming an instant elixir of happiness.

Giddy with excitement, Leah closed the car door and floated to her front steps. Dinner and a tour invitation were bold spur-of-the-moment decisions. She was pleased with herself for articulating her appreciation for Brent's aid and being assertive enough to invite him to dinner.

She fought to understand how she could have been so irresponsible in inviting Brent to tour, knowing Evan would be at the factory.

Everything's fine. Evan and I are just friends.

Leah hurried inside, pulling Amber's contact information from her phone as she walked. Amber was a new addition to Leah's life, but somehow, trust wasn't an issue. Besides, Amber was the only one she'd talked to about Brent Scott.

Leah found herself reassuring Amber.

"Yes, Amber, I promise. I'm okay. We still don't have a clue as to the cause of the explosion; however, the police are confident they will have some answers soon. Now, on to my real reason for calling. Guess who was at the town hall meeting?"

"Who?" she asked.

"Brent Scott." Dead silence engulfed their conversation.

"Have I rendered you speechless? I couldn't believe it either. He rescued me from danger this time instead of embarrassment."

"What do you mean Brent Scott was at the meeting? He wasn't injured, was he?" Amber's previous sleepy slur of words turned to curious concern.

"No. No injuries, which is a miracle. Not only was Brent my hero, but he was also my chauffeur. He offered me a ride home, during which we had some lovely conversations. He's visiting the factory tomorrow, and later we're having dinner. Can you believe it? I still can't figure out why he's in Bridgeport, but I'm ecstatic."

"Well, well, Brent's in Bridgeport. At least you both are safe. I'm happy about that outcome. You must call me after your dinner. I want to hear all about it, Leah."

Leah promised to provide details and ended their call, but something about their chat confused her. Amber's immediate concern for Brent's welfare puzzled her. She couldn't put her finger on the connection between the two. Nevertheless, her fears for Brent spoke volumes.

Maybe Brent and Amber are a couple, and he doesn't want me to know.

Eager to place the evening's horrific events behind her, Leah headed straight for a warm shower and her comfy pajamas. Everything else could wait until the morning.

Leah woke from a dream that replayed the explosion in vivid detail. Her meeting with Charlie Ashby was in just a few hours. Ms. Ashby seemed very cordial, yet, Leah was aware she didn't win all those awards for leniency in interviews. Yes, Charlie Ashby got answers to her questions, one way or another. It was one more ordeal to handle in a day that could possibly be full of them.

CHAPTER SEVENTEEN

The following morning, John Watts' office buzzed with activity. Leah bolted in and grabbed Carol in a bear hug. Carol began ranting about how she and Rhonda were safely away from the explosion when it occurred. Carol's watchful gaze fell on Leah.

"Someone has been very unsettled since he arrived this morning. He questioned where you were the minute he walked in." Carol said, arching one brow at her friend.

"I called Mr. Watts first thing this morning and informed him what time I would be here. I don't understand why he's so worried." Leah sighed.

"I'm not talking about Mr. Watts. I'm referring to Evan Holcomb. He's asked me twice when you were going to arrive. That's when he's not pacing the floor. Don't tell me that man doesn't want more than a business relationship with you, Leah Reynolds." Carol nodded her head toward the door ushering Leah into John's office.

She had one foot through the threshold when Evan marched up, grasped her by the waist, and parted her lips with a kiss that would arouse Sleeping Beauty. Overwhelmed by his heavenly cologne and proximity, Leah blinked, stunned.

I must be dreaming.

When Evan finally released her, Leah's first instinct was to assess her surroundings. Undoubtedly, being in John Watts' office like this could create a scandalous situation for them both.

Thank goodness John has not arrived yet.

"Well, that was quite a Good Morning!" she proclaimed.

Evan chuckled so hard he could barely speak. "I've wanted to do that from the first moment I saw you standing in my office in Charlotte. After last night, thinking about the "what ifs," now seemed like the perfect time."

In truth, Leah wondered if Evan was jealous of Brent. He didn't care for Brent's offer to drive her home. Yet, after that kiss, he left little doubt that he desired to be more than a business partner.

"Evan, things could have turned out much differently at the hall meeting, but don't allow what could have happened to make you crazy. We're all happy with the way things turned out."

"I can honestly say that was my first welcome-to-the-office kiss." Leah made her way to a chair. If she didn't sit, she risked falling.

"I may have to ensure it won't be your last." The sensuality of his tone caused Leah's heart to race.

"I won't push the issue now, but at least you're aware of my desire to explore more than a business relationship," Evan added, returning to his professional tone.

Leah had never been so happy to see someone enter a room as John Watts at that moment. She wasn't sure how to respond to Evan's comments, especially with Brent in town. Evan Holcomb was dashingly attractive. They were comfortable around each other and maintained the same work ethic. She'd felt something like this was brewing, but she'd shoved it to the back of her mind.

Brent would arrive around two, and things would get interesting when he did. Leah's heavy sigh of concern caught John Watt's attention.

"Leah, do you think the events from last night correlate with yesterday's phone call? Is someone out there willing to cause people physical harm over this merger?"

John's face, pale white, strained with despair as he questioned Evan.

"Evan, I don't know if we can take the chance of calling off the merger. How would we ever explain its collapse between the press releases, the town hall meeting, and the gala scheduled for next week? Still, I can't risk innocent lives for the sake of a business venture, no matter how productive it may be. So, what are we going to do?" He pleaded for an answer.

"John, we cannot panic. We're still not sure what the perpetrator's motive was last night. Was it meant to be a warning of some kind? Unfortunately, we can't confirm that the phone call is related to the explosion." Evan's words contradicted his heart.

"Mr. Watts, we can't jump to conclusions. Let's see what the local authorities find out about the incident. Surely, they will have a suspect or motive soon." Leah's attempt to reassure the men seemed futile. Then, without warning or introduction, Charlie Ashby, early again - caught them off guard.

"The cops have no idea why this happened, much less who might be responsible." Charlie spoke without preamble, diving into her interview. "The police found no clues on the scene, no fingerprints, no bomb fragments, nothing. Whoever was responsible for this knew what they were doing. What I'm trying to figure out is why. I think the three of you know more than you are saying. Am I correct?"

Their lingering silence prompted Charlie to utilize another tactic, "Look, I'm only trying to help. Any information you give me will remain strictly confidential. I will trace any possible leads personally, but you have to trust someone. I have a strange suspicion the three of you are holding something back. I can't help you if you don't tell me the truth."

Leah offered the most genuine smile she could muster for Charlie. "I'm sure you mean to be of assistance, Ms. Ashby; however, we have no idea what's going on. We are baffled, just like the police. One can only hope that they catch the individual quickly." Leah calmly folded her hands and continued.

"Now to the business at hand, is the article ready for print? We would prefer just the positive from last night, please. Enough confusion and rumor are floating around town at present." Leah tried to direct the conversation into safer territory.

"I'll have the story ready for print tomorrow morning, highlighting all of the positives, Ms. Reynolds. It will be in our best interests to mention the unexplained explosion as possibly a gas line issue. Emphasizing that it didn't put a damper on the success of the evening. Now, what's this about a gala?" Charlie asked curiously.

Leah wondered how Charlie Ashby learned about the gala. Her reporting skills far exceeded what they needed right now, which was a concern to Leah. If the threats were real, she had no desire to endanger anyone else's life.

"A charity gala in Charlotte next week will officially mark Holcomb Industries' welcome of Watts Enterprises to the corporation. The event allows employees from both companies to mingle and become better acquainted. Construction, training, and hiring will conclude a short time after the gala. Then, before we know it, it will be time for the ribbon cutting and grand reopening."

"Why don't you plan to attend, Ms. Ashby?" Evan interjected. "You could handle the press for the Bridgeport newspaper. It never hurts to have the hometown reporter give a personal perspective on things." Leah attained Evan's invitation was meant to keep Charlie Ashby close at hand.

"Thank you for the invitation, Mr. Holcomb. I may do that. First-hand news is always the best news, I say. Well, I greatly appreciate your time this morning, but I need to be on my way. It's apparent that no one in this room has any additional information about last night. I will keep you up to date on what the police find."

Leah escorted Charlie to the door, promising to notify her of any new developments.

Charlie Ashby offered her thanks and exited Watts Enterprises with two known facts. First, Evan Holcomb had offered up an invitation a little too quickly. Secondly, there was an underlying story to the companies' merger that no one was willing to disclose.

CHAPTER EIGHTEEN

Brent sat in his hotel room and sipped his morning cup of coffee. He replayed the previous night's events in his mind. All of his former training confirmed the explosion was a warning sign. Figuring out who was responsible, and their intended target was another story.

Troy Marshall had returned to the meeting with a bag retrieved from the trunk of a car. The image seared in Brent's mind.

What was in the bag?

Surely, Leah recognized Troy Marshall. After all, he was Evan Holcomb's right-hand man. He'd been on-site at Watts Enterprises for the past couple of weeks with the rest of the staff. Brent's brow creased in confusion. For now, Troy Marshall would remain on the suspect list.

Unable to avoid his work obligation, Brent decided it was time to call Steve Alexander. Nonetheless, he desperately needed more coffee before talking with Steve. Leah Reynolds had invaded his dreams in the early morning hours, ensuring he got little more than a restless night of sleep. Brent couldn't stop thinking about their ride to her apartment. Leah asked him for a lift home so they could talk, invited him to tour, and out to dinner. A reasonably good outcome for a surprise encounter.

Leah never appeared upset with him. On the contrary, she seemed happy to see him. The slight twinkle in her eye spoke volumes to Brent. Leah showed her willingness to spend time with him, even with Evan Holcomb around.

Brent was well aware he would have a battle on his hands for Leah's attention. Evan Holcomb seemed like a man who always got what he wanted. This time Brent was unwilling to oblige. He was tired of being alone.

Perhaps it's time for things to change.

Steve's call could no longer wait. Brent needed his expertise on the explosion.

Brent decided to forego the cup of lukewarm coffee. He reached for the phone and inhaled deeply. There was too much to tell Steve to delay any longer.

He answered on the first ring.

"Brent, are you saying what I think you're saying?" Steve fought to comprehend Brent's words.

"All the information you're giving me ties Watts Enterprises and Holcomb Industries together. The threat had to come from someone with inside knowledge. Everyone knows the airline is the common mode of travel between Charlotte and Bridgeport. If this person wanted to fabricate a merger disruption, the airline would be the perfect mechanism to use. Do you have any idea who could be behind this?"

"Steve, there are so many questions that need answering. Who knows where to start? I'm guessing it could be someone in either organization who has an unrelenting motive to stop the project. Which company would it affect more if the merger didn't take place? Right now, I can't answer that question. Leah Reynolds, a Watts Enterprises employee, has seen a peculiar individual on several occasions before some pretty bizarre things have happened. The latest was the explosion last night."

"After talking with Evan Holcomb, I feel he's baffled by all this, as well. Although, in his defense, I wouldn't care to admit one of my staff members could be responsible for wanting this merger terminated in such an unsavory manner."

"I think I'll hang around here a few more days. Hopefully, the police will release more information about the explosion by then. So, keep me posted, okay, Steve."

"I don't anticipate anything happening in Charlotte right now. I'll see you in a few days, and Brent, stay alert. Whoever this is means business." His warning stayed with Brent.

"I'll be fine, Steve. See you soon."

With the official business behind him, Brent began to think about his two o'clock appointment. He looked forward to spending more time with Leah.

CHAPTER NINETEEN

Leah peeked at her watch; only ten minutes before Brent Scott arrived. Evan made himself scarce after their encounter this morning, and Leah wasn't sure if that was to give her space or give him space. There would be no mistaking his intentions from here on out. Leah needed to determine how she would handle those intentions, but right now, Brent was coming.

Brent Scott was not a person easily forgotten. Leah couldn't decide the depth of Brent's attraction. Was it his dazzling smile, those smoky, sensual blue eyes, his southern drawl, or how he handled extremely awkward situations with such all-out testosterone-filled assurance? No matter the reason, Leah found herself enjoying it way too much. True, she was not as comfortable with him as she was with Evan, but that was part of the excitement. Leah felt like a schoolgirl in Brent's presence. Then again, perhaps she'd been out of the dating loop for too long. It wasn't that Evan lacked charisma, but Brent seemed to send her emotions into overdrive.

Leah Reynolds.

The overhead page lured her back to reality. Startled, she jumped into the elevator and made her way to the first floor. The elevator doors opened ever so slowly to reveal a vision that made her weak in the knees. There stood Brent Scott in all his casual masculine glory.

Does he have any idea how delectable he is?

The royal blue polo accentuated his mesmerizing eyes, while the simple khakis perfectly matched his personality.

Leah's stomach turned cartwheels as she produced a nervous smile. "Hi, Brent. Are you ready for the grand tour?"

"I'm more than ready to check out the exciting things my guide has in store for me. It's not every day I'm fortunate enough to visit one of Holcomb Industries up and coming projects." Brent was acutely aware of the importance of this opportunity.

"If boredom overcomes you, we can leave at any time. This industry can become a little dull. You either love it or hate it; there is no in-between." Leah smiled.

"Seems we have the same motto. I tend to move on from the things that don't interest me." His devilish grin spoke volumes.

Leah hoped her shy smile concealed her true feelings of fascination with Brent. "Well, let's hope you enjoy your afternoon. I wouldn't want you to make that love/hate decision based on this excursion."

"I promise to reserve my judgment until later. Shall we start?" Brent extended his arm in true escort fashion. Leah intertwined her arm with his, and they headed off down the hallway.

Halfway through the tour, they bumped into Rhonda. Surveying Brent from head to toe, Rhonda's actions forced Leah to make an introduction.

Typical Rhonda fashion!

"Rhonda. I'd like to introduce you to Mr. Brent Scott. A friend of mine from?" Leah turned to Brent for assistance. She had no clue where Brent lived.

"Atlanta, Georgia. Very nice to meet you, Rhonda. I guess you are pretty excited about the upcoming changes for the factory." Brent's arm remained linked with Leah's.

"Excited is not the proper adjective to describe what I

am. This upgrade has caused me more sleepless nights than I care to mention for all the wrong reasons. I'll be so glad when things settle down around here. So … how long are you staying in town, Brent?" Rhonda asked intimately, batting her lashes.

"I'll only be here for another day. Duty calls. After that, I need to be back on the road." Brent's words carried a frankness meant to squelch the familiar look in Rhonda's eyes.

"Well, if you desire some company at dinner, just let me know. Leah has my number." Rhonda's slow southern drawl carried a hidden meaning to her invitation.

Her comment left Leah feeling somewhat jealous. Leah knew she was no competition for Rhonda when it came to men. She was outgoing, beautiful, and loved the company of handsome men. Qualities most men flocked to immediately.

Brent grinned, "Thank you for the offer, Rhonda, but I already have plans with an exquisite woman tonight. I'm not sure my heart could withstand the pleasure of being accompanied by two."

Leah brimmed with confidence after hearing Brent's statement. She tightened her grip on his arm.

Rhonda's expression instantly infused with curiosity. "Well, it was a pleasure to meet you anyway. Call me, Leah. It sounds like we need to catch up!" She strolled away, moving straight in the direction of Carol's office.

"I'm sorry about that. Rhonda has always been a little outspoken, but I'm sure you're accustomed to women inviting you to dinner. I'd venture to guess your monthly food budget is quite meager." Leah smirked.

Brent responded casually, "It doesn't happen as often as you might think. Dinner can be quite boring sometimes. Are you willing to help me change that?"

"I'm willing to try depending on what that change might involve…for tonight anyway." Leah's best offense was a strong defense, a relaxed attitude.

Leah and Brent concluded their tour and started out the door to the parking area. The eerie sensation she had experienced several days ago encompassed her once again. The feeling of dread grabbed her, squeezing the air from her lungs. She was unprepared for what caught her attention. A broad figure peered down on them from the upper level of the factory. An icy shiver ran through her body while the shadowy figure stood motionless. Blinking to refocus, Leah opened her eyes slowly to discover the image had disappeared.

"Hey, are you coming?" The sound of Brent's voice jerked her back to the present.

Leah moved as if in quicksand toward the car, an inexplicable sense of doom riding her back the whole way.

Evan waited for Leah to return to the office for almost two hours. The internal struggle surrounding his assertive stunt this morning weighed on him throughout the day, and the need to talk to her was unbearable.

Walking over to the window, he gazed into the night to clear his head when he noticed two people in the parking lot. He realized it was Leah and Brent Scott. Another evening with Brent Scott was not something he counted on happening. However, the sight of the two pushed his previous thoughts aside. Perhaps he was not forward enough. Leah was one of a kind, and he knew it. He would have to up his game if he wanted a chance with her.

And soon.

Leah decided to take Brent to one of Bridgeport's "homegrown" restaurants. Supporting the local businesses made her feel like she was contributing to the town's survival in a small way.

Seated at their small table, Leah found herself only inches away from Brent. A brush of her hand when he reached for the menu disoriented her thoughts and her ability to speak.

Is he going to have this effect on me all night?

She counted to ten and inhaled.

"So, Brent, what type of business brings you to the outer confines of small-town Louisiana? Bridgeport is certainly not a tourist town. You spoke of traveling a lot with your job. You're acquainted with Amber, which I assume has you flying her airlines frequently. That's about the extent of my knowledge about you."

"On the other hand, you know a great deal about me. For example," Leah counted off the items on her fingers as she said them. "Where I live, my occupation, and I have a knack for embarrassing myself in front of people. So not a good character trait!" Her cheeks glowed with embarrassment.

"Where should I start? You're correct. I do travel excessively. I guess you could say I'm in the security business. My job's to ensure people are safe."

"Yes, I'm friendly with Amber on a somewhat personal basis. We are very often on the same flights together. She's beautiful, kind, and has an award-winning personality. When I saw her the other day, she told me that you two have kept in touch since you met. She's a wonderful person. You're fortunate to know her."

Brent's last statement set off caution lights for Leah.

Amber would be a true friend until the end, and she was lucky to have met her. Brent was right about that. How could she sit at dinner drooling over Brent when he and Amber were together? Amber would never do that to her. If Brent gave her the answer she hoped for to her next question, dinner would be a success. An incorrect response would prompt her to cut the evening short.

"This may seem personal, but I have to ask because I value Amber's friendship. I don't want her to get the wrong impression about us having dinner together. Are you and Amber involved?" Biting her lower lip, she waited for what seemed an eternity.

"The answer is no. Not in the way you are thinking. Is that a good thing?"

Tickled, Leah replied, "Well, Mr. Scott, I'd say that's an excellent thing. I never want to hurt Amber."

The evening flew by with conversations spilling into debates over anything from football to Atlanta's sights and sounds and Bridgeport's lack thereof. She hated for it to end.

As Brent drove Leah back to Watts Enterprises, he couldn't suppress the sense of loss.

How can I be so attracted to this woman in such a short time?

He remembered Cooper's comment about a bit of scenery over dinner. He would not be opposed to having dinner with her every night.

Brent parked the car and turned to face Leah, only to notice her hesitant gaze.

It's now or never.

He had waited for this since the moment he'd laid

eyes on her.

Staring into those captivating eyes, he brushed the hair from around her face. Then, He kissed her with unmatched gentleness. The connection between them stopped time. Leah returned his kiss with the same cherished tenderness. As their lips parted, he managed to speak.

"Sorry, but I couldn't leave town tomorrow without doing that. I'm not sure when I'll see you again, and I won't live with the regret of not having kissed you." Brent felt the truth of every word.

"Well, I can't have you leaving Bridgeport with regrets. Not after you saved me last night." Leah laughed, flushed from her honesty.

"I'll never complain about being your savior any day of the week, but I prefer it not to be life-threatening." Brent paused. It was time to be frank with her.

"Leah, you know that you need to be careful. There's something strange about this whole situation. I prefer you not get hurt." He couldn't tell her exactly how bizarre and dangerous it was becoming.

"Brent, I appreciate your concern. Everything's going to be fine. The police will have a suspect soon, and this whole thing will be over. I'm not sure where your travels will carry you next, but maybe we will cross paths again soon."

"You never know. Maybe we will."

Why do I have anxiety about leaving her again?

His lips parted, wanting to say more. He shoved aside the need.

"Thank you again for dinner, the tour, and the excellent company."

He gave her another quick kiss and watched as she walked to her car, consumed with a sense of euphoria he hadn't experienced for some time. Their paths would cross again. He would make sure of it.

CHAPTER TWENTY

Leah found herself perplexed the following day as she entered Watts Enterprises. Images from her night with Brent clouded her mind. His kiss exhilarated her. If honesty prevailed, she had to admit Brent surprised her. Nothing like she expected him to be, but everything she wanted him to be. He was caring, honest, engaging, and ever so handsome. If he had an ego, it remained very well-hidden last night. Leah prayed she would run into him again soon.

On the other hand, Leah couldn't ignore Evan's desire to be more than a business associate. His kiss had caught her off guard, but it was indeed enjoyable. She bounced between thoughts of the two men. Staring straight ahead as if in a trance, she found herself rendering a comparison.

Brent carried a rugged masculine physique with outright male charisma. His gentle kiss made her tingle from head to toe, but she was comfortable with Evan. She never sensed an uneasiness around him. They spent so much time working together; there was no time for nervousness. Brent's personality was mysterious and unknown. Even though their dinner discussion involved a few personal comments, there were still so many things she did not know about him. Those undiscovered things excited her. No question, both men were dashingly handsome, each in their own very different way. Writing a pro/con list crossed her mind, but she would ultimately require girlfriend support.

Speaking of girlfriends, Leah was unprepared for the sight of Carol and Rhonda standing in the doorway to her office, hands on their hips.

Here we go. Prepare for an onslaught of questions.

"Good morning, ladies. I trust you enjoyed a wonderful evening last night. Did you both sleep well? Anything going on this morning I need to be aware of?" Leah stifled a laugh.

"Anything going on? We should send that question right back to you. We need details, Leah. Why would you keep Brent Scott from us? All this time, we thought you were interested in Evan Holcomb. Now we discover you have two of them fawning over you. It is so not fair." Rhonda pouted, unable to contain her exasperation.

"Two, Leah? In Bridgeport? Both of them are undoubtedly interested in you. I'm not looking for a husband, but dinner and a movie would be nice. So tell me, how in the world you're going to handle two of them?" The mother in Carol surfaced.

Leah wanted to tell them her dilemma, but the office was not the place. "Calm down. There's nothing to handle. Brent and I enjoyed a pleasant dinner. We're friends who just wanted to catch up a little. As for Evan, we work very closely together and have also become great friends. That's all. You two are letting your imaginations run away with you."

"What I have seen in their eyes has nothing to do with friendship, and I should know!" Rhonda exclaimed.

"Come on, Rhonda; you only met Brent for a brief moment. You couldn't possibly tell that. Besides, you hit on him two seconds after meeting him. What do you have to say for yourself?" Leah said jokingly.

"Look, knowing a good thing when you lay eyes on it and being frank are not crimes. I see no sense in wasting time on a pointless conversation. Men like Brent don't stay unattached for long, especially if they are as nice as they are handsome." Rhonda's lips pursed in a particular show of clarity.

Leah never doubted Rhonda was correct in her analysis, but she couldn't control the outcome of a situation well out of her grasp.

"I'm quite sure that Brent has the opportunity to get extra attention frequently. However, you should be ashamed of yourself. Your actions did not present a good image, especially in the workplace." Leah huffed.

Both ladies gazed at each other, sporting an "I told you so" grin. "Sounds like someone may have been jealous, Rhonda! Maybe we were all wrong about Mr. Holcomb." Carol peered at Leah with prying eyes and waited for her to confess something, anything.

"Jealous is not the correct word, Carol. We must portray a professional image when conducting tours with our guests. The public must envision this merger's positive impact on the factory and its employees." Leah maintained an all-business attitude.

Rhonda piped in immediately, "Yep, she's jealous because that public image smokescreen's a load of crap. It seems more like a cover-up to me, but don't worry, he's not interested in anyone but you, dear. You don't need to worry about me; however, I can't speak for all the other women in the world," Rhonda and Carol chuckled at their friend's expense.

Exasperated, Leah issued a wave goodbye and promised to catch up with them later. The whole conversation unnerved her.

At least there was one positive thing exposed during their discussion. Rhonda recognized Brent was interested in her. An attraction she noticed during dinner. However, that realization only added to her confusion. Deep in thought, Leah heard a loud cough directly behind her.

"Hum. Hello, you seem rather preoccupied." Evan stated.

Turning around, one thing she'd determined for sure - the man was unapologetically handsome. He did something for a business suit no fashion designer could ever imagine.

"Hi. I'm sorry. I was thinking about a few things. How are you this morning?"

"Better now that you are here. I need to discuss something with you." Evan's presence cast its notorious spell.

Leah believed it was only a matter of time before the subject of their kiss came up. Life was suddenly going to become complicated. She played innocent.

"And what would that be? Is there something wrong with the merger plans?"

"No, things are going surprisingly well if you discount the fact that someone is willing to harm one or all three of us to stop it from happening. Didn't you say you saw the man from the airport in the meeting right before the explosion?"

"Yes, standing at the back of the room. The man willed me to notice him. I'll never forget his probing stare and continuous eye contact. I realize this sounds ridiculous, but it's almost as though he wanted me to know something was going to happen. Although Brent may have been right, maybe he did only intend to scare us. If you think about it, we could have seen dozens of injuries. Yet, the device exploded well away from everyone. Think Evan. Does anyone dislike you enough to do something on this grand of a scale?"

"Are you sure it is me they dislike? What about you or John? The individual did call John's direct line to make the initial threat. Are you sure there aren't any employees who want to enact revenge upon John for some reason? Or maybe it's someone who doesn't like you; look at you. You're beautiful, business savvy, excellent at your job, valued by John and those around you. It might be someone jealous of you, maybe even jealous of something you have.

Can you think of anyone who might want to harm you or prove a point?" His voice escalated with worry.

"Evan, I get we're all on edge, but please don't get too upset about this. I understand you're trying to protect John and me, but I cannot conceive of anyone who would want anything to happen to John. He's the pillar of the community. He and Martha are always assisting charities and donating funds to the community."

"As for me, while I appreciate the wonderful compliments, my life is boring. It always has been, even in my college days. I can't name a single reason why someone may be mad or resentful enough towards me to do this." Leah's sudden epiphany directed her attention back to Evan.

"Now, you, on the other hand, are a different story. Countless women desire your attention, your business's success inspires envy among your competitors, and you continue to grow your empire across the country. So, it seems you are the primary target, which concerns me deeply."

Evan smiled wickedly. "You're concerned about me?"

"Oh, stop. I'd never want to see anything happen to you or John."

"Too late to backtrack now, Ms. Reynolds, and don't go adding John into the mix. You're concerned about me. You just admitted it."

He's too attractive.

"Ok, I'm concerned. Are you happy?" Leah huffed.

"Yes, I am. For now, though, we have to figure this out. It won't take long for Charlie to discover there were other, let's say, issues before the explosion. I do not want anything in print regarding these threats. My siblings have enough trouble dealing with all the notoriety tied to the company. Something of this magnitude would cause them concern, or even worse, it might make them a target for this idiot. I won't tolerate that option. I have an idea. Why don't we grab some dinner tonight? Compiling a list of potential suspects seems the best place to start."

"I guess that makes sense if you think it would help. I'll check with you later this afternoon. Talk to you soon." Leah nervously answered.

Evan's tender grasp on her hand as she turned to walk away propelled her senses into overdrive. "And Leah, we'll have to discuss what happened the other morning. Even though you may not want to."

The sincerity on his face made him vulnerable and attractive.

"I guess we really should," Leah whispered, continuing down the hallway. She was sure of one thing. Her list of pros and cons between the two men was a necessity.

The uneasiness on Evan's face as they discussed the explosion was undeniable. His apprehension and restlessness reinforced hers. She could not dismiss the feeling that something else was going to happen - the unknown of where and when started to scare her.

Leah rambled through her daily routine, quite distracted about who would go on the suspect list, not only hers but also John and Evan's. She prayed Evan would invite John to accompany them to dinner. At least that would keep the two of them from being alone tonight. Furthermore, John's presence kept Evan from discussing the inevitable and provided her another day to grasp what was happening between them.

The unexpected ring of her cell phone caught Leah off guard since only her close friends and family had access to the number. The word "restricted" on the telephone alarmed her. Why would anyone in her inner circle need to hide the incoming number?

Lord, I have to stop this.

Her imagination was uncontrollable.

Inquisitively Leah uttered, "Hello?" No response caused her heart to skip a beat.

"Hello, is anyone there?" She questioned again, trying to keep her voice steady.

She knew "dead zones" within the factory prevented clear cell signals. Perhaps this was the case. When she heard the throaty voice, a short gasp escaped her lungs

"I have no desire to hurt you. You're not the one I'm after. Drop your involvement with this merger. If not, chances are you might be in the wrong place with the wrong people and get caught in the crossfire. Consider this your only warning. A courtesy call, you might say."

Leah stood speechless as the line went dead. Questions rifled through her head.

How did this person get her number?

Why was she being protected?

The call confirmed either Evan or John were the target.

Or was this just a ploy to cover the perpetrator's tracks?

Arctic blasts of fear invaded her body, filling her in terror as her phone rang again.

She answered frantically, screaming, "Why are you doing this? What do you want? We've never hurt anyone?" Pausing to catch a breath, she heard Evan's voice. Leah never realized she'd answered her office phone.

"Leah, what's wrong? What are you talking about, Leah? Don't move. I'm on my way to your office."

Evan arrived at Leah's office in a matter of minutes. As he entered the doorway, she lept into his arms. Shaking uncontrollably, she looked into his eyes with a fear he never wished to see again.

Unnerving terror tinged her voice, “Please stay here. Don’t leave me right now.”

“What is wrong, Leah? What happened? I promise I won’t leave you, but you must tell me what’s wrong.”

She pulled back from Evan’s embrace, peering up at him, weak with fright, “I received a telephone call similar to John. A male voice stated he didn’t want me to get hurt, that I wasn’t the focus of his plan. He told me to step away from the merger, or I could get caught in the middle. He stressed that this call was my only warning. I’d placed everything happening in the back of my mind, telling myself I was silly and there was no danger. How naïve we have been. His call clarified his intent to hurt someone. I’m sure now it’s either you or John, but I’m unsure why.”

Leah now understood this maniac could harm Evan. She gazed into his eyes, realizing this madness had the potential to destroy them. Without warning, Evan leaned forward and kissed her with passionate concern. Their kisses increased in intensity with every passing second - each anxiously aware of the danger that awaited them while seeking comfort in each other’s embrace. Evan’s safety overwhelmed her mind as she lost all concept of reality.

After what seemed an eternity, Leah broke their embrace. She backed away from Evan, straightening her clothes, her head still spinning.

Trembling, she gaped at Evan. “I’m sorry. I can’t imagine what came over me. I didn’t mean to attack you when you walked in.” Leah backed away, placing her desk between them for a barrier.

Evan stared eagerly at Leah, “Please feel free to ‘attack me’ any time you like. Hopefully, it will be under more inviting circumstances next time. I’m not complaining about this little interlude, but you realize we can no longer write these events off as coincidences.”

“We need security to pull all telephone records over

the past hour. We may have a slim chance of tracing the number. I promise, we will find out who called you."

"You can't," Leah expressed softly. "The man called my cell number; therefore, the call wouldn't go through the switchboard."

"Who has your number? I'm going to need to verify everyone with access to the number," Evan grimaced. Brent Scott would be one of those people.

"Only my close friends and family. I make a point not to give it out to business acquaintances; with you being the exception, no one else has it."

"After that little exchange, I would say we are more than acquaintances, Leah," Evan said frankly.

Leah rubbed her temple wishing she could ignore the comment. "Evan, you're fully aware of what I mean. I don't give my number out, ever. I told you I have a boring life. There's no reason for me to give out my number."

"I'm glad to hear that; however, we need to talk to John ASAP. It appears we're in more danger than we imagined. I think John should join us for dinner. The suspect lists are ever so important now."

They stared blankly at each other. Whoever was behind the calls would not wait long to issue another warning.

Or worse.

CHAPTER TWENTY-ONE

At the restaurant, the three sat silent, contemplating who could be considered a suspect. John struggled with names. He didn't have enemies, nor did Leah. Evan's list contained the names of several competitors against Holcomb Industries expanding their business to Louisiana. Still, no one offered a single name that carried any value.

"Evan, I have tried; truly, I have. I've racked my brain for possibilities and can't think of anyone. All of the employees seem happy. I even considered Martha. If someone's angry or upset with her, I'm not aware of it. We try to do right by everyone. Since our boys passed away, we've had a mission to help others whenever possible. The tragedy of losing a child is difficult to overcome. If you stay focused on the good, life's much better. We worked so hard to build the business." John's brow furrowed with frustration.

"I'm afraid it's the same with me," Leah interjected sullenly.

"Rhonda, Carol, and Amber are my friends. It can't be a family member. No one from college or high school stands out to me. Besides, it has to be someone affiliated with our companies.

"That's an excellent point, Leah. In all probability, you're right about the affiliation with both companies. It may be someone playing a major role in the merger, which points us more in my direction. This individual must want to harm either me or my business." Apprehension echoed in Evan's voice.

Could it be someone in the organization that wants to harm me?

He was so busy pointing a finger in John's direction that he never considered it could be someone working for him. He believed in the competitor theory more than the personal vendetta scenario. Evan hesitated to think it may be someone in his employ capable of committing evil acts so indiscriminately. Company policy dictated that he interview each employee. If this individual worked for him, he'd made a fatal judgment in character.

The evening concluded with the three vowing to investigate Evan's list immediately. John professed that he didn't like to be away from Martha, his high school sweetheart, who he loved deeply for a long time. He thanked Leah and Evan for dinner and rushed out the door.

The silent journey back to Leah's apartment placed them both in an awkward situation. Glancing at Evan, Leah noticed he was extremely uneasy. Their listing exercise proved one thing. This person was undoubtedly focused on Evan since he would suffer the most significant loss from the collapse of the merger. The thought scared her. She wasn't in love with Evan by any means, but there was an attraction she couldn't deny. Nevertheless, she remained confident that Evan knew way more than he was willing to share with John or her.

They walked to her door in insufferable silence.

"Ok, out with it. You've been preoccupied since we left the restaurant. Today's events are unsettling, but at least we have a starting point now. Your competitor list will help narrow the search." She blurted out the words, feeling guilty afterward for her tone.

Frustration, concern, helplessness, and anger all wrapped in one propelled Evan forward to close the gap between them, backing Leah against the door frame. He kissed her with a desperation that weakened her knees. One long demanding kiss was the compilation of every emotion she knew he felt. His tight hold on her seemed as though he was cherishing his last moments with her.

Leah attempted to catch her breath, somehow opening the door, forcing a separation between them. As Evan stumbled towards her, he realized what had just happened. Sadness now constricted his handsome features.

"Leah, today brought so many of my problems to the forefront. It doesn't take rocket science to figure out I'm the target. If our relationship caused you some misfortune, I couldn't live with myself. You mean more to me than you understand. My main focus is to figure this out, like 'yesterday.' I refuse to let this situation cause harm to you or anyone else I care to protect. I'm heading back to Charlotte in the morning. A little space between us will make it safer for you. I have several ideas that might help stop this madness. You and John can finish things up here before your trip to Charlotte. I'll see you at the gala. Then all we have left is the ribbon cutting for the new opening."

Leah heard the anguish in his voice.

"Evan, I know we have become great friends, and it would upset me so much for anything to happen to you. Don't worry about me; I can take care of myself. At least I've seen this maniac's face, and besides, he said it's not me he wishes to hurt. On the other hand, you have no clue."

"I have an idea, and before you say no, hear me out. We should tell Charlie Ashby what's happening. She already has the impression we're hiding something, so let's use her skills to our advantage. Her previous casework in New York provided her with numerous contacts. What if she could connect me with a sketch artist or someone that can provide a drawing based on my description? At least we would have an image in black and white."

"I will agree on one condition." Evan held up a finger as he delivered his ultimatum. "Charlie must assure us this will remain confidential. I can't risk the story going public. A nightmare like this would destroy the business and my family. You can notify me if Charlie accepts those terms." Evan cleared his throat, observing Leah.

"Now, we have to discuss the inevitable. You're aware of how I prefer this 'thing' between us to progress. My desire is to become more than your friend or colleague. My feelings for you increase with each passing day. However, I realize you may not be ready for a relationship, given that we've only known each other for a short time. I won't pressure you in any way, but I want you to understand I'm going to do everything in my power to help you see what a great team we could become. The only thing I ask is that you tell me how you feel. Please don't keep me waiting and wondering what's going on in that pretty head of yours. Deal?"

Leah nodded her head, signifying a yes, and remained silent.

Before Evan left, he made sure she had a clear correlation between how he felt and the direction he preferred her heart to take. The passionate kiss would undoubtedly leave her tossing and turning all night again.

Unable to sleep as predicted, Leah determined she needed reinforcement in the form of girl support. She dialed Amber's number, praying she would answer. Carol and Rhonda could never learn about the impending danger looming over them. They were factory employees, and it would only scare them to death. Trust wasn't an issue between the three, only their safety. Leah realized she couldn't share the full story with Amber, but right now, she needed a "non-stressful" conversation about anything besides the merger.

Amber's sleepy "hello" had Leah rethinking her actions.

"Oh, Amber, I should have waited until the morning to call you. I never dreamed you could be in a different time zone. Which you are, I bet." The stress of the day erased all concepts of time.

"Hi, Leah. What's going on?" Leah heard Amber release a long yawn.

"Oh my gosh. I'll call you later at a decent hour. Go back to sleep." Leah felt so selfish, thinking only of her needs.

"No, no, it's quite alright. I've wanted to catch up anyway. Tell me, what's going on in your fabulous world of mergers?"

"Oh, not much, same old boring stuff. You know the business world, a dull daily grind." Leah paused, fixated on the word dull. Of course, her job was anything but that right now.

"Your voice tells me something different. What are you holding back? We haven't known each other for very long, but I can tell there's tension in your voice. So what's wrong?"

"Nothing." Leah made a mistake calling Amber. She was too perceptive.

"Well, there is one thing. Brent and I had a wonderful dinner together while he was in town. We discussed his job in the security business. I wasn't surprised to find out his occupation consisted of keeping people safe. Look what he did for me."

Amber's tone livened up. "Give me all the juicy

details of the evening."

"What makes you think there are juicy details, Amber?"

"How could there not be? He is quite roguish! Like one of those tough cowboys from a romance novel."

"If I'm honest, his kiss was soft, slow, and smooth, like a case of fine red wine. It was most enjoyable. That man oozes sex appeal from his pores." Leah confessed.

Amber stifled a giggle. "A case, huh? Well, that must have been one heck of a kiss. Did you make plans to see each other again?"

"Not really. I think we both have a lot on our plate right now. We'll have to wait and see what happens. I'm aware that it sounds outrageous, Amber, but he carries this masculine aura around him. You feel safe and happy when you're with him. You know?"

"Yeah, I guess so." Amber's ears tuned into Leah's words.

"How's your friend Evan Holcomb by the way? During dinner, he appeared to have a strong personal interest in you. Are you attracted to him? If the answer is yes and Brent makes you feel like you are describing, you have a problem. Two guys are hard to handle, Leah."

Leah knew all too well she was playing with fire. "Evan and I are friends and do business together. I hope Brent and I will become good friends soon. I have to see what the future holds, I guess. Look at me rambling on like we have all night. Thanks for talking, Amber. Things have been highly stressful here, and I desperately needed a girlfriend chat."

"Any time, Leah. I'm always here for you. Something tells me you and Brent are going to become great friends. I'm sure of it."

"You think so? I hope. You take care, Amber. I hope to see you soon." Leah's goodbye held an ominous tone.

"You too. I'll talk to you soon, I promise."

Amber's concern for Leah overrode all credible logic. Brent would have to talk to her, now. Amber dialed Brent's number, casting aside any care regarding what he was doing. Angry that he didn't tell her he was headed to Bridgeport to visit Leah, she struggled to understand why. She and Brent were extremely close. He always shared everything with her.

Brent answered the phone to a barrage of questions spewing from the other end.

"Amber, hold on, give me a minute," he exclaimed. "I couldn't tell you that I was going to Bridgeport. You know the protocol. I didn't go to visit Leah; it just happened."

"Oh well, big brother, you better be glad there's a "protocol" that we must follow. Leah is a good friend. I don't want her to be another one of your random conquests. Just because I told you she thinks you're hot doesn't mean you can toy with her. Leah is way too sweet to be a passing interest, Brent." Amber's protective nature was unleashing in full force against her brother.

"Amber, I have no plan to make Leah a conquest. What has you so upset because you know I'm not that type of person? There has to be something else that started this tirade."

"You're right. I'm sorry. It's just that I'm worried about Leah. Something seemed peculiar when I talked to her a little while ago. She sounded scared, almost frightened for some reason. Normally, I'd tell you not to do this, but I think you should call her. Remind her that you are in the security business if she asks where you got her number. Security business, yeah, great cover that was!"

"What do you mean? Frightened? Did she tell you

what was wrong?"

"She actually said very little. Instead, she discussed how stressful her job is right now. Oh, she did say that your kisses were like fine wine!" Amber erupted with rolling laughter.

"You know I'll have to tell her you're my brother. I can't continue to keep something like this from her. She will feel betrayed, and I don't want that. She's a friend and has become like a sister to me."

"A sister? I didn't realize you two were that close. Can we move to the fine wine part? Why wine of all things?" Brent nervously awaited Amber's response.

"Brent, you know girls don't kiss and tell. Just call her NOW. I'm worried."

"Ok, give me her number. I will call in the morning, I promise. It's too late to call tonight. Amber, thanks for the "heads up. You're a great sister. I love you!"

"Yeah, yeah. Call Leah. Goodnight, big brother!"

CHAPTER TWENTY-TWO

Since his arrival back in Charlotte, Brent couldn't clear his mind of the events in Bridgeport. The local authorities, to date, were unable to provide any further information about the explosion, while the Bridgeport newspaper highlighted only positive aspects of the meeting. The article did not mention the blast or the possible circumstances surrounding it. Someone was doing a great job of weaving a different storyline for public perception.

Brent, without a doubt, sensed a tie between both companies still existed. Now there was this phone call from Amber about Leah. He figured Leah was too smart to provide Amber with any details about what was happening. The explosion occurred several days ago, yet Leah still sounded extremely upset. She didn't seem like a girl who would panic over minor things. When Brent left her the other night, her demeanor was one of calmness. Her faith was set on the authorities looking into the incident. If there was another threat against her, he wanted to know about it. The only way to tell would be to call her.

As he dialed the number, Brent possessed a feeling of "schoolboy" awkwardness, formulating a story in his head for the call.

"Hello, hello, who is this? Why are you calling me? Please stop." Leah's voice seized with terror.

"Hello, Leah. It's me, Brent Scott. Are you ok?" Brent's instincts kicked in.

"Brent? I'm fine. How are you? How did you get my number?" A lighter tone was instantly noticeable in her voice.

"I'm in the security business, remember? I wanted to check on you and tell you thanks again for dinner, but in truth, I needed an excuse to talk to you again." He was silent.

"I have to admit; I'm happy you called. I was thinking about you last night," she whispered.

Brent chuckled.

"I wish I'd called sooner since you feel that way. Seriously, Leah, how are you? Do you have any updates on who may have caused the explosion? I must admit I'm a little concerned about you but elated that nothing else has happened."

Leah's voice began to quiver.

"No, unfortunately, they don't have any leads." Her lips trembled as she spoke.

"Brent, something else has happened. I'm fine, Evan and John are fine too, but I'm deeply concerned."

Brent knew his sister had inherited keen instincts. He would listen to her more intently the next time she told him about one of her feelings.

He suppressed his anger. "What happened? Did you see the same guy again? Was he at the factory?"

"No. I haven't seen him. It's all quite strange. I received a phone call from a restricted number yesterday morning, and without a doubt, a male voice was on the other end. The man emphasized I'm not the target of his plan, but if I didn't separate myself from this merger, I could get hurt in the crossfire. He ended the call stressing that it was my only warning. Brent, I'm beginning to become very frightened."

Unable to hold his anger at bay any longer, Brent spewed several expletives she couldn't overhear.

This stupid man thinks he is untouchable.

Brent concentrated on offering Leah assurance and support. He would deal with his anger later in the gym; God bless anyone who got in his way.

"I can be on a flight to Bridgeport in the next hour if you need me. It distresses me that some maniac is making threats, and you can't identify him. Do you have any idea how he found your number?"

"No, I've been over this numerous times with Evan. I don't give out my telephone number. I have no idea how he got it."

Brent fought to comprehend anything else Leah said after hearing Evan's name. So Evan Holcomb was still in Bridgeport. He detested the idea that Evan was the one comforting Leah in Bridgeport, but he had to admit he appeared more than capable of protecting them both. Right now, his jealousy would need to go on the back burner. Leah's safety was more important than his petty envy.

"Brent, we have come to one conclusion. Evan, John, and I sat down last night and made a list of who has a motive and the possible intended target. We assumed it was not me since the caller was trying to warn me away from harm. It was clear to all of us that Evan's the target."

"Why Evan? What evidence pointed to Evan as the target?" Brent pushed for information that confirmed the company tie-in theory.

"John and I couldn't think of a soul who would despise us that much. We determined it must be someone who stands to gain a great deal from a failing merger. No one from our past would care what we are doing. There's no need for revenge against us. It has to be one of Evan's competitors."

"So, you've been doing some detective work, huh, Ms. Reynolds? Might I say I'm quite impressed with your investigative skills?" Everything Leah said made perfect sense. She used the same rationale as Brent had to draw his conclusions.

"Did Evan agree with your theory?" He presumed the answer would be yes.

"Yes, he did. Evan is on his way back to Charlotte now to follow through on some of his ideas. Brent, we have an event coming up next week in Charlotte. Holcomb Industries released the promotional information yesterday. We can't cancel now. You don't think this person will try something crazy at the gala, do you?" He suspected the bold statement wasn't off the mark. Anything was possible.

"Listen to me; I'm drawing you into our problems. I'm sure you have more important things consuming your time. I'm afraid to admit that I'm more comfortable and secure with you around. After all, you've saved me twice." Leah professed.

Brent, pleased with Leah's honesty, knew the attraction was mutual.

"You're not drawing me into your problems. If your safety is involved, I'm all in to help wherever I can. This event will have security, right?"

"Yes. Evan stressed that hiring extra security would be one of his priorities when he arrived in Charlotte."

He breathed a sigh of relief. "With that in mind, I wouldn't think this man plans to make a move during the gala. Besides, Evan's extra security will act as an added deterrent. An open area would allow too much exposure. Most people attending will view the additional security as normal."

"I hope you're right. By the way, did I tell you I'm glad you called? You have made me feel so much better." The smile on her face radiated through her words.

"I have a question. I may be in Charlotte while you're there on business. How would you like to have a glass of wine with me? I've heard about a great place that specializes in fine wines." Brent prayed she would make the connection and say yes.

Leah's elation was evident by her quick response. "I

can probably arrange something. Call me if it works out for you. Thanks again, Brent. I hope to talk to you soon."

"I like your answer. I'll talk with you soon, and Leah, you don't need to thank me. Promise you will call me if you need me sooner."

He hung up the phone to Leah's promises with a sense of accomplishment. Their telephone conversation confirmed his suspicions regarding the two companies. He needed to find the common thread that bound the group together. Plus, he'd managed to wrangle a commitment from Leah for drinks.

Today's a good day.

CHAPTER TWENTY-THREE

Securing Leah's promise to call him, if she needed to, would have to be enough for now. Brent was well aware of the "upcoming event" in Charlotte. The gala's formal introduction of Watts Enterprises into the corporation would be the perfect target for their menacing friend.

Brent hated lying to Leah about the additional security but telling her the truth would only frighten her more. Brent's intuition reinforced his concerns. The offender would thrive on the added challenge of the extra security. Being in Charlotte was no longer an option. Brent would secure an invitation to the gala one way or another.

There's no way I will leave Leah unprotected.

"Unprotected" was not the correct term. Leah would have protection. It would just be by the wrong person. Brent believed Evan would do everything possible to keep her safe. But, if honesty prevailed, Brent felt Evan's likely preoccupation with company business could leave an opening for disaster. Something he was unwilling to accept.

Steve Alexander awaited Brent's arrival back in Charlotte even as he dreaded meeting with his friend. The two had met back in their military days, serving the same Army division. Years of combat training and front-line action provided each of them with the ability to detect the other's feelings before they could vocalize them. Nevertheless, Steve saw the subtle signs signaling Brent's attachment to Leah Reynolds.

If his suspicions were correct, Watts Enterprises and Holcomb Industries had a terrorist with a vendetta against one or both companies. A valuable part of Watts Enterprises, Leah Reynolds, would also be an essential asset to Holcomb Industries after the merger. There was a high probability that Leah would be targeted if the situation escalated. Based on Steve's latest intel, things were rapidly moving in a dangerous direction.

Brent walked into the room, smiling from ear to ear, but Steve speculated his friend's cheerful grin would disappear in a matter of minutes.

"Morning, Steve, how's it going? It's way too early in the morning to look that serious. Is something happening I should know about?" Brent's words echoed his concern.

"Brent, sit down. You're not going to like this." Steve took a deep breath before continuing, hoping to bolster his confidence. "My contacts confirmed credible evidence concerning the connection between Watts's and Holcomb's companies. You were right. They narrowed the initial threat to flights between Charlotte and Louisiana. All data ties back to those two locations. There's no mistake. After what you told me happened in Bridgeport the other night, I know from previous experience that this guy will not stop until his plan's complete. Or he winds up dead."

"Yeah, but Steve, the problem is we don't have a clue as to WHAT he wants. All we know is that this lunatic doesn't want the merger to occur. What happens if it does go through on schedule? Both companies stand to make millions. The upgrade will enable them to make and distribute their products in half the time. New manufacturing jobs will provide Bridgeport with a thriving economy once again. Who would be against that?" Brent pressed Steve for an answer, any answer.

Steve remained void of emotion. He didn't have an answer, not a legitimate one anyway.

"The only conclusion I can draw is a rival company. They have much to gain and little to lose. Regrettably, we're fighting a losing battle until we can find the connection. I've instructed everyone to remain diligent in searching for a possible link."

"Brent, one other thing. If we don't get a lead soon, people could get hurt, one of them being Leah Reynolds."

"Believe me, Steve, I'm well aware of that. But I am doing all I can. I spoke with Leah this morning to check on her. She filled me in on an anonymous phone call she recently received during our conversation. The caller said he didn't want to harm her, but she should remove herself from the merger or risk being in the wrong place at the wrong time. This corporate gala is just a few days away. You know as well as I do, Steve, our new friend, will have something planned." Brent's gaze bore into Steve when he delivered his next statement. "That's why I'm going to be at the gala."

"Brent, remember you're an Air Marshall. Your jurisdiction doesn't involve civil events. They will have other security for that. Our job is to protect people on our airlines. The threat originated with a proposed attack on one of our flights. I still believe that."

"I understand what you are saying; however, somehow, I will be in attendance. There's no way I'll let Leah attend without me. This maniac will make a move. I'm sure of it. If we are lucky enough to catch him, the airline issue is null and void. Trust me on this, Steve." Brent placed added emphasis on the words "trust me."

"Hey. When have I ever not trusted you? Brent, you need to watch your step and tread lightly, though." Steve grimaced, aware it would never happen.

"Believe me, I realize what could go wrong. But my instincts have never failed me. We will either catch our perpetrator or have a good idea of who this character is. I'm confident we will stop this before anyone gets hurt. I'm going to go. I have someone I need to see. I'll check with you later." Brent walked out of the office on a mission, and Steve knew exactly where he was headed.

CHAPTER TWENTY-FOUR

Holcomb Industries definitely lives up to the hype, Brent thought. From the smooth, sleek silver curvature of the center's ceiling panels to the clean, crisp design encompassing the expansive building, the entire facility transported visitors to a setting only available in science fiction movies. Brent was quite impressed, as he witnessed first-hand why Evan Holcomb's competitors revered him.

As visitors entered the building, it was abundantly evident the Holcomb Industries staff enjoyed their job. Friendly smiles adorned their faces while they carried out their duties. In this work environment, who wouldn't take pleasure in their career? Employees loved their leader, Evan Holcomb. Their dedication was evident in homages placed throughout the first floor. Photos and articles lined the walls displaying the company's success stories.

Articles touted Evan Holcomb as "A CEO who leads by example."

The clippings described Evan's ability to perform any job or task within the company. Holcomb had mastered them all. The company's success seemed rooted in Evan Holcomb's vast knowledge base. His workforce held an undying appreciation for his honesty, factual input, and never-ending support. These people were not just employees; they were family.

Brent continued his journey through the fantastic world of "Holcomb Industries," traversing his way to the futuristic elevators.

As the elevator rose to the 14th floor of the sleek high-rise, Brent struggled to clear his head. The conversation with Holcomb would not be an easy one, but for Leah's sake, it was necessary. He knew they both cared for Leah more with each passing day. He witnessed Evan's protective nature and concern for her during the explosion. If Holcomb were anything like Brent imagined, their conversation would be difficult. At best.

He won't be happy with what I have to say.

The visit to Evan's office also provided Brent with an opportunity to analyze Steve's theory relating to a connection between the threats and Holcomb Industries.

Brent assumed he'd arrived on the 14th floor as the elevator came to a quick stop. The doors glided open slowly to reveal none other than Troy Marshall. Stunned by the sight, Brent's mouth gaped open as the man strolled casually through the doors.

Troy's quizzical eyes locked on Brent's, creating several moments of tense silence. Marshall scratched his head in confusion. He seemed baffled by the man with whom he shared the elevator.

Brent suspected Marshall was trying to recall their acquaintance, so he tossed a cheerful greeting.

"Morning"

Smiling, Troy replied, "Haven't we met? Yes, I'm sure we have. You're the guy from the airplane. Man, how are you doing? What brings you to our glorious Holcomb Industries?" His tone mimicked elements of the mystical karma Brent witnessed upon his arrival.

Astounded by Troy's zen attitude, Brent uttered. "You are correct. I wasn't sure you would remember me. I'm on my way to Evan Holcomb's office."

"Evan?" Marshall's expression twisted into a labyrinth of unspoken questions.

Brent strained to determine if the surprised expression

on Troy's face was one of curiosity or concern.

"Do you have a business meeting with him? Do the two of you know each other? I'm usually familiar with all of Evan's associates. What type of business are you in?" The back-to-back questions spewed rapidly from Troy.

This guy is too inquisitive.

"I'm in the security business. And yes, we're acquainted." Brent stated nonchalantly

"Security? Oh wow! Is Evan hiring additional security?" Troy questioned with eyebrows raised.

"Evan's very perceptive. If someone's interested in damaging relations with his new interest, Watts Enterprises, he'll take corrective action before the merger. People tend to go crazy when someone starts a new business venture. Evan's competitors are jealous of the success he's experienced before the age of 35." His voice trailed into a stern defensive tone.

The elevator came to a swift halt. Troy Marshall exited with a fast-paced stride calling out, "Have a good day," as he bolted down the hallway.

Before the doors could close, Brent noticed Troy had turned to peer back into the elevator.

Something is alarmingly disturbing about that guy.

Their conversation still played in Brent's head when the doors opened to the 14th floor. Stationed in the center of the room sat a stout-faced receptionist. Instantly aware this woman would die before she allowed a stranger into Evan Holcomb's office, Brent moved toward her desk.

Eyeing Brent from head to toe, glasses perched on the end of her nose, the woman launched into her well-rehearsed interrogation.

"May I help you, sir? This floor is for invited guests only. Do you have an appointment?" her face scrunched in disapproval.

This is going to be more complicated than I anticipated.

Issuing his warmest, most disarming smile, Brent spoke, "Morning. My name is Brent Scott. I would like to speak to Mr. Holcomb, please."

The assistant's lips pursed in a show of dominance as she uttered.

"I'm sorry. No one sees Mr. Holcomb without an appointment, and at present, you are not on my calendar for today." Her eyes peered over the top of her glasses.

"No, ma'am, I don't have an appointment. But if you could tell Mr. Holcomb, I'm here. I am relatively sure he will have time for me."

The woman's eyebrows arched in skepticism. Then, as she picked up the phone to notify Evan, his office door pitched open.

Out walked a man full of confidence and determination. Evan's six-foot frame filled the doorway and exuded strength. His broad shoulders and stance were indicative of a gladiator ready for battle. Brent squelched any doubt that Holcomb was incapable of protecting himself or Leah.

"Well, Mr. Scott, what are you doing here? I trust there are no issues back in Bridgeport that warrant your visit." Evan muttered.

"My work has me in Charlotte for a few days, so I thought it might be beneficial for us to have a brief one-on-one chat. Unfortunately, we didn't have a chance to talk during my visit to Bridgeport." Brent knew Evan would talk with him. Evan would be too curious to deny his request.

Extending an arm toward the door, Evan ushered Brent into the office. "Please come in. Joan, normal protocol, okay."

"Yes, of course. I'll hold all calls except for one should it occur." The woman returned to her other tasks, either unfazed or oblivious to the apparent tension circulating between the two men.

Brent entered the lush executive suite on guard, unsure of Evan's open welcome. He cleared his throat. "Thanks for seeing me today. Leah informed me that you were back in Charlotte. She also told me about the disturbing phone call she received." Brent sank back into the leather chair as Evan moved to a seat behind the large mahogany desk. Once comfortable, Brent continued. "I have to be honest. I'm getting a little concerned for Leah's safety. It would be beneficial if you could tell me your side of the story."

Evan leaned back in his chair, his tone turning defensive, "I'm unaware of what you know, Mr. Scott, but this involves our two companies. I am not sure the matter should be important to you. I'm aware the two of you are friends and are concerned for her safety. But let me assure you, no one, and I mean no one, will harm Leah while I'm around."

"Evan.... do you mind if I call you Evan?" Brent questioned.

"By all means," Evan retorted.

"Evan, I believe you would do everything in your power to ensure Leah's safety. I'm also aware that you're more than capable of protecting her under certain circumstances. However, it appears the threats point toward you and your company. With that in mind, let's be clear." Brent leaned forward to drive his point home. "Leah's more than just a friend to me, much more. If the caller had his way, the closer Leah gets to you, the greater her risk of harm. She's an extraordinary woman. I don't want her to get hurt, and if I'm correct, she could also be more than a friend to you. Am I correct?" Brent leaned forward, closing the gap between the two men.

"Since we are on a first-name basis... Brent. I, too, am aware you hold Leah in high regard. It was undeniable from the moment we met. Unfortunately, that's not something easy to conceal. Once you meet Leah, she's a hard woman to forget."

"Frankly, Brent, I've protected myself for years from caring about anyone other than my immediate family. However, meeting Leah has changed my perspective. With that said, it appears we have a problem." Evan steepled his fingers in front of his mouth. "We've both made the mistake of falling for the same woman. However, I may have a solution if you agree."

Brent hesitated, waiting for the inspired solution Evan had devised in 30 seconds, "I'm listening."

"We have to allow Leah to decide which one of us she prefers. Then, once the merger is complete and all danger has subsided, Leah's heart will lead her in one direction or the other. After that, there'll be no need for a debate."

Brent was impressed. Evan Holcomb never suggested he would utilize his money or influence to sway Leah in his direction. Instead, it appeared he only wanted the best for Leah.

"I have to admit. I like you, Evan, and I actually agree with your solution. But I do need to tell you, I won't give up trying to persuade her to choose me."

"And neither will I," Evan quipped.

Rising from their chairs, each man extended their hand, indicative of an old-fashioned gentleman's agreement.

"Now, Evan, why don't we compare notes? Let's figure out how we can capture this nut job." Evan agreed with Brent's sentiment and pointed him in the direction of a conference room.

Brent left Evan Holcomb's office feeling accomplished and optimistic. He and Evan understood the rules. Leah would make her own decisions regarding her love life, and they would keep her safe. Secretly, each understood the other would do everything possible to sway her heart in their direction.

Regrettably, their brainstorming session had failed to produce a definitive suspect. They were back at the drawing board without credible evidence pointing to a specific competitor. Brent knew breaching policy to advise Evan of the airline threat would only worsen matters. He would continue to rely on the explosion and Leah's phone call to gather additional clues.

Brent beamed as he strolled out of the building, quite confident after his one big takeaway from the meeting with Evan Holcomb - he'd scored his "plus one" invitation to the gala.

CHAPTER TWENTY-FIVE

Watts Enterprises hummed with excitement in preparation for the executive gala in Charlotte. Leah, Rhonda, and Carol flopped down in the stiff cafeteria chairs simultaneously. Exhaustion and apprehension absorbed their essence. Carol's face, tense with worry and dread, propelled Rhonda into a tangent.

"This is ridiculous. Here we sit, grown women, acting like schoolchildren. Carol, you need to get over the fact that you have to attend the gala and focus on the idea that we all need new dresses. What woman doesn't love to shop for something new?" Rhonda's blunt statement brought Carol to tears. Carol dabbed at the droplets, straining to hold back the flood, waiting to escape.

"Carol, don't cry. The gala is our chance to live like celebrities. You could meet lots of new people in Charlotte. It'll be like walking the red carpet in Hollywood. Plus, we'll all be there together to support one another." Leah smiled her sweetest smile as an encouragement to Carol to think positively.

"I hear what you're saying, both of you, but it still doesn't quiet my nerves." Carol's voice cracked with emotion. "I would love a new dress, but let's face it, where will we find something glamourous in Bridgeport?"

She counted silently, awaiting their reply. "There, silence from you both. How am I supposed to remain calm when neither of you can answer a simple question? This is so not happening!" Tears streamed down her cheeks once again.

"We can drive to Baton Rouge a few days before our flight and find something there. It will be a wonderful girls' adventure. Come on, Carol. Stop crying and say yes. Besides, I'm ecstatic about who might be in Charlotte. I hope they resemble their hot boss. I want to be ravishing. Say yes, or we'll have to leave you. It's just that simple." Rhonda's harsh words expressed her exasperation with Carol.

"Leave it to you, Rhonda; always trying to find an eligible bachelor. Ok, I'll go." Carol huffed.

Jumping out of her seat, Rhonda squealed with joy so loudly that everyone in the cafeteria turned their way. Shrugging her shoulders, Rhonda flicked her hands outward, urging the other employees to mind their own business.

"Besides, it's not like I have a choice anyway, so I may as well look my best." Carol lifted her head high, sporting a renewed sense of purpose.

"It will be fun. You'll see, and we promise not to leave you alone at the gala. Right, Rhonda?" Dragging out the syllables of each word to make a point, Leah's eyes turned to Rhonda.

"Oh yeah, right, Leah. We promise; providing a hot guy doesn't sweep me off my feet!" They all laughed because they were well aware Rhonda spoke truthfully.

After a delightful lunch, Leah decided to handle the next task at hand. She dreaded talking to Charlie Ashby. Leah liked Charlie's perky attitude and quirkiness. On the other hand, Charlie's inquisitive nature posed a problem.

Their meeting would only reinforce Charlie's earlier suspicions, but it could also prove very beneficial. Drawing a deep breath, Leah dialed Charlie's number. Just as Leah entered the last digit, her cell phone rang. Chills ran down her back.

What if it's him again?

Consumed with fear, she glanced at the telephone number. Charlie's call would need to wait.

Filled with relief, Leah answered, "Well, hello, stranger. How are things in the big city?"

"Honestly, they would be much better if you were in the big city with me," Evan uttered.

"Please tell me everything is okay in Charlotte. You're not calling with bad news, right?"

"Ms. Reynolds, do I detect worry in your voice? You wouldn't be concerned about me, would you?" Evan teased.

"No, no bad news. But I'm sorry to say no good news either. We've been unsuccessful in finding a lead here. Don't worry. I'll continue searching. Now, how are you and John? No problems there, I presume?" His questions begged for encouraging answers.

"John is fine. Problems? I'm happy to say my biggest problem at the moment is trying to find a dress for the gala in a town like Bridgeport. Carol and Rhonda are experiencing the same dilemma. You men have it so easy. A black tuxedo, fresh haircut, and you're dashing in the matter of an hour." Leah laughed.

"Yeah, a good black tux, and we all look like the same penguin," he joked.

"Besides, everyone knows that the men aren't the main attraction. It's the beautiful women who adorn their arm that makes the evening more enjoyable. I have an idea. What if I could help you out with your wardrobe predicament? Are you willing to trust me?"

Puzzled, Leah pursued the idea, "Of course, I trust

you. I'm just not sure you realize what you're getting yourself into by offering to help."

"Don't worry about a thing. Consider your attire for the evening handled. I will take care of everything. Tell Carol and Rhonda not to worry either. I'll forward the details when they are available. All of you are going to be gorgeous. Not that you need a new dress to make you that way. You are always beautiful."

"Stop. Flattery will get you everywhere! It sounds like you have a trick up your sleeve, Mr. Holcomb."

"I most certainly do, Ms. Reynolds. I hope you like it."

Evan's soft, deep voice peppered with sincerity caused Leah's heart to flutter. Memories of his passionate kiss flooded her mind.

"Leah, are you there? Don't tell me I've left you speechless again?"

"Umm. No, I'm listening. But I must admit your wardrobe surprise has me quite mystified."

Leah directed their conversation to business, unwilling to linger on her previous thoughts.

"On a business note, just before you called, I was in the process of contacting Charlie Ashby. Charlie's experience may be our best option for finding a lead. Although, I'm not sure we should be entirely transparent with her. Too much information may cause an uproar. Nevertheless, I'll do my best to meet with her today and call you with the outcome tonight. That is if I'm not going to interrupt any plans you may have this evening." Saturated with curiosity, Leah paused.

"I only have one plan for tonight, and that's to await your call. My plans would include much more if you were here working with me. However, since that's not the case, I'll talk with you later this evening."

"All right then, enough of your plans, business-related or otherwise. We will talk soon."

Their conversation ended with images of Evan Holcomb in his masculine glory. Leah wasn't sure she would object to his "proposed" plans. Were these vivid scenes that played in her head attributed to a sense of vulnerability? Or had she somehow developed feelings for Evan?

But why do I feel as though I'm betraying Brent somehow?

Leah closed the male drama door quickly and moved on to Charlie Ashby.

Charlie Ashby didn't understand what prompted Leah Reynolds to contact her. She only knew her instincts surrounding the bombing were right on track. Charlie's previous career in New York accorded her the keen ability to pick up on hidden signals during investigations. Signs most people preferred to remain suppressed.

Leah's request for acquiring a forensic artist indicated something or someone had made an impression on her. Charlie decided to honor Leah's request. Watts Enterprises and Holcomb Industries had a secret, and she needed to find out what it was.

She turned to a former colleague for help. A renowned artist in Chicago. Best known for solving cold cases. Anything Leah remembered, down to the smallest detail, would be captured in black and white.

Two o'clock could not come soon enough.

Charlie entered Leah's office with an increased sense of urgency. Although she'd met with Leah just a few short days ago, it was abundantly clear that the strained look on Leah's face warranted an immediate action.

"Hello, Leah. I must admit I was a little surprised by

your call earlier today. During our last meeting, you informed me Watts Industries would be unable to provide any details regarding the explosion. And now you're requesting the assistance of a forensic artist. You must realize I'm a little suspicious that you know more than you stated." Leah remained silent, biting her bottom lip.

"Before we start this process," Charlie continued, unperturbed by Leah's restraint. "I need your confirmation of complete disclosure. I'll need all of the facts, not just the convenient ones. All of them. That's the only way I can help. I take it you want my help since you called me." Charlie stood her ground, determined not to budge an inch until she received an honest answer.

Leah cleared her throat. "Yes, Ms. Ashby, I called you. We desperately need your assistance. First, however, I've been instructed to clarify that anything we discuss remains confidential. What I'm going to tell you must not leave this office. If this information leaked out, we would have a crisis on our hands that would affect this company, Holcomb Industries, and hundreds of people. Do I have your promise?"

"I've solved dozens of police cases that required the same confidentiality. I assure you whatever you tell me will not be released to the public or anyone else unless you authorize the release. Now explain why you need a sketch artist and start from the beginning."

Charlie listened intently to Leah recount the nightmare she, Evan, and John were experiencing. Amazed by the honesty with which Leah divulged the background information, Charlie understood the reason for their fear. Charlie's coaching helped Leah recall several imperative details. After hours of discussion, the sketch artist provided a realistic composite of their only suspect. Charlie saw the cold, callous attitude portrayed in black and white. Determination, bitterness, and anger filled his face. Charlie had seen this before, and she was confident the man Leah described wouldn't stop until he completed his mission.

Unfortunately, Charlie agreed with Leah that all roads led back to Evan Holcomb and a jealous competitor.

"You know, Leah, we're fortunate you kept such a vivid picture in your mind of this guy. I'm sure it seems like a slight lead, but a small one is better than nothing."

"His face haunts me whenever I close my eyes. I don't think I'll ever forget his face. Seeing it on paper only reminds me how real this is. He's out there somewhere planning his next move. You can count on it. Remember, Ms. Ashby, that sketch must remain hidden from prying eyes."

"You have my word. It will not leave my sight. I wish you'd made me aware of all this during our earlier meetings. Sadly, we've lost valuable time. Promise me you'll notify me if anything else happens. An objective opinion can be more helpful than you realize. Cases like this tend to lead you back to a close connection between the offender and the victim. By the way, please start calling me Charlie. Ms. Ashby makes me sound old." Charlie giggled.

"I promise I'll tell you if anything happens, Charlie. I will be forwarding the sketch to one other person outside our group. He's a good friend who's familiar with everything happening. I feel quite sorry for him. Poor guy, he was thrust into this situation by default. His name is Brent Scott."

"That's interesting in itself. Thrust is a thought-provoking word, Leah. Do you trust Mr. Scott?"

"Oh yes. I trust Brent completely." Leah spoke without hesitation. "Anyway, the gala is coming soon, and we'll have something to celebrate. I'm not sure about you, but I'm ready for a party. Anything to change the mood and take our minds off all this."

"Agreed. A change of scenery will do us all some good. I'm looking forward to it. I probably won't see you again until then. Keep me abreast of any changes, and I will do the same."

Oh, how I love a mystery, Charlie admitted to herself. Her small-town reporter job had just placed her smack in the middle of a good one.

Leah's confidence level soared several notches after the meeting with Charlie. Acquiring her assistance seemed to be the right move.

Leah stared at the sketch Charlie placed on her desk. She couldn't deny the fear that engulfed her every time she looked into his eyes. But on the flip side, the drawing also evoked a strange sense of familiarity. Leah struggled to recall if, by chance, she had seen him somewhere before this nightmare started.

The bleached tips of hair encircled his narrow eyes, forcing instant attention to their mystic meaning. Leah's mother had always told her, "the eyes are the windows to a person's soul." Shivering, she knew this person's soul reeked of darkness and wanted to figure out why.

Leah contemplated calling Evan first, but her heart ushered her in another direction. Her stomach quivered at the thought of talking to him. Ripples of excitement rushed through her veins when she dialed the number. The pleasant twinges of excitement that had lain dormant for so long now had her thinking of his kisses. She couldn't deny the instant attraction she felt when Brent picked her up off the floor of that silly airplane. Joy surged through her at the sound of his voice.

"Hello there. I was just thinking about you." Brent cheerfully answered.

Her heart leaped. He'd given her the perfect answer. "Really, should I be afraid to ask you exactly what you're thinking? Considering our time spent together, that could be a loaded question."

"You're right about that one. I wouldn't call our time together conventional. But I would call it enjoyable, even if there were extenuating circumstances. Do I need to give you a hint?"

"Maybe you better. I'm at a bit of a loss," Leah searched for an answer.

"It involves you, me, a quiet corner in a quaint little cafe having a glass of wine." Dead silence filled the phone.

"Don't tell me you have forgotten that you promised to have a glass of wine with me while you're in Charlotte?"

"No, of course, I haven't forgotten. I was unsure if your work schedule permitted us to be in Charlotte at the same time." Brent's reference to "wine" forced Leah to gasp for air. Memories of her conversation with Amber flooded her mind.

Leah stammered for words. "It would be my pleasure. Do you have a particular night in mind?"

"Well, if it meets your approval, I'd like to see you as soon as possible. Unfortunately, we were unable to finish our conversation before I needed to leave Bridgeport."

Conversation, what conversation?

Leah only remembered the undeniable, luscious kiss they shared before Brent drove off.

Is he referring to our kiss?

"I'm flying in early Thursday morning. We can meet Thursday night if you would like. Do you have a place picked out?" Leah tried with all her might to calm both her nerves and her voice.

"That sounds great to me. There is no place in mind yet, but I will check some things out and find the perfect spot. Tell me where you're staying, and I'll pick you up."

Leah's anxiety skyrocketed. If she allowed Brent to pick her up, trouble would immediately follow.

Since security was an issue, Evan had insisted that

she, John, and Martha stay at his apartment while in town. However, Leah knew allowing Brent to pick her up there could cause problems.

"We're still ironing out the final details. What if I let you know?" Leah muttered cautiously.

"I'll await your direction. But, Leah, there's something else you need to tell me, isn't there?"

Had her hesitancy placed Brent on alert?

"How can you always tell when I have something else on my mind? This is the third time you sensed my need to tell you something. Do you have someone spying on me, Brent Scott?"

"If I wanted to spy on you, I wouldn't send someone else to do it. I'd have the pleasure of performing that task myself. I have a heightened sense of awareness, that's all. Go ahead, tell me, what's up?" Brent awaited Leah's confession.

"Okay. Okay. I've collaborated with a local reporter and sketch artist to render a composite of the suspect from the bombing. The drawing is strictly from memory, but I think it is pretty accurate. I want to share it with you if you're interested. I'm sorry you've been immediately drawn into this terrible situation by default, but I thought you might like to see his face." Leah waited, unsure if the offer overwhelmed him or enticed him.

He may never call again. Or maybe he'd run. Why would anyone want to be involved in this mess?

"Please, send it over. I'd love to look at the sketch and your recollection of the man's facial details. Are you alright with all this? Everything comes back to the forefront when placed before you in black and white. Those memories can be very unsettling."

"Do you recall ever seeing him before? For this man to warn you of impending danger tells me you know him or mean something to him. Could it be someone from your past?"

"Brent, the eyes look so familiar. I can't place the face as a whole, but those eyes keep haunting me. I'm certain I've seen him somewhere. But where?" Remembering terrified her.

Do I know him?

"I'm sure we will figure it out soon. Nevertheless, it does concern me that you're in Bridgeport, and I'm so far away. Should anything else happen, I pray it doesn't, but I won't be able to help you, Leah. We're just getting to know each other. I don't want this to end. So be cautious. Don't assume anything." Brent's cautious, caring nature resonated in his words.

"I'll be fine, Brent. Can I tell you I feel the same way? I'd like to spend more time with you too. Besides, you're my guardian angel, remember! I can't let you off the hook that easy. I'll see you in a few days. And Brent, thanks for the moral support. It means a lot."

"I'm always here. See you soon, Leah."

Smiling, Leah ended the call with a lighter spirit. The promise of their plans in Charlotte carried her through the day.

Brent hung up the phone, astonished that one woman in a dead-end town could acquire more intel on the case than Steve Alexander's entire office. Leah was unique, indeed. Every time Brent heard her voice, he detected a sense of confidence. Leah's innocent sex appeal had cast a spell over him. It was an unwelcome addition in the beginning. However, Brent realized that was no longer true. He vowed to make the most of his time with Leah in Charlotte and turned his attention to the new email on the screen.

When Brent opened the message Leah forwarded of the artist's sketch, his eyes sprang open. The figure carried an uncanny resemblance to Troy Marshall. The drawing wasn't an exact match to Marshall, but there were definite similarities.

Why wouldn't Leah remember Troy's face?

He knew Leah remained committed to the familiarity in the eyes. But, perhaps she had overlooked the connection to Holcomb Industries and Marshall.

It all made sense to Brent. He was suspicious of Troy Marshall from the beginning. But what were his motives? Evan gave Troy his start in the business and was more than a boss. He was his friend. Evan befriended all of his employees to a certain extent. The camaraderie they shared ensured the success of the business. Hopefully, Evan would contact Brent once he found out Leah shared the copy.

CHAPTER TWENTY-SIX

Evan breathed a sigh of relief. With his sister Pam's help, they persuaded Suzanne Harper and Kimberly Vega to style the ladies of Watts Industries for the gala. It was no easy feat convincing the world-renowned fashion designer and Hollywood's famous makeup artist to assist him. The corporate gala was not an event that generally commanded their attention. Hollywood and New York were their prime locations, not Charlotte. Evan would never finish paying this debt back to Pam. He knew it. In the end, he felt it would all be worth it.

With Leah's surprise secured, Evan turned to the unpleasant business of increasing security for the gala. His responsibility to protect everyone from the imposing danger that faced them weighed on him. Additional protection deterred the average paparazzi on any given day, but they were dealing with a madman. A madman who was unconcerned about spectators or crowds. And who seemed to love a challenge.

He struggled to swallow the idea Brent Scott would be in attendance but admitted an extra set of trained eyes was a helpful asset. The gala offered significant PR for the city and the company. However, the evening also carried troublesome opportunities should their "friend" wish to take advantage of one. The additional security provided a limited amount of extra protection.

Evan focused relentlessly on the sketch. The charcoal

drawing rendered an ominous-looking soul with deep grooves in the forehead and a broad nose. He tossed around the idea that the picture vaguely resembled one of his employees. His theories regarding why this employee wanted to stop the merger were unfounded. There was no logical reason for his involvement in something of this magnitude. After all, it was just a sketch drawn from Leah's memory. Maybe Leah gave the artist an inaccurate description of the assailant. The explosion occurred several days ago. Leah's mind may have played tricks on her. He strained to produce a legitimate reason for his defense of the employee; however, he would keep a close eye on his suspect and everyone else in attendance. Frustrated, Evan moved on to other details for the gala.

Leah was excited about the gala even though she didn't want to admit it. This time tomorrow, they would all be in Charlotte enjoying a little downtime. She hoped.

Evan went out of his way to provide attire for the ladies of Watts Industries. She couldn't wait to tell Carol and Rhonda about their enormous surprise. Pampering by a famous fashion designer would be as much fun as the party itself. Evan even encouraged Leah to invite Amber to the gala when he found out she would be in town. Leah had to hand it to him; he wanted to make everyone from Bridgeport feel comfortable in his city. By all appearances, Evan only desired the best for everyone. Why else would he rescue a small remote little company from the brink of disaster? Evan Holcomb was a rare man, indeed. He possessed the heart of a lamb and the body of a lion. The deadly combination could set any girl's heart aflutter.

Leah struggled to decide who made her heart flutter

more. Evan brought out her practical business side; organized, structured, secure, and sexy in a subtle way. Brent was all risk, spontaneous, and oozing testosterone. How in the world did she get into such a dilemma? She'd never been one to play the field. Dating numerous guys was just not her cup of tea. Now two unbelievably handsome men interested in her simultaneously was almost more than she could handle. A decision must come soon. Fortunately, she had a plan. And the plan would be put into action this weekend.

Leah stretched, forcing herself up from the comfort of the plush sofa. She needed to start planning her attire for the trip. Every single article of clothing she owned lay strewn around her bedroom floor. The winner was a little black dress. Quite an out-of-character purchase for Leah at the time. The sheath's tight fit, sculpted waist, and low neckline screamed, "Look at me." Leah knew if she wanted attention, this dress commanded it. Her black heels and modest jewelry rounding out the ensemble finished the look. Leah prayed she'd be ready to handle the results the dress could provide.

Due to their varied schedules, the Watts Enterprise staff would be flying to Charlotte at different intervals. Leah wasn't brave enough to tell Carol and Rhonda why she wouldn't be flying later that evening with them. She loved them, but some things needed to remain private.

With her wardrobe selected and her travel plans for the morning complete, a sense of accomplishment seized her. Leah focused on sleep.

Leah felt positively euphoric as she stepped onto the plane. There, in the aisle, stood Amber. Noting the presence of the other, simultaneously, the women screamed and ran to hug each other.

"What are you doing here? I thought your flight didn't leave until this evening. I'm so excited to see you. Now I don't have to call you tonight. I have a surprise for you." Leah giggled.

"The airline needed me for an earlier flight. Call me tonight, for what? What surprise? You certainly have my curiosity up, Leah Reynolds. I'll come back once we're in the air. Hang tight." Amber issued a warm smile and moved on to help the other passengers.

Leah scanned the plane, familiarizing herself with the passengers around her, when she spotted a bearded gentleman sitting in the back of the aircraft. Something about the man garnered her attention. His persona of calmness lent no credibility to the sneaky look masking his face. Instead, his expression brought back memories from Leah's childhood, flooding her mind of being a kid in school, listening to the jeers of classmates, "I know something you don't know."

He appeared unfazed by Leah's stares. Smiling at her, he nodded. Fear clutched Leah's heart. She was too far away to obtain a more unmistakable look, but something deep inside her screamed it was him.

Is that the guy from our sketch?

The beard confused her, and there was no way to tell if it was a disguise or natural. Leah could not be sure unless she looked deep into those dark eyes. Her body stiffened, unable to move a muscle. The man smirked as he stared in her direction while her thoughts ran wild.

Does he think I recognize him?

His face indicated if so, he didn't care. Leah needed to find a way to get closer to him. It was the only way she could be sure.

Amber bolted to Leah's seat immediately after takeoff. "Now, tell me all about this big surprise. I love surprises, most of the time."

Leah remained silent and pale despite Amber's excited rambling.

"Hey, don't tell me you have air sickness. You're white as a sheet. Can I bring you a bottle of water or something?" Anxiously awaiting her reply, Amber touched Leah's hand.

Leah gathered her thoughts quickly. Amber mustn't be involved in this ugly mess. Sharing her concerns about the other passenger would place Amber in danger too.

"Oh, I'm sorry. No, I'm fine. Too much work and stress lately. Back to your surprise. When you told me you would be in Charlotte this weekend, I took the liberty of making plans for you. I hope you don't mind." A wicked grin crossed Leah's face.

Amber placed her hands firmly on her hips. "Leah Reynolds, please don't tell me you've set me up on some silly blind date with one of your co-workers.".

"No, something even better. How would you like to attend the corporate festivities tomorrow night in a gown designed by one of the fashion industry's top designers?"

"What? Are you kidding me? That's not something you should tease about, Leah." Amber's eyes widened with anticipation.

"I'm not teasing. Evan set the whole thing up for some of us, and when he found out that you would be in town, he wanted me to make sure you participated in the fun. So are you in?"

"In, are you kidding? Tell me when, where, and I'll be there. I'll have to make sure I thank Evan for his generous invitation. It will be a first for me. Leah, I don't know how to thank you." She squealed.

"You're welcome. We haven't known each other very long, but I feel like we're old friends. Everyone will have so much fun."

Without warning, the plane violently jerked before

Amber could respond, hurling her to the ceiling and then slamming her to the floor. Passengers screamed while the aircraft lurched in a sharp descent. Amber promptly regained her footing, directing all passengers to fasten their seatbelts. The captain's voice boomed over the speakers assuring everyone things were under control. They were merely experiencing some minor engine trouble.

Leah turned to Amber for direction, but her expression said all Leah needed to know. She hastily buckled her seatbelt as Amber struggled to help other passengers. Unsure about what caused the engine trouble, Leah imagined who created them. It couldn't be a coincidence. She contemplated turning to see if the man remained seated when she heard a deep voice from behind.

"Don't turn around. There's no need to worry. I would never dream of crashing the plane with us on it. I only want to send another message to the right people. I instructed you to remove yourself from the situation, and you haven't done that. Consider yourself lucky. Next time I won't be responsible for your safety. Be smart, and don't tell anyone I'm on this plane if you value your friendship with that pretty flight attendant. It would be a shame for something to happen to her. Now sit back and relax. Things will straighten themselves out in just a few minutes."

Paralyzed with fear, Leah couldn't utter a word. When she mustered her courage enough to turn around, he was gone. The plane was still in a panic, making it impossible for her to remove her seat belt and find him. Time moved so slowly, she felt as if she were in a vortex. What seemed like an hour for the captain to regain control was, in reality, just minutes. The passengers listened intently as the captain explained a slight electrical problem had caused the engine to malfunction. Things were under control, and their flight would arrive in Charlotte on time.

When she could, Leah turned to view the rear of the plane. The vision of him sitting there smiling like the cat that swallowed the canary angered her, but her hands were tied. Now was not the time to alert the authorities. Amber, along with countless others, remained in danger. She would never risk the life of her friend. Leah stayed quiet as requested for now, but more importantly, she'd never forget the sound of his voice.

Brent sat with Steve Alexander and Cooper, reviewing their notes and the artist's composite when a staff member burst into the room. "Sir, an urgent call requires your immediate attention." The young messenger's demeanor proclaimed "trouble."

Snatching the phone from its cradle, Steve listened closely before roaring, "Keep your eyes on the flight all the way into the airport. Are you sure the captain feels things are now under control? Notify me the second the flight lands. Find me the passenger list ASAP." Steve slammed the phone down.

Brent's senses heightened when he overheard the end of Steve's conversation. This maniac was going to make good on his word.

Expressionless, Steve looked to Brent and Cooper. "There's been an occurrence on Flight 1020 from Baton Rouge to Charlotte. The captain reported an electrical malfunction to the tower. The traffic controller's impression at the time was that it was serious. Then within minutes, per the captain, the problem corrected itself."

A staff member hurriedly returned with the passenger list. Jerking the list from her hand, Steve began reviewing the names. A look of shock and horror engulfed his face.

"Steve, did you say Baton Rouge to Charlotte? Who's on the list? Steve, is she on that plane?" Brent bellowed in anguish. Afraid to discover the answer.

"They're both on the plane," Steve uttered grimly.

"Both? What do you mean both?" Brent pounded his fists on the desk. His voice escalated into a yell.

"Amber and Leah are on that plane. Amber diverted from her normal layover. She was supposed to be on a return flight to Charlotte tomorrow."

Pure horror rolled over Brent's face. If he had not asked Leah to arrive a day early for their date, she wouldn't be in harm's way. It was bad enough that Leah was on the plane, but his sister was too. He figured it was their guy. How the man managed to short out the electrical system remained a mystery. One thing was for sure, if Amber and Leah were hurt, he would kill this guy with his bare hands when he found him.

"Brent, I know what you're thinking. The captain assured the tower everything was under control. They're being watched like hawks all the way in. We'll find out what happened. Everyone on that flight is going to be fine." Steve tried everything he could to reassure his friend.

"I know why he did this. He needed to make good on his original threat. To show that he's still in control. He's playing the dominance game with us. He's letting us see firsthand that he dictates what happens next, not us." Brent had seen these tactics before. Someone always played the superiority game.

Steve urged Cooper, "Get to those monitors. You've seen the sketch of this guy. If he's anywhere around this airport, I want him located now."

"I got it, boss. If he's here, I'll find him. I promise you that." Cooper didn't walk. He ran out the door.

"Brent, it's a good thing you brought in a copy of the sketch. At least we have something to reference. It may not be our guy, but it gives us an excellent place to start. Stop worrying. They're going to be all right."

Brent's face filled with worry. "Steve, you realize I'm

going to have to tell her what I do for a living after this. I can't lie to her. Our relationship is just getting started. I care way too much about this girl to build a relationship on lies. I'll swear her to secrecy, but I'm going to tell her. If you're not ok with that, you need to tell me now." He waited for Steve's answer.

"Hey, this is the first mention of a relationship I've heard about from you in years. No way I'm interfering with that. You've been by yourself far too long. Swear her to secrecy. If she cannot abide by that, you understand she'll be putting her life in more danger if she tells anyone. It'll have to be a judgment call on your part, but I trust you, Brent. You'll make the right decision. Now get down to the terminal; that plane will be arriving soon. Keep me informed on what you find out from the captain and crew."

"On my way." Brent raced to the terminal. If he happened to catch a glimpse of their man, all hell was going to break loose.

Who does he think he is, putting all those lives in danger?

As the plane's doors opened, passengers rushed onto the walkway. Each clueless to the degree of peril they were in during the flight.

Where are they?

Brent panicked.

Unwilling to wait any longer, Brent moved in the opposite direction of the departing passengers forcing his way onto the plane. With no sign of Amber or Leah, he entered the aircraft's interior, pushing his way back to the crew area. All of the flight attendants gathered in the rear of the plane. Amber stood in the middle with Leah, just to her right, chattering away about their experience.

Brent walked straight to Leah, hoisted her into his arms, and kissed her passionately, not caring who saw them. When he eventually released her, her look of surprise spoke volumes. Desire, shock, fear, and relief all rolled into one stretched across her face. Brent then grabbed Amber, hugged her tightly, and planted a kiss right on her lips.

Dazed and confused, Leah stood still, her mouth gaped open.

"Brent, what are you doing here? How did you know we were on this flight? But, wait, you better check on Leah. I think she's in shock. Maybe she requires mouth-to-mouth." Amber burst into laughter.

"Amber, why are you laughing at this? He's playing both of us. Who walks on a plane and kisses two women at the same time? By the way, how are you even here right now?" The look on Leah's face announced her difficulty in processing the situation, which Brent guessed was also preventing her from speaking intelligently.

"Leah, it's perfectly all right. Although, I must admit he kissed you much differently than he kissed me."

"Are you serious? You're questioning the intensity of the kiss versus the fact that he did it at all." Her eyes flashed daggers in Brent's direction.

"Brent, we need to tell her, now." Brent nodded his head in agreement.

"Tell me what?" Her arms crossed in anger.

"Leah, I have to talk to you. Privately" Brent gently tugged her arm, leading her toward the exit when Amber's voice echoed from the back."I love you, Brent. Leah, I'll call you later."

Leah walked toward the small airport office in a trance. Amber's admission that she loved Brent and the joyous kiss he issued her placed Leah in a whirlwind of emotions. She blindly followed Brent through the door, unsure of what he would say once inside. In mere seconds,

Leah found her back against the wall. Brent's arms extended to either side of her shoulders, leaving no room for escape. Inches away, his eyes peered into hers, searching her soul, reading her mind. No longer able to hide the attraction wrapped with fury and betrayal in her eyes, Leah blinked, restraining a tear.

The sudden softness in Brent's eyes carried a measure of understanding. Bending, he kissed her softly. Wrapped in the subtle affection that flickered between them, Leah submitted to his kiss. When their lips parted, she knew it was now her time to issue a warning.

"I hate to admit, while that was extremely pleasant, it doesn't dismiss what just happened on the plane. If you were going to play two people at one time, why would you pick Amber? She's become like a sister to me."

Leah felt like such a hypocrite. Wasn't she playing the same game between Evan and Brent? The cold hard reality of the situation slammed into her like a blast of arctic air. Not until she listened to her own words did she realize the predicament she'd placed herself in. Sorrow and shame filled her as she lowered her head.

Lifting her chin, so she had to look at him, Brent began, "Leah, listen to me. It's not what you think, honest. I have a lot to tell you, but first, you must promise that our conversation will not leave this room. If you think you cannot uphold that promise, I'm afraid we have nothing more to talk about." A look of sincerity crossed his face.

"Talk about an ultimatum. I'll never understand why you picked Amber over me if I say no. On the other hand, if I say yes, I'm afraid I will learn something that breaks my heart." Fighting back the tears, Leah steadied herself.

"I'd prefer not to break your heart only to make you happy, but I can't lie. What I tell you may place you in more danger. I'll leave the decision up to you. I can walk away now, and we never have to see each other again if that is what you choose."

Leah gazed into Brent's eyes. "Well, I've never been a huge risk-taker. I always figured there were too many things that could go wrong. My entire life, I've stayed with the safe decisions. But my heart tells me it's time I started playing the odds. Besides, I can't imagine not seeing you again. Be honest and forthcoming, don't leave out any of the details. If I'm going to promise complete secrecy, I want to know everything." She breathed deeply, bracing herself for whatever he had to say.

Brent leaned into her, wrapping Leah in a bear hug, a radiant smile replacing the stern set of features from a moment before.

"You have no idea how glad I am to hear you say that. You might want to sit down. This could take a few minutes. I'm not sure where I should start."

Leah poised herself for the onslaught of bad news.

"First, let me say, Amber wasn't aware that I was seeing you until just a few days ago. Seeing you, um, that has a funny ring to it. I'm not sure how to categorize our relationship. In Amber's defense, she wanted to tell you immediately. But due to the nature of my job, she knew telling you would break protocol." Brent paused.

"Your job, what do you mean? Are you like some spy or something?" Leah struggled to comprehend.

"Umm… I'm a U.S. Air Marshall for the airlines. My anonymity is essential. Passengers can't find out who I am or what I do. If something were to happen, it's imperative people think I'm just another passenger. Without that, I'm a target and rendered completely ineffective. People's lives depend on me in a dangerous situation."

Things began to make sense as this first bit of information sank in. That's why all the flight attendants knew him. His charismatic behavior with them would fool anyone. She certainly believed his cover.

Clearing his throat, Brent continued. "There's more. If anyone knew my real identity and intended to harm me in any way, their first thought might be to hurt my family. Which is why we are so careful not to let anyone learn about the type of relationship we have."

"We…who is we?"

What was he talking about?

"You see, Amber and I are brother and sister," Brent admitted sheepishly.

"Amber is your sister!" Leah wanted to turn cartwheels over the news, but she decided not to let Brent off the hook that easy. Instead, her face contorted into a mask of anger.

"Please don't be mad at Amber. She had no idea that you two were going to become fast friends. It all happened so fast. Please tell me you understand why neither of us could tell you the truth." His eyes were pleading for understanding.

"I'm not mad at Amber. Really, I'm not. But you, Brent Scott, are another story." Brent bowed his head in anticipation of what would come next. Leah fought hard to maintain the ruse, only to be betrayed by the giggle that bubbled from her lips.

"I guess, now that I think about it, that beautiful smile of yours and those baby blue eyes should've been a dead giveaway. Besides, both of you are insanely gorgeous. I'm not sure why I didn't figure it out sooner." Leah erupted with laughter over the irony of the whole thing.

"Insanely gorgeous, huh?!" Deep chuckles rumbled in Brent's broad chest.

"Enough. I'm afraid I may have said too much already. Don't start inflating your ego with my words."

"Me, never. You should know better than that." His bright smile weakened her defenses.

"One thing I don't understand, how would knowing you and Amber are brother and sister put me in danger?"

"As I said, if there were any problems, someone might consider retaliating by harming the people close to me. All anyone needs to do is see how I look at you. Hurting you would be a deadly blow to me and possibly their first option."

Leah's willpower waned. His frank confession, coupled with those piercing blue eyes and pearly white smile, had her reaching for him. Her subtle kiss evoked a gasp of relief from Brent as he reciprocated with a deep kiss of his own. Leah drew back to take in the sight of this extraordinary man. Then, smiling, she returned to his arms and placed her head on his chest.

"Leah, one more thing. It's ironic how we met. Almost like fate or destiny. Are you ready to hear the rest?" Brent whispered.

"I said I wanted to know everything, so out with it."

Leah listened carefully to Brent's account of the past few weeks. He began with their chance meeting on the plane. Then, he recounted everything from the airline threat to the explosion in Bridgeport and the connection between the two companies. Images spun through Leah's mind.

"Leah, what is it? You look as though you've had a revelation of some sort. A very frightening one."

"Brent, the threat regarding one of the flights, was there a specific flight number or date mentioned in the threat?" She wondered if he would mention her flight number.

"No. Nothing specific related to flight numbers. Only the departure or arrival destination of Charlotte. Why?"

Leah began describing her frightening midair experience. The vulnerability she experienced when the cold, evil whisper rang in her ears from behind. How she was terrified to approach anyone, especially the authorities, fearing the maniac would make good on his threat to harm Amber.

Leah noticed an immediate shift in Brent's demeanor. Redness crept up his neck, inflaming his face in a visual display of anger and guilt.

"Don't worry. I'm fine; Amber's fine," Leah tried to reassure him. "The plane landed safely. I'm sure your co-workers will be able to obtain some evidence that brings you closer to catching this criminal."

"Let's hope they picked up something on the security monitors. Everyone was on high alert. I should've focused on my job instead of personal interests." His sense of guilt was evident in his words.

"As a passenger, I'm glad you were concerned for my safety. You were doing your job." But unfortunately, the statement didn't have the impact she'd hoped. Brent had become very distant.

"Let's go retrieve your bags and get you to your hotel. I still have a lot of work to do here. What time shall I pick you up this evening and where?"

"How does seven o'clock sound? I'll send you the address. John, Martha, and I are staying with Evan. That doesn't make you uncomfortable, does it?"

"No, not at all. Forward me the address. Now let's get you out of here." Leah stood waiting for a hug or something from him. Instead, Brent opened the door, escorted her to baggage claim, and placed her in a cab without a word. What changed from the time they had entered the small office? Brent seemed happy over the outcome of their discussion. Was it all a dream?

Confusion once more clouded Leah's thoughts.

Brent issued strict instructions to the taxi driver and sent Leah on her way. Watching Leah's cab depart from the airport brought him feelings of hurt and regret. He knew tonight with Leah would be his last. Memories of why he stayed single flooded his mind. His job demanded too much, and people were counting on him. Today only reinforced his theory. His preoccupation with Leah's safety had prevented him from searching for their man.

Yes, the best way to ensure Leah's safety was by never seeing her again. Of course, Evan Holcomb would be elated about his decision.

Brent reentered the terminal and hustled to reach the security office. "Cooper, stop what you're doing! You're looking for the wrong guy. Our suspect wore a disguise. Natural or fake, he now has a full black beard. Review the video footage for men with black beards but match the eyes to our sketch. Leah said he threatened her on the plane."

Steve's ears perked up. "Leah, what?"

"You heard me correctly. Our perp seated himself behind Leah issuing strict instructions. First, he reassured her he would never crash the plane with them on it. Secondly, our guy issued her another warning to remove herself from the merger. Finally, he forbade Leah to alert anyone about her situation. He threatened to harm Amber if she did. I promise both of you I will catch this maniac if it's the last thing I do. No one threatens the people I love and gets away with it."

Did I admit I love Leah?

Cooper and Steve's faces paled as they locked eyes.

"You guys get what I mean. Don't stand there with your mouths hanging open. Amber's my sister." Brent's face reddened from his admission.

Cooper mocked, "Yeah, sure, Brent, we get you. It's just Amber's safety that concerns you."

"Continue watching the monitors, Cooper. He may have picked up baggage, although I doubt it. He'd be crazy to check a bag. But, if we're lucky, we may catch a glimpse of him. Steve, what's next? How do you want us to proceed?"

"Sounds like you're on a good track, Brent. Let's examine the footage. It worries me that his actions reflect an untouchable attitude. He's daring and carefree at the same time. Not a good combination since fear and defeat typically never crosses the mind of someone like that. They have one goal: the success of their mission. We have to solve this mystery quickly."

"Don't worry; I plan to. These scare tactics have gone on way too long. Call me if you come up with any leads. I have a dinner engagement that's probably my last."

Cooper shrugged his shoulders, "What's that supposed to mean?"

"Nothing. I'll keep in touch." Brent left the office, dreading what must be done. Forgetting Leah Reynolds wasn't going to be easy. But it was definitely necessary.

CHAPTER TWENTY-SEVEN

Evan awaited Leah's arrival at the apartment with bated breath. Tonight offered the opportunity of an evening alone with Leah before John and Martha flew in tomorrow. It had been several weeks since their last meeting, and he was anxious to know if she missed him as much as he had her. The sound of the doorbell ringing pulled his mind back to the present. Evan jerked the door open, hoping to catch a joyous expression on Leah's face, but instead found one of despair and concern. She wandered through the door as the taxi driver placed her bags in the foyer. Without a word, she moved toward a chair.

"Well, hello. I'm glad to see you too!" Evan stared at her, curious about her mood.

"Oh, Evan. I apologize. I'm glad to see you. Thank you so much for your hospitality. You're so generous to open your home to us. John and Martha will be arriving early tomorrow morning." Leah slowly sank into the chair.

"Leah Reynolds. I know you well enough now to recognize when something is wrong. And something wrong."

Emotions played across Leah's face, hinting at some sort of inner turmoil. Evan intended to get to the bottom of it, but Leah sighed.

"My flight was a little rough, and I'm tired. That's all." She was a terrible liar avoiding direct eye contact with him.

"I don't believe that, but I'll let it go for now. Why don't I show you to your room? So you can rest some before we make arrangements for dinner."

Leah reached for a strand of hair rolling it between her fingers, answering hesitantly. "Evan, I'm afraid I already have dinner plans. Brent informed me he would be in town tonight, and we made plans several days ago. I hope you don't mind. I knew we would be attending the gala together. I'm sorry. I hope you don't think I'm unappreciative of your generosity."

"Please don't worry yourself. You're certainly not acting unappreciative. We have tomorrow night. Now let's get you to your room for some rest."

Evan returned to the foyer disheartened. His duel with Brent for Leah's affections would be more challenging than he anticipated.

Leah tossed and turned in the fluffy oversized king bed, but rest escaped her. The sudden shift in Brent's attitude lingered in her thoughts, causing her further distress.

Why would he turn on a dime like that?

Unwilling to surrender so quickly to the possibility of defeat, Leah jumped from the bed and pulled the secret weapon from her bag. There was no time for rest. Brent would arrive soon, and she needed to be ready.

As Leah rested, Evan's brain worked overtime. Brent must have called Leah on the same day of their meeting. Brent made it clear he wouldn't stand back and give Evan free rein with Leah. By golly, he meant every word. Things were about to get very complicated. Evan would not go down without a fight. Admittedly, Brent won tonight's battle. But tomorrow was the gala, and he would make the most of his time with Leah.

Once again, Evan answered the ringing doorbell, only this time, he wasn't eager to face the person on the other side. His instincts told him Brent would be gloating over the accomplishment of seeing Leah on her first night in Charlotte. Unexpectedly, the open door gave way to an expression far from the sneer Evan imagined. Instead, Brent's drawn features filled his face with despair.

"Good evening Mr. Scott. Nice to see you again. Please come in." Evan uttered grimly.

"Mr. Holcomb." Brent entered, cautiously scanning the room. With Leah nowhere in sight, he spoke frankly, his words abrupt and to the point. "We need to talk as soon as possible. Something happened today. I'll contact you first thing in the morning."

Evan now understood the probable cause for Leah's preoccupation when she arrived earlier. The risk of Leah gaining knowledge of Brent and Evan's previous meeting loomed over them. Evan indicated his understanding with a nod toward Brent just as Leah rounded the corner. Both men focused on the image before them, stopping them dead in their tracks. Leah's appearance oozing raw beauty rendered them speechless.

"I'm sorry, did I interrupt something? If you two need some time alone, I can come back in a few minutes."

Both men gaped, unable to blink. Or think. Or speak.

"I'm not sure how I should interpret your silence. Do I have something on my face or what? Is something wrong?" She nervously shifted her stance.

Brent eventually uttered. “I think it’s the ‘or what’ part that I’m trying to control.”

Leah smoothed her dress and smiled. Her simple swept-up hairstyle enhanced the outfit’s plunging neckline and modest earrings. Evan became acutely aware her whole ensemble was meant to make an impression.

“Well, I guess I should take that as a compliment.” Leah chuckled as she guided Brent toward the door.

“Brent, are you ready to go? Evan, thank you again for allowing me to stay with you. I will try my best not to disturb you when I return. I won’t be in late, I promise. You and I have a big night tomorrow night.”

“Yes, of course, no problem. I hope you have an enjoyable evening. I’ll see you in the morning. Mr. Scott, it was nice to see you again.” Evan’s tone echoed uneasiness. Truth be known, it bothered him a great deal to see the two of them leave.

Evan could not control the feeling that he’d lost the battle for Leah. A woman only wears a dress like that for one reason: attention. His sudden realization that it was not his attention she tried to capture sent pains of regret coursing through his body.

Did I take things too slowly? Should I have been more open about my feelings?

He continued to ask himself questions that were of little importance now. However, he had no plans to concede defeat so quickly. Round one went to Brent. Round two would be his for the taking since the gala was only 18 hours away.

CHAPTER TWENTY-EIGHT

Brent's intimate café selection set the mood for a perfect evening. Their table sat in the rear of the restaurant, where it was private and cozy. The small café oozed romance, transporting its guests to the streets of Venice. Friendly musicians played soft romantic tunes. Couples cuddled at their tables, relishing the intimacy of the dim lighting as they enjoyed their wine. Leah soaked in the ambiance.

Leah noticed Brent's quiet, withdrawn demeanor.

"This place is quite fantastic. Thank you for picking it out." She saw him smile.

"I would say you're quite fantastic in that dress. Let's say it's very flattering."

"Well, thank you, Mr. Scott. I'm glad you approve. Can we make a vow tonight not to talk about anything serious? Nothing related to business. I don't care what happened today. All I care about is what's happening right now. I want to focus on you and me and an enjoyable evening. Do you agree?" Leah prayed he agreed. Today's events unsettled her more than she wanted to admit. But tonight, she wanted to have fun.

"I agree, Ms. Reynolds. Business can wait."

They talked for hours between bites of sumptuous Italian dishes orchestrated by the kitchen's renowned chef.

Each relaxing as the evening progressed. Maybe it was the wine, or perhaps it was the fact they just seemed to have so much in common. Their conversation flowed without interruption as they talked about anything and everything, from football to their favorite ice cream. Minutes turned into hours.

Noticing the time, Brent interjected, "We really should be getting you back to the apartment. I'm sure you have a lot to do in preparation for the gala. I don't want to be the one who keeps you from enjoying your success with this merger." He knew he had to end this. It would only become more painful later on.

Leah began to speak, surprisingly, the words flowing out made sense. "Brent, would you like to come to the gala? Evan has already invited Amber. No one would be suspicious if you showed up as Amber's date. I guess I'm being selfish, but I'd like you to be there."

Could it be destiny for them to be together? Brent stared at her in disbelief. Leah wanted him there. Her alibi paired perfectly with the plan he and Evan had manufactured earlier.

"I won't make any promises, but I'll talk to Amber." Amber had no choice; Brent would convince his sister to agree to be his date.

"Well, I will take that as a yes!" Her warm smile was more than he could bear. Brent took her by the shoulders and stared deeply into her eyes. Brent had seen the look on Leah's face before. It was in their best interest to pay the bill and get moving. It took everything in him to release her as he planted a quick kiss on her lips.

The ride back to Evan's apartment provided more

interesting conversation and laughter. However, their conversation suddenly ceased when Brent eased the car into the apartment parking lot, and they turned to face each other. They hesitated to vocalize the feelings of attraction while their eyes portrayed all the emotions their mouths dared not confess.

Brent's plan for their final night together fell into the shadows. Everything had changed. His feelings for Leah could no longer be suppressed by his denial. He would die for this woman. Brent intended to let Leah know just how much she meant to him here and now.

He leaned in, trickling kisses across her cheek. As he crossed over to her mouth, she breathed intensely. Brent covered her mouth with a long kiss. Grasping for air, Leah broke their kiss, eyes wide. Before he realized it, her dress had slipped off her shoulder. As much as this woman meant to him, he could not allow this to happen.

Brent pulled away and pushed the corner of her dress back over her shoulder. Leah suddenly realized just how far they had gone in a short amount of time, so caught up in the moment as they were. Leah began straightening her clothes while Brent watched, smiling. Her swollen, red, pouty lips bore witness to her enjoyment of their interlude. A cute curl of hair escaped her bun and covered her left eye. Brent knew he could never give this woman up.

"What is so funny?" Leah muttered when she caught Brent smiling.

"You. Do you even know how beautiful you are?" His eyes twinkled with pleasure.

"Well, I don't hear that very often. Thank you for the compliment, Mr. Scott." She snickered. "I really should be going in. Evan will wonder what has happened to me."

Brent laughed. Her comments could not be more accurate.

"Leah, in case you can't tell it by now, you mean a great deal to me. I've thoroughly enjoyed our time together.

So much so that I can only think about taking you away from here. But the gentleman in me is preventing that. Please, promise me one thing." Brent gently clasped her hand in his.

"I'll need to think about that. It depends on what the promise involves." Leah's answered coyly.

"Don't ever wear that dress again unless you are with me, deal?"

"On that, Mr. Scott, I can give my promise. Besides, no one else would appreciate it the way you do. I'll talk to you soon. Please call Amber. You two need to make arrangements for the gala." Leah opened the door and hurried into the apartment.

Brent smiled while he watched her walk towards the door. He struggled to comprehend how this woman consumed his heart in such a short amount of time. Brent hoped Amber was awake. He needed to make plans with his "date" for the gala tomorrow night.

CHAPTER TWENTY-NINE

Leah woke the following day to a bright ray of sunshine shimmering through the window. A visual display of her current attitude. All smiles, she touched her lips, remembering Brent's passionate kisses from last night. She reminded herself the evening was real and not a dream. In her eyes, Brent was almost perfect. Being the utmost gentleman when he felt things progressed a little too far. He'd stepped back, controlling the situation to protect her. Her quiet morning reflections assured her of one thing. She cared for Brent more than she'd realized.

Of course, she needed to consider Evan's feelings also. He openly admitted his desire to become more than co-workers. The last thing she wanted to do was to hurt anyone. But there was no denying who held a firmer grip on her heart.

Leah longed for tonight's festivities to begin. She knew Amber would help Brent with the charade for the gala. What fun they were all going to have. Leah drafted a short message to Rhonda, Carol, Amber, and Charlie, setting things in motion. The ladies had no clue about the surprise that awaited them. Jumping from the bed, she headed to shower.

Meanwhile, Evan paced the kitchen floor waiting for Leah to come down for breakfast. His inability to sleep stemmed from Leah's late return to the apartment, which resulted in the need for a morning of caffeine overload. Unwilling to linger on negative thoughts out of his control, Evan spent time planning their evening. Hopefully, the night would solidify his intentions.

Bouncing into the breakfast nook, Leah issued a cheerful greeting.

"Good morning, Evan. I hope you're ready for an evening that defies all social logic. We're going to have a party that will make history. Gathering the staff from both companies together in a social setting will benefit all of us. The break will do everyone good. Don't you agree?" All smiles, Leah reached for the coffee pot.

"Yes, I agree. But, Leah, you need to remain aware we are in a dangerous situation with our terrorist friend still on the loose. The downtime will be wonderful; however, we need to stay alert. I've increased the security personnel as a deterrent. Without a lead on this man's identity, we're back to square one. It is all very frustrating."

"Evan, please don't ruin the gala by worrying about this. Too many people are working to find a lead. The extra security will do their job. We've worked too hard to make the gala a success, and so it shall be."

He loved her positive outlook and determination. It was one of the characteristics that initially attracted him to her. "I hear you, Ms. Optimistic. Just don't forget one thing, you are my date tonight, and we are going to dance the night away."

Leah smiled in agreement. "Dancing always solves the world's problems, even if only for a short time."

"Now, you remember, everything's arranged for you and the other ladies to meet Suzanne and Kimberly at the Centennial Building three hours before the gala, right?"

"They're all aware of the arrangements. Thank you again for planning such a wonderful surprise. It's not every day a girl gets pampered in such style. They will love you forever."

"I hope you enjoy your day, but there's only one person I need to love me. You're well aware of who that is." An awkward silence filled the air.

"I need to head to the office for a little while. Please make yourself at home. I'll see you at seven. Don't be late!" His words commanded compliance.

Leah laughed at the stern tone. "Yes, sir, boss."

It took all of Evan's resolve to leave the room before questioning Leah about her night out with Brent. His body said, grab her and kiss her before you go, but his mind said, don't pressure her. In the end, he knew tonight would be their night.

CHAPTER THIRTY

Leah, Amber, Charlie, Carol, and Rhonda entered the Centennial Building to a bustle of activity. Decorators, caterers, and staff worked feverishly. The atmosphere heightened the upcoming evening's excitement for each lady, except Carol. She remained furious about having to attend the party at all.

"Come along, ladies, enough of this. We need to make our way up to the penthouse. Evan arranged a huge surprise for all of us." Leah felt like a kid at Christmas. She couldn't wait to see her friend's reactions.

As the penthouse doors swung open, the vision inside spurred gasps from the ladies as they stared in awe of the room's contents. Against one wall, an enormous buffet stocked with champagne, fruit, cheeses, and an array of other delectable goodies beckoned their attention. An elevated platform with rows of mirrors and a small runway sat on the left side of the spacious penthouse. Numerous clothing racks were neatly lined up next to the runway, displaying dozens of gowns in every color, fabric, cut, and design. Luxurious sofas and chairs rounded out the décor in their fantasy surroundings. Adding to the ladies' disbelief stood two extraordinary women who welcomed them with warm smiles and open arms.

Leah had only seen her picture in various society publications, but there was no mistaking Kimberly Vega. Suzanne Crawford stood beside her. The women were polar opposites. Kimberly Vega's petite frame and flaming red locks contrasted Suzanne Crawford's towering stature and California beach blonde hair. Each possessed prominent features that made them extraordinarily beautiful.

While the other women exclaimed their jubilation, Leah approached the two women.

"Hello, I'm Leah Reynolds. I can't thank you enough for your generosity. It is so wonderful to meet each of you." Leah's face glowed.

"I'm Kimberly Vega, and this is Suzanne Crawford. It's our pleasure to be here. After meeting you and seeing how beautiful you are, I can see why Evan has gone to so much trouble to impress you. He is quite enamored with you, you know."

Blushing, Leah responded, attempting to sidestep the infatuation comment, "I know he worked very hard to provide this surprise, and so have the two of you. We're extremely grateful and appreciative. Let me introduce you to the rest of the ladies so you can get started working your magic. You will need all the time you can get to make us gala glamourous."

With the introductions completed, each woman provided Kimberly and Suzanne with their idea of a gown style. Of course, Rhonda wanted sultry and sexy. Carol just needed to survive the night and look decent. Charlie preferred something simple that allowed her the freedom to move and take pictures. Amber desired a gown that would cause heads to turn. As for Leah, she wanted something discretely alluring that would leave a lasting, unforgettable impression.

The women sipped champagne while pampered with hair, makeup, and gown selections. Leah lightly touched Amber's arm, pulling her aside from the other ladies.

"Amber, we haven't talked since I was enlightened about your relationship with Brent."

"Please don't be mad at him. Brent told you why we

couldn't tell you the truth. Tell me you are happy. I don't want you mad at me either."

"Amber, I'm far from mad. I'm ecstatic! My new best friend is the sister of the guy I can't get off my mind. What more could I ask for?" They squealed while the others looked on. Rhonda's suspicious stare outwardly confessed she thought the two were drunk. Both women ignored her and continued hugging and smiling.

"Please tell me he's coming, Amber. You two have the perfect alibi." Bright eyes and wishful thinking had Leah hanging on Amber's every word.

"Yes, he's coming. He'll be downstairs when we arrive. I'm sure you're not happy about that, are you?" Amber giggled.

Leah coughed, "Oh no, I'm not; whatever gave you that idea." Laughter erupted again.

Rhonda suddenly stood up, eyeing the two, "I want some of what they're having. It must be better than what I'm drinking." Everyone roared with laughter and carried on with their preparations. The festivities started in an hour.

Kimberly and Suzanne strived to make each lady's makeover experience special. Kimberly had to admit she was having more fun than she had in a long time. It could become quite dull, outfitting the Hollywood crowd. The ability to have anything they wanted at any time resulted in entitled boring clients. However, these women were genuinely honored by what she and Suzanne were doing for them. Each woman shined with infectious dreams and ideas, utterly different from the usual stuffy California crowd. It would be fun to get to know them better.

Returning to her task at hand, Kimberly bellowed to

the women from the front of the runway, "Come on, ladies, the time has come. Let's see what we have here."

Rhonda was the first to appear in a bright red gown with a profound "V" neckline and a high slit. Evermore the siren. Carol emerged next in her gold-toned modest ball gown that coordinated perfectly with her hair color and body type. Carol bashfully walked the runway to the sound of Rhonda's cheers.

"Wahoo, Carol, you may find your next husband wearing that tonight!"

As Carol departed the runway to more catcalls and laughter, Charlie appeared. Charlie's look portrayed professionalism in a black jumpsuit and black heels, mirroring her sophistication. Her outfit afforded her the freedom of movement she'd requested. Next, Amber emerged in a dazzling green, heavily embellished, high-necked gown. The gown's bodice had a keyhole cutout and a modest slit down the side. The color complemented her gorgeous brown hair ensuring Amber would turn heads.

Finally, Leah stepped through the curtains. Kimberly had placed Leah in a royal blue, form-fitting, low-back gown. The lace front strategically held bits of beautiful fabric that provided ample coverage. Her hair had been piled high upon her head, enhanced by tiny loose tendrils that framed her face. Bold earrings complimented the look. The sight of her left the group speechless. Uncomfortable with the silence, Leah looked around at her friends, concerned.

Is this dress giving a wrong impression?

It had taken some convincing from Kimberly even to get her to try the dress on. However, once Kimberly saw her in it, she refused to let Leah wear anything else.

Worried that the dress was inappropriate, Leah spoke up, "Well…."

As she turned to grab another gown, the room erupted with cheers and clapping. Tears filled her eyes. "Really?

Lasting impression material?" she said, shrugging her shoulders. The cheering grew louder as water continued to pool in her eyes.

Suzanne stepped in front of Leah. "If you start crying, I'll kill you. I worked too hard on your makeup." Laughing, the two women embraced.

Leah was thrilled that Kimberly and Suzanne also decided to attend the gala. In just a few hours, the two transformed each of the ladies into a vision of beauty. Their outing had managed to form a tight bond among all the women. Leah hoped their bond continued to grow into everlasting friendships and future adventures for all of them. As the ladies headed toward the door, Leah shouted,

"Look out, world. Here come the Sisters Seven. I certainly hope you are ready!"

Echoing their sentiments, sounds of "Yeah" roared around Leah as the ladies piled into the elevator and started their descent to the festivities.

CHAPTER THIRTY-ONE

He laughed inwardly. It was almost too easy to gain access to the building. He'd mingled with the different vendors and skated right past the extra security, undetected.

Some security personnel.

It was early in the day; finding a hiding place would be imperative until the ideal time arrived to emerge later in the evening. Scouting for the perfect spot, he watched the group of giggling women walk to the elevator.

Well, of all the luck.

Leah, her friend Amber and the other ladies, had walked right past him. His brain raced with ideas. He never intended to hurt Leah, but it was absurd how they kept turning up in the same place. Recognizing she was an innocent party in his grand scheme didn't change the fact she was an extremely valuable innocent party. Both companies depended heavily on her knowledge and ability. Not to mention, it wasn't a secret Holcomb held a fond attachment to her. *He* watched as the ladies boarded the elevator, absorbed in their plans. A devious thought entered his mind. It would be easy for him to rig an accident on the elevator's return to the lobby. That would certainly make a statement. War waged within him as he thought through the merits of each path forward. *He* hurriedly decided to stick with the original plan. The ladies' safety would remain secure for now. Besides, his mission tonight involved observation. Those observations would help inflict the final blow on his enemies. All the warnings to stop the merger had fallen on deaf ears, and now they must pay for their blind ignorance.

Brent and Evan agreed earlier to avoid each other until the ladies arrived. Neither of them could afford people forming a connection between the two.

John and Martha Watts rolled into the square, all smiles as they exited the back of the black limousine. The loving couple walked hand in hand, blushing from the roaring welcome showered on them by their employees. Shortly after their arrival, the hall filled quickly with the usual socialites, reporters, and local dignitaries, all on a quest to experience the lavish festivities planned by Charlotte's youngest entrepreneur.

Evan and Brent, endlessly watching for suspicious activity, scanned the room. Each abundantly aware that everyone had arrived, excluding the ladies. Worry contorted their expressions.

Unable to wait any longer, both men gravitated toward the entrance, approaching from opposite sides. They paused at the musical sound of ladies' laughter echoing outside the door. Charlie Ashby started the procession into the ballroom, followed by Carol and Rhonda.

Carol's temperament, overhauled by the joyous adventures thus far, resulted in an enormous and uncharacteristic grin on her face. Ever on the prowl for single men, Rhonda tugged Carol's arm, pulling her forward. Charlie started her photo montage for the evening, snapping pictures from the second she entered.

Finally, Leah and Amber waltzed into the room. Arm-in-arm, giggling and engrossed in their conversation, the women were oblivious to the effect they seemed to have on every male in the room. Transfixed by their beauty, Evan and Brent's attempt to speak became fruitless. Mere words failed to reach their lips.

"Hello, gentlemen. Don't you both look dashing? You two are the most handsome men in the room." Leah's eyes lingered a few seconds longer on Brent, unaware that Evan noticed her gaze.

Perceptive as ever, Amber interjected and broke the silence, "Evan, I'd like to thank you for your gracious invitation to attend tonight. I must think of a way to show my appreciation. It's not every day a girl gets treated like a queen by her host." Smiling, Amber bumped Leah's elbow.

"A thank you isn't necessary. It was my pleasure to arrange things with Kimberly and Suzanne. However, I must say, I look forward to your show of appreciation when you decide just what it shall be." Evan responded with a devilish smile, obviously an attempt to stir Leah's jealousy.

"We should thank you, ladies, for allowing us to accompany you to this grand event," Brent interjected.

"Well, Mr. Scott, you're my date for the evening, and with that obligation, there's the responsibility of dancing with me at least once, so shall we?" Brent turned to escort Amber to the dance floor but not before offering Leah a flirtatious wink and a sly smile. Brent's actions prompted Evan to reach for Leah's arm and pull her to the side of the room.

"Leah, you are stunning in that dress," Evan whispered in her ear, sighing as he tried to breathe. "I'm not sure I can leave you alone tonight. Every man in the place broke into a sweat the moment you and Amber entered the room."

"Surely not every man here feels that way." She chuckled.

"But I do feel quite like a princess. Kimberly and Suzanne were so attentive and helpful. We had a wonderful time, all because of your generosity. I can't thank you enough for everything." Leah's warm, appreciative smile only added to her allure.

"Right now, you can express your appreciation by dancing with me. We'll think of another way later." Extending his hand, Evan and Leah made their way to the dance floor.

Twirling about the floor, Leah took a moment to observe her friends. Rhonda was undoubtedly on cloud nine, enjoying her conversation with a tall, handsome blonde man. Charlie moved around the ballroom, discretely snapping pictures of everyone in attendance. Even Carol seemed to be having a good time - drink in hand, chatting away with some of the Holcomb Industries associates. But it was John and Martha who made Leah's heart leap with happiness when they breezed by her on the dance floor, all smiles. Leah hadn't seen them this at ease in several years.

"Isn't it wonderful to see everyone relaxed and having a good time? This party was just what we all needed. Things are running smoothly. The extra security appears to be doing its job. So, let's enjoy!"

Evan pulled her closer and gazed deeply into her eyes, uttering a saucy, "I plan to" before he twirled her full circle, moving about the floor.

Evan's throaty promise made Leah fully aware tonight would be the night she must choose between him and Brent. They had a right to know how she felt about them. There was just one problem: she wasn't entirely sure which one controlled her heart.

When the music stopped, Amber appeared over Evan's shoulder and placed her hand on his arm.

"I think it's time for my dance Mr. Holcomb. You can't corner one woman all night. You should share your time." Smiling brightly, Amber pulled Evan toward her and the music while Brent assumed Evan's place by Leah's side.

Brent moved closer seizing his opportun
"date" was on the dance floor. Grasping her
Brent led Leah to an empty table. Maneuveri
closer together, he placed his seat slightly behina ne.
they sat down.

"Now that we're alone for a few moments, I must tell you, Ms. Reynolds, you're the most beautiful woman I've ever seen. You look ravishing in that dress. I'm not sure who selected your gown but remind me to thank them." Brent's comment sent a warm flush to Leah's cheeks.

"No need to blush now. You knew that dress would send me over the edge, didn't you?" He said, offering his most dashing smile.

"A girl can always hope, can't she?" Leah giggled.

Leaning so close she could feel his breath, Brent whispered, "You must know if we weren't in a room full of people, it would be in our best interest to move to one." He teased.

Brent's positioning of the seats provided him full access to Leah's back. He began massaging her neck. "You need to relax, Ms. Reynolds. Have some fun." His fingers on her skin forced a gasp from her lips. Powerless to bear the weight of Brent's closeness any longer, Leah leaned forward to issue a quick kiss when Rhonda's voice broke the spell.

Lifting their eyes, Evan, Amber, Carol, and Rhonda stood before them.

"What in the world are you two doing over here in the corner? Don't tell me you're tired already?" Searching Leah's face for an answer, Rhonda remained exasperated. Eyes wide, Leah only shook her head no.

Brent hastily interjected, "No, of course not. Who could be tired this early? Rhonda, would you like to accompany me to the dance floor?" Brent extended his hand, executed a gentlemanly bow, and escorted the utterly thrilled Rhonda to the ballroom floor.

Evan, Amber, and Carol took a seat. The four sat in silence for several moments, unsure what to say. Finally, Leah broke the silence, quietly asking, "Carol, are you having a good time?"

Carol beamed, her whole face alight with happiness, "Oh, Leah, I simply can't understand why I was so worried about this gala. I'm having a grand time. Evan, I have to say everyone on your staff has been so welcoming and friendly, especially a young man named Troy Marshall. He was certainly interested in learning more about all of us."

Evan's jaw tensed. "Well, I'm happy he's trying to make everyone comfortable. Troy is one of my best software technicians. He generally tends to shy away from crowds and keeps very quiet most of the time, so I'm surprised by his interest. Exactly, what type of questions was Troy asking, Carol? I certainly hope he wasn't quizzing you on company business. Tonight's supposed to be relaxing and fun. No work discussions allowed."

"Oh no, nothing about software and such; I really wouldn't know where to begin with all that stuff." Carol fanned her face and laughed. "He asked simple things about our personal lives. Please don't misunderstand. He wasn't prying or anything. He inquired about our families, where we lived, how long we had been with the company, what John and Martha were like, and things like that. It seems to me he's just trying to familiarize himself with the people he'll be working around. If you'll excuse me, I'm in dire need of a cool drink." Carol continued to fan her face while she walked away, swaying to the background music.

Leah instantly detected a definite shift in Evan's expression and demeanor. He moved from lighthearted and happy to confused and concerned in a few seconds. Leah's body stiffened, noting the difference. Her eyes locked with Brent's as he escorted Rhonda back to their table. Tension stabbed the air like jagged knives. Leah half-heartedly smiled at Rhonda when Amber piped in.

"Well, Rhonda, I hate to do this, but we have two handsome gentlemen that need to spend a little one-on-one time with their dates. So, if you'll excuse us, we'll return soon." Smiling, Amber grabbed Brent's hand; Evan followed suit with Leah. As they took their position in the center of the dance floor, Leah, Evan, and Brent hesitantly glanced at each other.

"Ok," Amber huffed. "Does someone in this group want to tell me what's going on? You three know something, and I'm smart enough to figure out it's not good. So we will stand right here until someone tells me what the hell is going on." Amber's eyes flashed with the fury to match her voice.

Brent's soft hushed tone tried to soothe his sister. "Amber, will you please lower your voice and stay calm. Everything's fine. I'm not quite sure what you're talking about." Unfortunately, his tactics failed to defuse the situation.

"Brent Scott, did you forget I grew up in the same household as you. I can read you like a book. Especially when you aren't being straightforward with me." Amber turned to Leah in exasperation. "You know what's going on, don't you?"

Leah found herself unable to lie to her friend. "All I can say is yes, something's going on, but everything's under control, right guys?" Nodding her head, she looked to the men for support.

"Amber, she's right," Evan agreed. "It's just a slight problem with the merger. Nothing big; there's no need to worry. Wait, where did growing up in the same house come into play? Were you two childhood friends?" Evan waited. Confusion playing across his face. No one responded.

Amber's anger threw her into a tangent as she pointed her finger at them. "Do I have stupid written on my forehead? When you're trying not to lie, the expression on your face, Brent Scott, gives way to an even bigger lie. I care about each of you, and if something is going on, I need someone to tell me now." She stomped her foot, driving her point home.

What? Did I hear that correctly? Amber cares about all three of us!

Leah scratched her temple. Amber just possibly let the cat out of the bag in the heat of her anger. Leah sensed Amber's fondness for Evan since their meeting in Baton Rouge. No one else caught the hidden meaning of Amber's statement, not even Amber. Well, that further explained her friend's dress selection for the evening.

Unable to maintain a straight face any longer, Leah stifled a snicker that evolved into uncontrolled laughter.

"Excuse me. Just what are you laughing about?" Amber's lethal glare demanded an explanation.

Leah's infectious rumble spilled over to Brent, who began his own round of chuckles. Evan, as confused as Amber over the whole fiasco playing out in the middle of the dance floor, began to smile. Leah and Brent bent over, grasping their sides from the hysterical chuckles. Amber, furious at the entire scenario, stomped her foot again. Amber's attempt to issue another stern warning was interrupted by Charlie Ashby's sudden appearance on the dance floor.

"I'm sorry. I hate to break up a good time, but we may have a problem. Can we find a quiet spot? I need to show you something." Pivoting to lead the way, Charlie stopped in midstride to the sound of Amber's protest.

"If you expect to leave me standing here while the three of you sneak off, you're dead wrong. Lead the way." Left with no option but to allow Amber to accompany them, the group fell in line behind Charlie and exited the ballroom.

Evan nodded toward the elevator.

"Let's head to the penthouse. We'll have complete privacy there."

The group boarded, exchanging glances indicative of fear, worry, danger, and the unknown as the elevator ascended to the penthouse.

Charlie exited first, turning to Evan, Brent, and Leah. "Do you want Amber to hear all this? You're aware it could put her in danger too."

Brent knew Charlie was right. However, Amber's part in this sick state of affairs became more significant when she and Leah encountered the terrorist on their Baton Rouge flight. It was time she knew what was going on.

"She'll be fine. I'll fill her in on the details later. Go ahead, Charlie, tell us why we're here." His gut lurched, waiting for the news.

"You all know my role tonight involves taking photos for the newspaper article. So, I decided to examine some of the pictures for content on a whim. During my review, I came across this." Angling the camera for everyone to see, Charlie pointed to the picture in focus.

"Your faces echo my thoughts exactly. The man in this picture looks scarily familiar to our artist's sketch, right? Guys, he's here, or should I say he was here. Who knows if he's still downstairs? I took this photo like two hours ago."

"Leah, is it him?" Evan awaited Leah's answer. He looked at Brent, and both realized that it wasn't a picture of Troy Marshall, but the two strongly favored each other.

Leah nodded her head in agreement. Tears pooled in her now sad eyes. "How could he be here, and none of us observed him moving about the rooms? We let our guard down. What do we do now?"

"Wait," Charlie exclaimed, "there's something else. Look at the image. Notice how close he is to John and Martha? I find that a little strange. This group's entire sequence of photos has him in the same area. It's almost as if he's shadowing them." Charlie pointed out the man's positioning in several photos of John and Martha.

Leah's face turned ghostly white. "If he's here, John and Martha are alone downstairs. They have no idea what's happening. We've kept them out of the briefings to spare them anguish. Now our short-sighted wisdom could cause them harm … or even death. We have to find them, now." Leah sprinted for the elevator doors.

Evan chased after her, calling out, "Leah, wait." Reaching her, he clasped her arm. "We can't make him aware that we know he's here. The element of surprise is on our side. Brent and I will go down. You circle one side, Brent, while I start on the other. Try to find John and Martha as quickly as possible. Once we're certain they're safe, we'll search for our guy. Amber and Leah, you stay here where it's safe with Charlie. We will be back in a little while." The two men moved toward the elevator.

The women smiled at each other, signaling their agreement, while Leah quickly assumed the role of spokesperson.

"I know you don't think you're leaving us here. Five people searching a room is much better than two. Besides, the rooms are full of additional security. They'll help protect us if needed. Let's go. We have to get to John and Martha."

The women marched past Brent and Evan, stepping into the elevator on a mission. In unison, the three barked, "Are you coming?" Knowing there was no sense in fighting a losing battle, Brent and Evan joined the ladies and headed to the ballroom.

The gang re-entered the room, splintering off in

different directions, taking a room section. Each believed *He* would be watching for any sign of questionable activity if still in attendance. Aggressively searching the room would tip him off. Their decision to move through the crowd socially, chit-chatting seemed to work in their favor.

Leah spotted John and Martha first, sitting near the band. All smiles, oblivious to any possible danger, John and Martha tapped their feet in time to the music. Leah headed in their direction, with Brent and Evan following closely behind.

Frozen in place, Leah spied the man. There *He* stood, perched against the wall trying to make himself invisible. She knew their actions had put him on alert. His recognition of their approach brought a sinister smile to his lips. *He* callously nodded, in no hurry to move, acknowledging Brent, Evan, and Leah's approach as he strolled to the exit.

Leah reached the exit door first. Then, in an attempt to block his departure and alert security, she placed her entire body in the doorway.

There's no way he'd risk causing an uproar, would he?

Too late, sensing his approach, Leah found herself unprepared for the sheer terror that consumed her by simply having him within mere feet of her. His cold, indifferent features matched her sketch perfectly. The blonde tips from her previous encounters with the man no longer highlighted his hair. He'd changed the color to an auburn hue to conceal his identity. Still, she couldn't deny the frighteningly familiar eyes. Concentrating on his eyes diverted her attention from his relentless, continued approach toward her.

Suddenly, Leah felt a tight, painful grip on her arm before being roughly jerked out of the exit. Standing her ground, she pulled back with a hard thrust. Feeling her vigorous resistance, *He* shoved her to the door frame floor and bolted out of the building. Evan and Brent helplessly watched the whole scene from where they stood. Forcing his way through the crowd of partygoers, Evan arrived first and scanned her body for injuries. Short of a small cut to the side of her head, Leah seemed unharmed. Scooping her up, he moved toward a chair when Leah kicked, jumping from his arms. Her feet rooted to the floor; balance regained, she rushed into Brent's arms. Fighting back the tears, she clung to him.

Brent clutched her tight before planting a desperate kiss on her trembling lips. Then, finally, he broke their kiss, chastising her.

"Leah, what in the world did you think you were doing? Have you lost your mind? You're lucky you weren't hurt or worse. What were you thinking?"

Brent's barrage continued as Amber and Charlie arrived in the corner of the ballroom.

"Are you sure you're okay?" Brent clasped her shoulders.

John and Martha joined the group brimming with concern.

"What's happening? Leah, are you all right? We saw you fall, and that gentleman didn't even stop to help you." Martha quipped.

"Martha, I'm fine. These things happen when you put a girl in five-inch heels and a beautiful gown. I'm sure even Cinderella had her issues. My ego's just a little bruised. That wasn't my most elegant move." Leah chuckled.

"Can we try not to draw any further attention to my little mishap and go sit down? It's quite embarrassing." Leah motioned toward the nearest table, quivering as she walked.

Rhonda, Carol, Kimberly, and Suzanne rushed to the table. Kimberly began apologizing, "Leah, I'm so sorry that I coerced you into wearing that dress. I should've let you pick something you were more comfortable in."

"Will you all please calm down? This is not your fault, Kimberly. It was just a silly misstep. I've been dancing the night away with no problems until now. Ask Brent and Amber; I'm notorious for this type of thing. Right?" Leah gazed at Amber for support.

"She's telling the truth. You should've seen her stunt on one of my flights. So not graceful!" Leah laughed at her own clumsiness, and everyone joined her.

"Now, continue with your evening. We still have hours of partying and fun. Go, everyone!" Leah commanded, shooing them away with her vibrant hand motions. The group dispersed, satisfied that Leah wasn't hurt. Only the five who knew the real story remained by Leah's side.

Concealed in the surroundings of the only people who understood her peril, Leah remained silent.

"Did he say anything to you?" Charlie questioned.

"No. That's what's so eerie. *He* sneered at me and threw me to the floor, muttering something. I guess his failed attempt to drag me out the door didn't faze him. All I could hear were his evil snickers after he'd bolted through the exit. It was almost as if he'd gotten the best of us somehow."

"Well, he certainly wasn't intimidated by the extra security. Who knows how long he was here, blending in, watching. I've seen this before during my work with the Chicago police. Some people have no fear of death or defeat. Instead, their mind is consumed with their plan's fulfillment, garnering the cherished result. We have to find him before he seriously injures someone. I'll start searching the remaining photos for additional clues. And Leah, I'm glad you're okay." Smiling, Charlie quickly headed to retrieve her camera.

Evan ran his fingers through his thick black hair, visibly filled with apprehension.

"Leah, why don't you and Brent go to the penthouse

and take care of that cut on your head. It doesn't look too serious. There should be bandages and cleansers in the bathroom. Amber and I will stay here and ensure things remain calm. We can't afford another incident tonight. Although I'm quite sure our "friend" is far away from here by now. If you'll excuse me for a moment, I need to have a word of prayer with the security staff." Anger and hurt gripped him. His fists clenched so tight his knuckles turned pale white.

Leah saw the recognition of her feelings for Brent on Evan's face. She respected him for being ever more the gentleman and ignoring the issue. However, she gathered the nodding acknowledgment between the two men signaled a "male code of honor." The concession Evan made offered Brent a clear path to her heart. Leah's direct eye contact with Amber confirmed her earlier suspicions. Amber would make sure Evan wasn't too lonely if he allowed her to get to know him better.

On the ride up to the penthouse, neither Leah nor Brent uttered a word. They both struggled to grasp the events of the past hour. The whole scene could have produced a disastrous outcome. Luckily, Leah and Charlie thwarted whatever plans the villain devised.

The elevator doors opened, prompting Brent's loving upsweep of Leah into his arms. Carrying her to the plush sofa, he lowered her body gently onto the cool leather.

"Your head's still bleeding a little. Don't move. I'll be right back." Leah stared at him as he walked to the bathroom. The vivid images of the past hour danced in her mind. The rush to leave Evan's embrace and run to Brent for comfort made blatantly evident to anyone watching what her true feelings were. The reality that she and Evan would be business colleagues who are close friends was never more apparent than now. Leah's heart skipped a beat at the thought of Brent. The excitement. The attraction. The unexpected joy that enveloped her when she was with him told her he was the one.

Watching him return juggling a cold compress, antiseptic, and bandages sent quivers down her spine.

How can I be lucky enough to have this gorgeous man interested in me?

Brent leaned over, nursing her like a small child, carefully placing the bandage on her cut.

"You should probably put some ice on your head for a little while." Handing her the compress, he smiled. "Leah, are you afraid of anything? You placed yourself between the door and that guy like a 300-pound defensive lineman. What were you thinking?"

"At the time, it made sense. It was the only way to slow him down until you could get there." A sharp grimace crossed her face when the cold compress found its mark atop the tiny bump forming on her scalp.

"But you could've been seriously hurt, or worse, taken. You were right by the door. There was no way for us to reach you in time. I'd never forgive myself if something happened to you."

"Brent, there would be nothing to forgive. It was my choice." Sincerity dripped from her words.

Leah raised her head, lashes fluttering from the cold of the compress and pain. She peered deep into Brent's eyes, seeking some admission of his feelings. Instead, she saw the instant division between duty and pleasure. He'd expressed a physical desire for her but never the longing to keep her in his life forever. Leah became acutely aware that Brent quite possibly read her mind when he lowered his mouth to hers. Their kiss released a gentle sigh of relief. Pent feelings exploded into a lengthy kiss. The moment seemed to last a lifetime. Only the sound of the compress hitting the floor jarred them from the fog that had enveloped them. Pushing against Brent's chest, Leah whispered,

"I guess I'd better change out of this expensive dress before I get water spots on it. Then Kimberly may want to kill me. I'll be right back."

Watching her move toward the changing screens Kimberly set in place for their earlier transformations, Brent willed himself to look away, but his will faltered. The shadows of Leah's body against the screen were too confounding. The slim figure enhanced by her long legs sent his imagination into a tailspin. Focused, unable to blink, he noticed Leah's struggle with the dress zipper.

Without even thinking, Brent moved blindly, eyes squeezed tightly shut, to join Leah behind the screen. Unaware of his presence, she continued to tug until his hands found their way and wrapped over hers. Brent felt the surprise in her body and heard the catch of her breath. He slowly worked the zipper, gently easing it down. Next, Brent trailed his fingers back to her neck, unfastening the two buttons from their clasps. The release of the buttons allowed the entire bodice to fall to Leah's waist. He heard her quick movements as she grabbed for the gown. His other senses went on high alert due to the darkness that engulfed his vision. Her every move reverberated the sound of the gown's swishing satin. Quickly repositioning her dress for cover, Leah slowly turned toward Brent, releasing a giggle at the sight of Brent's squinched eyes.

Leah placed her hands on his strong jawline, enjoying the full view of his pearly white teeth. She kissed him so profoundly Brent had to lean back to regain his footing. Instinctively, his eyes began to ease open. Brent jerked his hand upward to shield his eyes once again.

The images of their time together since the airplane encounter raced through his mind reinforcing his feelings. Leah was the only woman he would ever allow into his heart again. Brent decided now was the time to tell this woman how he felt.

Turning his back to her, he began. “Leah, I love you. I think I have since I picked you up off the floor of that airplane. Most people don’t believe in love at first sight, but I felt it the first time you smiled at me. You do realize there’s no turning back. I’ll never let you go now that I have you.” He waited. Wrapped in uncertainty after his declaration, he never sensed her movements toward the robe rack.

“I agree; no turning back. I don’t ever want you to let me go. When you walked off the plane that day, I just knew I’d never see you again. My heart broke at that moment, and I didn’t know a thing about you. Brent, you’re my whole world now. Everything I do, I want you there with me. Brent, you can open your eyes now.”

Blinking, he turned around and moved toward her. Leah had donned a thick comfy spa robe. Squeezing her tight, Brent pulled back and stared into Leah’s innocent, loving eyes. Then, baring his soul, he divulged, “You are the most beautiful woman I’ve ever seen, but do we want to rush things? I care too much for you to think that only intimacy is all that interests me.”

Hearing the words flow from the lips of a true gentleman, Leah whispered,

“Well, if you think it will be easy for me, you overestimate my restraint ability. But I agree with you. Our relationship is so much more than that to me. Would you like to hand me my clothes? I can’t very well return to the ballroom in this robe.” She giggled.

Consumed with thoughts of the nights ahead, Leah swiftly dressed, and they headed back downstairs.

At the gala, Evan's security staff received a severe tongue-lashing for letting their suspect slip into the celebration unseen. Amber's curious eyes followed his every move from across the room. Pausing a moment from his rant, he offered her a quick smile and then returned to the issue at hand, threatening to strangle his security team.

When the group meeting ended, Evan strode toward Amber, leaving the security team shaking their heads in disbelief. Taking a seat beside her, Evan grumbled under his breath.

"I'm guessing they're aware you are highly upset about the security breach," she said, smiling.

"You better believe they know. I cannot tolerate incompetence. We're fortunate Leah wasn't hurt worse, or heaven forbid another explosion occurred." Evan's face reddened with anger. Raw emotion from the evening's events tightened his features.

Amber spoke up, addressing the elephant in the room. "I'm sorry about Leah and Brent. I feel certain you have feelings for her. It's quite undeniable. I've been aware of them since I first met you in Baton Rouge. She's a very lovable person."

"Yes, she is. I probably should be offering you my support since Brent was your date. His display of feelings for another woman right in front of you couldn't be easy for you to handle."

Amber laughed. "Oh, that doesn't bother me. Brent and I are very close, but not in a romantic sort of way. We've known each other since we were young. I'm very sorry for your pain, and this may be hard for you to hear, but they really do suit each other. If you ever need a friend to talk to or confide in, please know that you can count on me. I love both of them, so I can't say I'm sad they're together. Consider this, though; once you've sorted through your feelings, let me know. Your newfound availability might open doors for others who may be interested in you." She proclaimed, smiling warmly.

Evan had to admit Amber was gorgeous. He'd taken note of her beauty both times they met. Being Leah's best friend spoke volumes for Amber's character. Maybe he and Amber could explore a friendship once he regained control of his emotions. Or more.

Arriving back in the ballroom, Leah and Brent rejoined the guests still lolling around. The gala was a smashing success, made evident by a lack of concern for time. The early morning hours had arrived without notice. As Leah scanned the room for her friends, her eyes drifted over to Amber and Evan. Seated at the same table, they appeared deeply engrossed in conversation. Smiles crossed their lips, giving way to a chuckle or two. Seeing the two of them together made Leah happy. She was probably the only one who knew about Amber's interest in Evan.

Leah hastily gathered Amber, Carol, and Rhonda together, reminding them to return their gowns to Kimberley's collection in the penthouse. Kimberly and Suzanne volunteered to go and assist the ladies. Before their departure, Leah showered the two stylists with an onslaught of verbal appreciation for their kindness, followed by Evan and Amber's echoed sentiments. Evan's declarations to repay the women somehow were interrupted by Kimberly's chuckle.

"Remember, Evan you owe your sister the big favor, not me. I did it for Pam. She's invaluable. I don't know what I would do without her. And I have a good inclination you'll be paying dearly." Laughing again, Kimberly headed to the elevator with Brent by her side.

Leah was well aware Brent's offer to escort the ladies upstairs served as a ruse to allow her private time with Evan. Postponing the inevitable would only make their relationship more awkward.

In between the thankful comments from guests, as they made their way out of the building, Leah glanced at Evan. "I guess I should've told you sooner about my feelings for Brent. I never meant for you to find out the way you did. I lost my head in all the excitement. I would never do anything to hurt you. It's just that I don't feel the way I should for the type of relationship you desire. I hope we will forever be friends."

"In all honesty, I wish it had turned out differently, but you can count on one thing. I'll make it a priority always to be a dependable friend that you can rely on and trust."

Jumping to hug him, Leah smiled. "Thank you, Evan. That means more to me than you realize. Besides, I think someone's waiting in the wings to console you when you are ready." Leah tilted her head toward Amber entering the room, yawning.

Evan smiled back at Leah. "So, you say! We have bigger fish to catch, Ms. Reynolds, before I can even consider that route. Our first priority is to focus on a plan to catch our 'friend,' just not tonight. Everyone's exhausted, and we need to consider our next move carefully."

Their conversation was interrupted by the group's return from the penthouse.

Rhonda, Carol, and Charlie exited the building and headed to their car, shouting their thanks to Evan for a lovely evening. Brent had promised Evan he'd escort Amber and Leah back to his apartment. After a wave of hugs, Evan sent Leah and Amber on their way with Brent. Unfortunately, he needed to stay behind and rid the building of stragglers. The Centennial Center cost the company a fortune for the evening. Unwilling to experience more screw-ups, Evan decided to stay and secure the facility himself. The sun would cross the horizon before he headed home.

CHAPTER THIRTY-TWO

The golden opportunity had passed by for the sinister man. Leah Reynolds was a lot stronger than he'd imagined. Once they spotted him, his plan changed. *He* knew dragging Leah through the exit door into the night with him made her the perfect pawn in the game. Unfortunately, her strength knocked him off balance, and the only option left was to toss her to the floor to ensure his escape. Still, the night was a success. He'd mingled with the crowd and observed his targets without being spotted by the security staff. Laughter coursed through his body, thinking about the clueless clowns Evan Holcomb had wasted his money on for security.

Basking in the night's accomplishments, a voice within the man told him to make his way back to the Centennial Center. It was late, the crowd would be sparse, and maybe he'd spot one of the prime targets heading out alone or, better yet, inside.

What could it hurt?

All his previous attempts to thwart their plans failed. The merger remained on schedule. They'd ignored his prior warnings. Maybe saving the life of a hostage would give cause for a cancellation, or so one would think.

After reviewing the access points to the building, he decided the loading dock would be the best place to start. It provided a quick entry to a secluded area if the need arose.

During his slow drive into the alley, *He* saw Evan

Holcomb exiting the loading dock door and rounding the corner. Accompanied by two new women, Evan followed behind, arms overflowing with gowns. As *He* inched closer, *He* picked up on the usual chatter; thank you, it was a great party. After one final "thank you," the women climbed into the van and headed down the alleyway.

I'm one lucky cuss!

Another ideal opportunity presented itself right in front of him. The secluded alleyway guaranteed privacy, but it wouldn't be easy to take Holcomb down. Evan was large, strong, and self-assured, but *He* held an element of surprise. Besides, his former training taught him profound ways to immobilize someone in seconds. Getting Holcomb back to the car would be the biggest challenge.

Evan returned to the loading dock and jerked the door closed. His back turned to the alleyway; he fought with the key. Cussing, he jiggled the mechanism forcing the key further into the lock.

Now! *He* rushed the dock, jumping on Evan's back, encircling his arms in a chokehold around his neck. As expected, the fight to maintain a firm grasp was no easy feat. Evan struggled, grabbing the man as he tried to pull him to his front side. But *He* won. Evan Holcomb lay before him on the ground like a sleeping baby. Time was of the essence to ensure the success of his spontaneous decision. He hauled Evan into the alleyway, tossing him callously into the darkness, and sprinted for the car. The medium-sized sedan contained all the tools necessary to ensure Holcomb slept on their journey, even a sizable trunk to house Holcomb's tall frame. *He* chuckled. They would be well on their way out of town before anyone ever noticed Evan Holcomb was missing.

Leah sprang to life the following day, full of hope. She felt as though she'd been living in a dream the last twenty-four hours. It had been quite an evening, or should she say morning. Brent escorted the ladies up to the apartment close to 5 a.m. Amber headed straight to bed, unable to hold her eyes open any longer. Brent's goodbye kiss resonated with the hidden promise of never having to wonder if she would see him again. Leah was astonished at the depth of her love for this man. Even she was unsure of the magnitude until she verbalized it. Her words of devotion echoed in her mind. Smiling, she changed and headed for a cup of strong coffee.

Making her way toward the study, Leah heard John and Martha's voices stream through the doorway. Excitement lingered in their tone. Both were chattering about how much fun they had at the gala.

"A wife should thank a husband when thanks are due. And you, John Watts, deserve a huge thank you. I'm so happy you convinced me to attend the gala. It's been years since I've enjoyed such a wonderful night out. I journeyed back to my younger days in the beautiful gown Kimberly provided." Martha's smile radiated warmth.

"You, dear, were the 'belle' of the ball. The most beautiful woman in the room, and I'm lucky to say you're mine." Chuckling, John leaned toward Martha and planted a hefty kiss on her cheek.

Pushing against the door lightly, Leah gave a big "hmmm."

"Hey, hey, you two. Should I leave the room!" Leah snickered.

"You most certainly should not. It's all because of you that this wonderful venture is taking place. I was so stubborn and hardheaded about merging the two companies. Everyone involved should offer you their thanks, not just me. Speaking of thanks, where's Evan this morning? I wanted to thank him for his hospitality before we leave."

"What do you mean? Haven't you seen him this morning? I think he stayed to secure the building last night, but he said he wouldn't be far behind us. Maybe he's still sleeping. Did you try his room?" Leah's mind began to wander.

Did he go to talk to Amber? Is he in her room?

No, she knew better than that. They weren't one-night stand types.

"I tried his room earlier, knocked, and knocked but no answer. He may have headed to the office early this morning." John uttered casually, engrossed in the morning paper.

"I don't think so. We all had a very late night. Besides, he wouldn't rush off and leave us here without a note or something." Leah's stomach tightened, and her heart raced.

"I think I'll go make a couple of phone calls. You and Martha finish your breakfast. Let me see if I can locate Evan." Leah exited the room, dialing Brent's number before crossing the threshold.

A groggy hello indicated he was sound asleep. "Brent? It's Leah."

"Believe me. I know who it is. There's no mistaking your angelic voice. I can't wait to wake up to the sound of your voice every morning. However, I'd prefer you were two feet away instead of two miles." Brent's sexy banter caused a flurry of love and emotion, but now wasn't the time.

"Brent, I think something's wrong. We can't find Evan. I don't think he came home last night. I called Joan, and she hasn't seen him, so he's not at the office. If he's not there and not here, where can he be? I have a terrible suspicion something's wrong." Leah's breath caught in her throat, unable to continue.

"What? Did you check with the security staff? Of course, he could've decided to stay in the penthouse instead of coming back to the apartment so late. After all, he had the center's master key and free rein."

"I called. Evan's not in the penthouse, and his car's still in the parking lot. Tell me this doesn't seem strange to you."

"Leah, calm down. Evan's quite capable of taking care of himself. He's a strong, level-headed guy. Any sign of trouble, he would've contacted someone. He'd never try to handle it on his own." Brent's words reeked of half-truths.

"I'm sure he's fine, but I'll head down to the center and see what I can find out. Why don't you, Amber, and Martha enjoy a girl's day. Find a spa somewhere. Do something fun. Get the royal treatment, and I'll find Evan. He's probably sound asleep somewhere. Don't worry, beautiful."

"If you're sure that everything's okay… I guess the girls could use a good massage to round out our dream weekend. There's no sense in worrying until we have a reason. Call me as soon as you find Evan. And tell him when you do that, I'm going to kill him for upsetting us. Be careful. I love you too much for anything to happen to you."

"That's music to my ears. I love you too. You girls, enjoy your day. We'll talk later this afternoon. I'm sure of it." Brent hung up the phone and immediately dialed Steve Alexander's number. Uncomfortable with his and Leah's conversation, Brent needed backup to help in his search.

CHAPTER THIRTY-THREE

Steve Alexander and Cooper met Brent at the Centennial Center. A quick check of the building's lower interior floors showed no signs of a breach or Evan. The three agreed to divide the search area among them. Cooper headed to the security office to review the previous night's camera footage. Steve prepared to check Evan's car in the parking lot and the outside perimeter while Brent proceeded to the penthouse.

Walking into the lavish penthouse, vivid images of the special moments he spent with Leah only a few short hours ago flashed in his mind, and now Evan was missing. How could things go awry so quickly? Everything in him said Evan was in trouble. And unfortunately, his thorough search of the empty penthouse offered no consolation.

Shaking his head in disbelief, Brent was on his way back down to the lobby when a call from Steve ordered him to the loading dock. Fast.

"We may have a problem" were the only words Brent comprehended when he arrived at the dock.

"Do you see the shoe prints by the door threshold? Footsteps toward the door and then away would leave a specific pattern. These appear to shuffle here and there. Another strange thing involves the marks on the ground over here." Steve jumped from the dock, pointing to the dirt surrounding them.

"Those ruts indicate someone pulled a rather heavy

object through the dirt for a short distance, then the marks disappear. The numerous tire imprints surrounding the area make it impossible to match all the marks with every vehicle that was probably loaded in and out of here yesterday. Evan's car is still in the parking lot and appears untouched since he left it yesterday. And that's not all, Brent. I found the master key dangling in the lock when I arrived." Steve swung the set of keys in the air.

"If I had to go with my gut, I'd say it's possible Evan was taken by surprise back here. What happened after that, I can't say." Steve lowered his head in frustration.

"Yeah, I agree with one thing. Someone would need to take Evan by surprise to immobilize him. Evan's a sizeable guy, fully capable of defending himself." Brent knew Steve's theory was more than probable.

Brent prayed Cooper had found something on the cameras. Then, as if on cue, Cooper approached the men, scratching his chin, bewildered.

"What do you have, Coop?" Brent asked.

"It seems Evan helped the ladies carry out all the gowns. Then the security cameras show Evan turning to lock the door when someone closes in behind him and gets a chokehold around his neck. This person had skills because Evan went down quickly. Anything else that may have happened back here was out of view of the cameras. So, what do we do now?" He questioned.

"Cooper, get a copy of that tape and head back to the office. Make sure the staff doesn't tell anyone what's happening. Brent, if our 'friend' took Evan, he's all about threats and intimidation. He'll most likely try to contact Leah or John with his demands. Notify me as soon as that happens. Make sure as few people as possible are aware of what's happening. The kidnapper won't harm him; he's too valuable alive."

Brent dreaded telling Leah and John that Evan was missing. Surprise, guilt, and worry would consume them even though it was not their fault. Truth be known, he was somewhat responsible. He liked Evan. And had his attempts to locate this villain sooner been effective, none of this would have happened.

Leah had taken Brent's advice and called the "Sisters Seven" together for a spa day before everyone headed in a different direction tomorrow morning. The women sat drinking mimosas at the luscious little spa, reminiscing about the prior evening. Deep in conversation and laughter with the ladies, Leah answered her ringing phone in a cheerful voice,

"Hello, love of my life. Did you find him?" Roars of laughter bellowed in the background as the "sisters" mimicked signs of nausea with their hands.

"I'm so glad to hear of your affection for me, but the answer is no. It should have been you and not Evan," the disturbing voice grumbled.

Leah froze in horror at the sound of *his* cold, callous voice again. "What are you saying? Why?"

"It was going to be you that I had in my snare, but you were able to escape from my grasp. Holcomb wasn't quite so lucky. I haven't hurt him yet, but I will if you don't cancel the ribbon-cutting in Bridgeport and stop this merger."

Leah whispered, "Please, don't hurt him. I'll resolve this somehow, I promise. Just tell me why you're doing this?"

"All of you will find out soon enough. I'll be back in touch. Hugs and kisses." And the line went dead.

Mother hen Carol suddenly piped up, "Leah, this has been happening way too much. First, weird calls, pale looks, horrified eyes, and now a secret phone conversation. You have to tell us what's going on. Do you have a stalker or something?"

Leah's eyes filled with panic as the group looked on. Charlie and Amber held their breath in wait for answers. As for Rhonda and Carol, keeping them in the dark for their safety could be a mistake. The room swelled with questions after her outburst. Leah saw it on the women's faces. Kimberly and Suzanne, once innocent bystanders, found themselves now involved due to the conversation they overheard.

Leah only told the women certain aspects of their drama. She determined it was in everyone's best interest to withhold essential points that might place them in danger, especially things related to Brent's job and his relationship with Amber. The ladies, sworn to secrecy, vowed to help in any way possible. Somehow Leah managed to convince them that the police were very close to catching the criminal. The ribbon-cutting would go on without interruption.

Before the ladies hurried out the door, Kimberly and Suzanne promised to visit Bridgeport. Since their spa outing was abruptly cut short, Leah headed straight to find Brent. If Evan's life was in danger, she must tell John and Brent immediately. Charlie and Amber followed close behind her.

Brent's choice to forego calling Leah and head straight to Evan's apartment proved to be the best decision. John Watts needed to hear the truth. Brent knew time was up waiting on a "catch me if you can" game now that Evan had gone missing. Leah and Amber were too curious to be kept in the dark. He would update them once they arrived at the apartment.

Brent knocked on the apartment door, feeling a tinge of selfishness over the timing of this crisis. He and Leah finally admitted their feelings for each other, and now their relationship was in a holding pattern until they found this maniac.

John opened the front door displaying a toothy grin and offering a generous welcome.

"Brent. How in the world are you this morning? Great day, isn't it! Come in, come in."

"Good morning, Mr. Watts. I trust you're having an enjoyable morning. I'm sorry to burst in like this, but we need to talk privately. Unless you feel our conversation should include Martha. That will be your decision."

"Well, that sounds rather ominous. I'm not sure what we need to talk about, but you have my attention. Let's discuss what is going on, and then I'll determine if Martha needs to be involved." John ushered Brent into the study.

"Please sit down. I'm listening."

"Mr. Watts, are you aware that I know about the phone call you received regarding canceling the merger?"

Drawn with curiosity, John muttered, "How could you? Did Leah tell you?"

"Yes, but not to betray your confidence. Several other incidents have occurred that you're unaware of regarding the merger. Things that Evan and Leah concealed from you for your protection. I'm telling you all this because, unfortunately, things have taken a turn for the worse. Evan has disappeared."

Standing until now, John grabbed the arm of a chair and eased down onto the seat. In a state of shock, his eyes widened, questioning Brent, "It was all genuine? Someone's going to get hurt because of this merger. But why?"

"I'd like to say no, but I can't be sure at this point.

There's a lot you need to know. But, in my opinion, Martha should also be privy to the truth. Only you can make that decision."

John's mouth gaped open; his decision was interrupted when Leah, Charlie, and Amber rushed through the door. Leah hurried into Brent's arms, trembling, unable to speak. Brent's fear for her safety gave way to desperation for her closeness when she feverishly kissed him sharing her unbridled concern in one long kiss. Unapologetic to anyone in the room for his display of raw emotion, Brent steadied himself, kissing her back. Relief that Leah wasn't the one missing flooded his heart.

Coughing sounds rolled throughout the room. Finally, Brent released Leah when she screamed, "*He* kidnapped Evan!"

"What? How do you know?" Brent questioned.

"The fiend called me again. His voice, confident and unconcerned, teased me. Saying it was supposed to be me, but I was stronger than he thought. I'm so worried about Evan. *He* emphasized that we'd all understand why this is happening soon enough. His instructions were clear. We must cancel the ribbon cutting if we want to see Evan again. What should we do?"

Leah turned to John. His resilience was waning. "John, I'm so sorry; we never should have concealed this from you. Evan and I only wanted to protect you and Martha. Now Evan is missing, and we have no clue where he is." Leah gasped for air. "Do you think *He* will hurt him?" No one spoke.

Brent watched as the two women in his life turned ghostly white. He loved them both dearly and vowed to protect them no matter the cost. It was clear that it would take them all, Steve, Cooper, John, Amber, and Leah, to apprehend this maniac. No more secrets. They were out of time. The terrorist had toyed with them long enough. Each of his warnings displayed more aggression and agitation.

Now, *He* was at the point where killing Evan meant nothing to him if his demands remained unmet.

The next few hours revolved around bringing John and Martha up to speed on the nightmare they were living. Brent and Leah decided to withhold the composite sketch from them. Brent suspected once John and Martha laid eyes upon the drawing, they would spot the guy on every street corner. Scaring them to death could only make the situation worse for everyone.

"I still have the same question. Why? Why would anyone want to cancel the merger? A successful merger means so much to so many people." John Watts rubbed his forehead, bewildered by their situation. Martha remained quiet, patting John's knee in humble support of her husband.

Steve and Cooper arrived, completing the "brain trust." The six people standing before Brent must now accomplish the overwhelming task of somehow keeping Evan alive, including himself. Leah's earlier conversation with the kidnapper indicated he would contact her again. *He* felt drawn to Leah, and they were unsure why.

Everyone agreed the ribbon-cutting must go on as planned. But, knowing *He* would be livid about the scheduled event, Brent figured it was just a matter of time before *He* contacted Leah to express his anger. And when *He* did, they would be ready.

Their organized plan awaited implementation. Leah needed to coax Evan's assailant into meeting with her face-to-face to talk about his anger surrounding the merger. She'd insist Evan remain unharmed and present at their meeting. Everything hinged on her ability to reassure him that she maintained all the power to cancel the merger if she saw Evan wasn't hurt. Leah's believability needed to be on point since it was essential to drawing him out. Brent knew the man was deranged. *He* was too sure of himself to give up an opportunity to boast about his motives, especially to Leah.

Fear seized Brent's heart. The best law enforcement officers in the country would track Leah's every move from the moment she stepped onto the Watts Enterprises property. Yet, his concern for her safety remained at the forefront. Everyone in the group had a part to play, but Leah's was extremely dangerous. Her bravery made him love her even more. In the end, Brent remained confident that nothing would happen to Leah. He'd sacrifice his own life first.

Looking forward to future days filled with love and laughter, Brent mustered the courage to initiate their plan.

CHAPTER THIRTY-FOUR

Evan awoke to the roaring of tires on asphalt. Slowly gaining recognition of his surroundings, Evan determined he'd been stuffed into the trunk of a car, a crappy one. His feet and wrists were bound tightly, leaving him no way to maneuver his large frame into a different position. Beneath him laid mounds of empty jugs, bottles, and cans strewn around, poking him. Evan figured the owner must live in the mobile piece of scrap iron based on the smell that encompassed him and the bulk of junk. Wiggling to gain an ounce of legroom proved impossible. His positioning in the small area had been no accident. His assailant wanted to immobilize him, preventing a glimpse of anything but the trunk roof.

The reality of who owned the car instantly stabbed him in the chest. The timing, the location, and the surprise attack left no doubt in his mind. Evan was now in the grip of their stalker. The attack occurred so fast that he had no time to react. The pressure on his windpipe constricted all his airflow, rendering him unconscious in seconds. His assailant held the upper hand for now. However, Evan welcomed the opportunity for a face-to-face conversation. Time. He needed a little time. He'd wait until the right moment presented itself, and then his attacker would experience a dose of his own medicine.

I'll end this once and for all!

By now, Leah, Amber, and Brent must know

something was wrong. Brent's intuitive disposition was now a weapon in Evan's arsenal. Brent would do everything in his power to find him. Evan just needed to stall until either an excellent opportunity presented itself or they located him, whichever came first.

Hearing the rumbling in the trunk, *He* assumed Holcomb had regained consciousness. *He* prayed the ropes kept his captive contained. Evan Holcomb was a big man and quite capable of defending himself. The luxury of taking Evan down rapidly by surprise wouldn't happen again. Evan's guard being up presented numerous issues for him. It would be more important than ever to keep Evan securely restrained.

Peering out the window at the rising sun, his decision to drive straight through the night proved beneficial. Their destination was just up ahead. *He* was well aware that people were scouring Charlotte in search of Holcomb by now. Nighttime provided the cover of darkness and their anonymity in addition to several hours of downtime. The drive and the endless visions of empty highways fueled his anger, provoking unsavory thoughts. Images of the happy smiling group at the gala only nourished his hatred. They had no idea who he was. Within steps of him, they never looked at him twice until he reached for Leah. How quickly people forget, but *He* would remind them. Then, they, too, would experience the pain he'd felt so long ago.

I will hit them where it hurts the most.

Twenty-four hours had passed since *He* issued his demands to Leah. The instructions were straightforward: cancel the ribbon-cutting, which meant a merger cancellation. The newspapers were undoubtedly filled with news of the merger collapse by now. Holding Evan captive increased his leverage. No one was dumb enough to risk Evan's life by disregarding his wishes. Everything would work out as planned, allowing him to move on to a new place that might provide better memories.

The vehicle maneuvered onto a gravel driveway, stopping abruptly and slamming Evan into the rear of the trunk. Cursing, he grimaced in pain from the blow to his head. Evan flinched as the cover above him cracked open. Unprepared for the captor's next move, he braced himself against the sides of the car. Then, he watched as a man, every bit the image of Leah's sketch, opened the hatch guardedly. The evil eyes that held Evan's attention weeks ago peeped into the trunk.

"Ok. Out, Holcomb. This is where the party will start." Waving his hand in a sweeping gesture toward the house and grounds, the man kept a watchful eye on his captive.

"You'll find the accommodations quite different from your normal furnishings, but I'm sure you'll find a way to cope. And before you think about making a move to disarm me, you should know this isn't the only gun trained on a target. Another one's watching every move your friend Leah makes." The concern on Evan's face fueled the indignant tone in his abductor's voice. "Yes, that's right, she's quite easy to reach, so no sudden movements. If you cooperate, there's a chance you all may survive this." *He* snickered.

Evan's intuition told him now wasn't the time to cause any trouble. The hatred radiating from the maniac indicated everything he said was probably true, and Evan refused to risk Leah's life. Evan would play the game as instructed for now. Nonetheless, he wanted answers in the meantime.

"You want to tell me where we are and why I'm here? I understand you want the merger stopped, but you've failed to explain why. What makes you think kidnapping me will force John Watts to cancel anything? Hundreds of lives will change for the better by the project's success. My life isn't that important in the grand scheme of things. I assure you the merger will go on." Staring into black eyes, Evan searched for even the slightest weakness in him.

He laughed. "Well, let's start by answering your first question…you're here because Leah escaped my grasp the other night. We both know that you and John Watts harbor a warm fondness for her and would do anything to protect her. She was my golden ticket to stop the merger. Since that didn't work out, you're here - by should I say - default. Call it, if you will, being in the wrong place at the right time."

"On the flip side, your safety's essential to Leah. She has feelings for you, and she holds the power to convince John Watts to stop the merger. You better hope your life means something to Watts, too, for your sake. I have no problem killing you to ensure my end goal is a success."

Evan analyzed his captor's every move and expression. *He* was no dummy. He'd devised a comprehensive, well-thought plan. Unfortunately, the man had managed to elude them at every turn, and capture was not an option in his vision. Still, something screamed familiarity about his captor. Racking his brain to remember, Evan goaded him to provide more information.

"You never answered my question about where we are?" An escape plan required knowledge of his location.

"In Bridgeport, of course, the location for the final event. The highly touted ribbon cutting for Watts Enterprises. There'll be hundreds of people in attendance.

I'm glad it's not my decision whether they will be in danger or enjoying a safe family outing. Bridgeport is the perfect setting for my last stand if Leah disappoints me. I may not survive, but I'm certain a few other people won't either." Evan sensed a hint of sorrow in his statement.

"Why is it necessary to stop something that benefits Bridgeport's citizens? This merger is lucrative for everyone involved. Do you have a vendetta against helping people and making money? The increased funding will make the entire town a better place. Doors will open across the country for new imports. In addition, Watts Enterprises will join the corporation and become part of a new family that cares for each other. Why would you be against that?"

He slammed the trunk closed. Streaks of anger transformed his face into a twisted mask. "Watts Enterprises helped everyone but the people who needed it, people who should have come first above all the others. Enough discussion. Get inside."

Shoving Evan forward, the two moved toward a dilapidated house, walking in silence. *He* casually opened the door and kicked Evan in the back, thrusting him into the room. Evan's eyes flamed with anger as he surveyed every inch of their humble surroundings. The leaky roof and crumbled walls gave way to an interior with minimal furniture. No pictures adorned the walls. Dirty, ragged curtains clung to the rotten window frames. The floors creaked from the aged wood beneath their weight.

Evan quickly searched for a newspaper, map, magazine, anything that might reveal their location. Unsuccessful, he pushed for one last bit of information.

"Tell me, have we ever met? Are you angry because I don't remember you? Is that why you want to punish Holcomb Industries?"

Laughing loudly, *He* turned around. "You keep staring, Holcomb. You're scouring your memory, trying to place my face. Something about me looks familiar, right?

You have no idea how close you are to the truth. You'll all know soon enough who I am. Right now, I have a phone call to make. Have a seat."

He ushered Evan to a small, straight-back chair, firmly binding his hands and feet to it. Evan knew his only choice was to remain compliant.

What did he mean about recognizing him?

Time was ticking away. Evan calculated he had a maximum of 48 hours to figure out the meaning of his comments. Not just to save his own life but to save Leah's, also.

He yanked a phone from his pocket and began entering numbers. Straining to see the numbers, Evan suddenly realized who *He* was calling. It was Leah!

He spoke in a tone that made Evan livid and sick to his stomach.

"Hello, beautiful. I bet you didn't think you'd hear from me again so soon. But you see, I have something I need you to do for me. If you don't, your friend Evan Holcomb dies along with whoever else gets in my way." Sinister chuckles filled the air, followed by further demands.

"You know what you need to do. Make sure it gets done. I'll be in touch again soon."

Evan presumed *He* cut the call short to avoid a possible trace. His kidnapper reinforced Evan's belief that the man was intelligent and capable of success. This knowledge heightened Evan's senses.

He moved toward Evan, scratching his head. "You know, I think she really cares for you. By the way, if it makes you feel better, Leah was on the verge of tears. You may live, after all. Guess we'll see if she can follow directions. Now I need to sleep. You'll have to sleep sitting straight up, but that's the only way to keep you secured."

"Meanwhile, I'll be in the car, all nice and comfy. You can't steal the car if I'm in it, and there's nowhere for you to run out here. Sleep tight." He smirked, walking out the door with an arrogant nod.

He was very sure of himself, and Evan liked that. It may prove helpful in the coming days. Evan hoped his extreme level of arrogance contributed to careless mistakes in judgment. Evan made himself as comfortable as possible and waited for tomorrow.

CHAPTER THIRTY-FIVE

The startling sound of Leah's phone placed everyone on high alert. Terrified the call would come and terrified it wouldn't, Leah squelched her inner fears. Answering cautiously, she uttered, "Yes." She tried hard to sound braver than she felt.

"You disappoint me, Leah. If anyone believed I'd carry out my threats, I thought it would be you. Remember, it's all your fault if your friend Evan winds up dead. I may or may not be back in touch." The infuriated voice on the other end told Leah their plan had worked.

Brent and Steve Alexander overheard every word. Charlie played her part superbly by writing a feature article boasting of the festivities for the ribbon cutting. They knew *He* would check the papers or news media for reports of a cancellation. The article excluded any mention of Evan's disappearance. Instead, the piece boasted food, fireworks, carnival games, and fun for the entire town and visitors. Things appeared to be going according to plan; everything except Leah's belief she could pull this off. *He* gave her no opportunity to respond during the call. What if *He* didn't call back? She couldn't live with herself if something happened to Evan.

Until two days ago, her feelings for Evan had wavered between a close business colleague and a possible romantic relationship. Her open admission of her love for Brent made her realize Evan was more of a best friend.

One person captured her attention throughout the whole ordeal. Amber. Amber appeared as worried as Leah. Quietly waiting in the wings on a request for help, Amber remained attentive. How lucky could a girl be to meet the man of her dreams and have his sister as a best friend? Yes, God smiled at her the day she fell into that airplane.

The man of her dreams stood before her, full of determination and strength. Brent certainly had a knack for making her weak in the knees. Constantly aware of her presence, he issued a quick wink and naughty smile, offering the reassurance she craved. The man was the epitome of sexy, kind, caring, and confident. Leah tried not to dwell on the fact that dozens of women would do anything to catch his attention. He loved her, and she loved him more than she ever thought possible.

Taking a deep breath, Leah shelved her selfish thoughts. Right now, Evan's safety must be her primary focus. She blinked and returned to the conversation taking place around her.

"Steve, as soon as we establish a meeting place, it will be pivotal that all the agents are in place to ensure Leah's safety. I'll remain as close to her as possible without making it obvious. But if things go bad, your agents will need to save them both. I don't intend to let anything happen to her, no matter what the cost." Brent's bold statement required no explanation. Everyone knew exactly what he meant.

"I have everything and everyone on standby. Rest assured, we'll catch this guy. Leah will not be hurt. The frustrating part is sitting and waiting while our suspect's playing cat and mouse with us. I suggest everyone find a comfortable place to get a little sleep. It'll be morning before you know it, and we need to be ready for whatever it brings."

No one wanted to leave the apartment, so Steve and Cooper found a plush sofa and oversized chair and made themselves comfortable. John and Martha headed to their room while Charlie bedded down on another couch. Amber made her way to Evan's room. Leah reached for Brent's hand, guiding him down the hallway. She gently turned the doorknob as they walked into the room. Her wandering mind evoked images of their interlude in the penthouse. Leah found herself stressing over little things in hopes of being discreet. She fluffed the pillows numerous times before turning the covers back on the bed. Next, she headed to the expansive chaise lounge outfitting it with blankets and a pillow.

Fatigue overrode any more prudence. Her tired body shrugged off her slacks and unbuttoned her shirt, tossing them to the floor. Reaching into her luggage, Leah pulled a t-shirt and boxers from her bag. She yawned, dragging the boxers up to her hips. As she popped her head into the shirt, she noticed Brent returning from the lavatory. Quickly, sliding her arms through the holes, Leah stood motionless, smiling.

Without a word, Brent crossed the room in an instant. Leah felt warm hands on either side of her cheeks, angling her head upward to his loving gaze.

"You know that I would die before I'd let anything happen to you. You're my entire world now. If he tries to harm you, I'll kill this maniac. My love life was nonexistent when I met you. I vowed I would never fall in love again after someone who professed to love me trampled my heart. But then you showed up out of nowhere. You fell right into my arms, and I don't intend to let you go. So, Leah Reynolds, I'll be damned if our life together will be cut short by this deranged idiot." He leaned into Leah and kissed her. His kiss created sensations of comfort, love, and joy – all at once. The longer their kiss, the tighter her grasp became around his neck.

Effortlessly, Brent scooped her up, placing her softly on the bed. Breaking their kiss to brush the hair from her face, their eyes locked when she slid her fingers through his dark hair. Brent carefully pushed away from her. A raspy exhale squeezed free from his lungs.

"You know this is very hard for me to say. But…"

Leah placed her index finger to his lips, quieting his statement. "I agree. Now isn't the right time."

"Sadly, you're right. The instant all this is resolved, we will focus on ourselves and our future. Are you ok with that?"

"Brent Scott, I love you so much. I'd be upset if you told me I'd never get to be alone with you again. However, for now, I agree with you. Evan's safety is our number one priority. I'm afraid it won't be this quiet again for a while." Brent hugged her, kissed the top of her head, and tucked her in for some desperately needed rest. He turned out the lights and made his way over to the chaise for a few hours of rest of his own.

The group's few hours of sleep only made them aware of how much rest they needed. Their weary bodies were exhausted from carrying the burden of the unknown. Red eyes, sleepy scowls, and a weak "good morning" welcomed Leah and Brent to the kitchen gathering. Cooper lazily pointed to the coffee pot, directing Brent to the fresh brew.

Brent's wake-up call arrived way too early. All the caffeine in the world couldn't return him to his blissful dreams of Leah. Watching Leah make her way toward his sister made his heart leap. He knew his life would never be the same, trying to control two strong-willed women, but he wouldn't change it for the world. Brent chuckled as Leah tapped Amber on the shoulder. Coffee, he needed coffee. There was no way he was interrupting those two on just one cup.

Leah smiled, pulling Amber to the side.

"Let's go have our coffee somewhere we can talk privately." Nodding in agreement, Amber grabbed her steaming cup and followed her friend, but not before sticking her tongue out at her brother, giggling.

The women crossed into the study, huffing a sigh, anxious to be alone. The oversized wingback chairs wrapped around them, welcoming them to a few moments of girl time. Unsure how to start the conversation, Leah cleared her throat.

"Amber, I need to talk to you. I hope you don't think me too forward, but I know how close you are to Brent." Breathing in deeply, Leah continued.

"In case you can't tell, I love your brother with all my heart. I get that it's been just the two of you for a long time, and we have become very close friends. I think of you as the sister I never had. If you're not comfortable with where Brent and I are heading in this relationship, please tell me. I wouldn't want to do anything to upset you or make you angry. We can talk about anything and resolve any issue; however, I need to tell you that there will be no resolution involving me giving up Brent. My desire isn't to be contrite or mean. I'm telling you, out of pure unadulterated, heart-pounding, everlasting love for him."

Amber began laughing. "Leah, so many adjectives used to describe one explanation of love. What am I to do? Your pledge of love was something out of Romeo and Juliet. But, of course, I want you in our lives. You have brought joy to both of us, although I'd venture to say more to his life than mine!" Amber's bright smile spoke volumes. Leah tossed the closest pillow in the direction of Amber's head.

"You and I are, and forever will be, best friends and now sisters. I wouldn't want anyone else sharing Brent's life except for you." At that moment, Amber's attitude turned somber, her head bowed.

Leah detected the change right away. “Hey, why the look of desperation? This whole thing is going to work out fine. You may have fooled most people around here, but not me. I know that no one wants Evan back safe and sound more than you. At our first dinner meeting, I saw the ‘love at first sight’ in your eyes. It closely resembles mine and is hard to dismiss once you recognize it. Don't worry. Evan can take care of himself.”

Amber sighed. “I keep telling myself I just met him and that he probably still has feelings for you, but I feel drawn to him. I can’t explain why. Can we keep this just between us, Leah? He may not want to get to know me better. The fewer people who detect my true feelings, the better.”

Leah could sympathize with Amber. Her heart was hanging on a thread only a short time ago. But, Leah wondered, why was it the women who always fell so hard and so fast?

“All I can say is if Evan doesn’t at least try to get to know you better, it will be his loss. Although knowing Evan the way I do, my gut tells me he’ll take the chance. Just give him a little time.”

Amber jumped from her chair and gave her friend the biggest hug she could muster, bringing both women to tears. Two crying women are what Brent found when he walked in.

“Well, well, what do we have here? A ‘cry fest or a hug-fest’? Because if it’s the latter, I’m in!” Amber and Leah grabbed any pillow within reach and tossed them at Brent. Covering his head with both arms, he ran from the room.

CHAPTER THIRTY-SIX

He woke with a sore neck and a small moment of panic.

What if Holcomb escaped in the night? It would ruin all my plans.

Shaking his head to clear his thoughts, *He* knew Evan was right where he'd left him. Holcomb would never try to break free or jeopardize his precious Leah's safety. Struggling to unfold his achy limbs from the car, *He* headed toward the wooden shack. Evan watched the door like a hawk, just as *He* expected.

"Forgive me for not providing breakfast, but we're on a fasting diet. No need to stock food when we aren't here long enough to eat it." Evan remained silent.

He began to smile. "Let's find out what the world has to say about the sudden disappearance of the most sought-after bachelor in Charlotte." His cell phone browser offered the only updated news available since there was no electricity in the shack. His fingers tapped at the phone screen over and over but continued to come up with zero references to Evan's disappearance. Anger, hate, and vengeance contorted his face. Those idiots disregarded his orders. Again.

Evan arched his eyebrows, his curiosity piqued at his captor's expression.

A vile chuckle echoed in the bare room. "You have to be kidding. I'm not sure who should be more upset, you or me. It appears you don't mean a thing to any of them. Unfortunately, the ribbon cutting will go on as planned, so will the merger. It must be hard for you to swallow the fact that Watts Enterprises only wanted your company's name and investments. You're simply the means to help them make more money for themselves. Leah and John Watts didn't even report your disappearance. Now that I think about it, the news is worse for you. I can still go to the ribbon cutting and exact my vengeance. You, however, won't be alive to worry about the outcome."

Evan smirked. "Didn't I tell you yesterday that my disappearance wouldn't matter to them? The merger impacts too many people. They can function without me."

"This would be a whole different story if I'd gotten my hands on Leah Reynolds. All of you would have moved heaven and earth to save her. Why don't we call Leah to see if she has any last words for you? She needs to be aware that she's the one who put the nails in your coffin. I think I may even let her tell you goodbye. Enjoy it; this will be the last time you hear her voice."

Leah and the others anxiously awaited the inevitable call. Charlie Ashby promised the stories would make today's editions, and now they laid before them in black and white. Everyone in the room knew *He* would be furious. The articles reflected the exact opposite of what *He* had wanted to happen. When Leah's phone rang, she immediately glanced at Brent for support. His loving smile and nod were all the reassurance she needed.

"Yes, hello…."

"It seems we have a problem, Leah. Please tell me which is it, that you don't care what happens to Holcomb, or you didn't believe me when I told you I would kill him. The ribbon-cutting remains scheduled. Do you have a problem taking my threats seriously?"

Steadying her voice, Leah answered, "I'm sorry; I don't understand what you're saying. I've taken care of that issue."

He began laughing. "That's not what I'm reading in the Charlotte and Bridgeport papers."

"But they promised me. Please don't be hasty. I haven't seen the papers this morning. Let me make one phone call to find out what's going on. PLEASE." She cried.

His snickers now became even more insidious, "So they duped you too! Is it difficult to swallow they don't care about you or Evan? You're only a means to getting what they want. Since I'm not surprised they've lied to you also, I'll think about giving you a few hours to straighten this out. But in the meantime, I think I would be remiss if I didn't let you say your last goodbyes to Holcomb. Just in case I make a decision that displeases you. Enjoy your two seconds because it's all you will have." *He* placed the phone on Evan's shoulder, enabling him to cradle it between his chin and shoulder.

"Evan, are you ok?" Leah held her breath.

"I'm fine. Are you?"

Whispering ever so faintly, Leah responded, "Evan, listen to me. We have a plan. No matter what *He* says or what happens, we have this under control. We will get you back safely, I promise."

Irritated with himself for the moment of weakness, *He* jerked the phone away. His inability to hear their conversation only infuriated him more.

"Times up, sweetheart. I hope you said all you needed to say." Smirking at Evan as he spoke.

"Please give me an hour. I'll convince John to change his mind." Her meek response screamed fear, and he loved making people fearful.

He knew Leah's sweet personality and dedication to the company meant a lot to John Watts. His original plan hinged on Leah's convincing John Watts to do what she wanted. She was renowned for getting people to listen to reason. That skill made this her most important job.

"Alright, one hour, no more. If you don't have positive news for me when I call back, it won't just be Holcomb that suffers. One hour." *He* looked at his captive. "I certainly hope Leah has the power she thinks she does over Watts because your life depends on it."

Leah ended the call feeling victorious. "He bought it. So far, so good. I think we can do this."

Brent and Amber, the telepathy twins, questioned simultaneously, "How did he sound? Is Evan okay?"

"He sounded in control, as always. Evan's voice carries a distinct sound of determination when he's hell-bent on achieving a goal. I've heard it many times. I also recognize that if we have a plan, he, too, has an agenda to gain his freedom. I only hope the two don't conflict, placing his life in greater danger."

Steve reassured Leah. "An hour will pass quickly. Do you remember the details of the proposed meeting location and time? Once he agrees to your requests, I'll put everyone in motion."

"I have it. I know what to do. I'll be fine. How could anything happen when we have all of you looking out for us." Leah trusted the entire group to ensure her and Evans's safety.

In precisely 50 minutes, Leah received the return call. "You better tell me you have everything in order." *He* growled.

"It hasn't been an hour yet, but I think I have John on my side. There are a couple of things."

"Things? What things? You still don't understand who's in charge, do you?"

"No, no, I do. It is just that all the festivities involve the community. We can't panic an entire town. All publicity information regarding the event will stay the same to control the situation. Everyone can enjoy the activities for a little while. Then right before the ribbon-cutting, we'll announce its cancellation for reasons beyond our control. The next morning, the papers will report the rescinded merger. It's the safest and easiest way for everyone to obtain what they want. Children and families will be in attendance. I don't want anyone hurt." Leah inhaled deeply.

He sat very still, listening to the details of Leah's plan. It came as no surprise that everything must happen in a "business proper" way, even when it came to Holcomb's life. Leah's plea fits the mold for corporate business. He'd seen the same thing all too often. *He* heard the faint whisper of Leah's voice on the other end. Another quivering request exposed her fear,

"There's one other thing. While the community enjoys the food and fun, I need to ensure that Evan's still alive. So if we can arrange a location for the two of us to meet at the factory, I can confirm he's alive and well. Then I'll make the announcement myself regarding the cancellations. No one else will be allowed to do it."

Playing her words over in his head, *He* felt relatively sure Leah harbored intense feelings for Holcomb.

What could it hurt to let her get together with him and grab a final kiss before making the announcement?

He'd decided to kill Evan anyway, then disappear quickly, so what could be the harm?

"Since you asked so sweetly, I can buy into that. Watts Enterprises was always more interested in public opinion and community needs than anything else. Let the 'kiddies' enjoy their day. As for you, we're both aware you know that factory inside and out, so I'll pick the meeting location. Holcomb's dead if I detect one sign of the cops or anyone else. You got me?"

Her voice holding more self-assurance, Leah replied, "Yes, of course. I just need to see Evan. I don't care where we meet at the factory."

"Good thing you don't care because when I decide, you'll only have five minutes to reach the location. We'll talk again soon." Smiling, *He* ended the call.

Leah slowly placed the phone down and began apologizing. "I'm sorry. *He* wouldn't allow me to select the location. *He* said I was too familiar with the factory, and the location would be of his choosing. Now the bad news." Steve and Evan exchanged glances riddled with concern.

"When *He* provides a meeting location, I'll only have five minutes to get there." Leah shook her head in exasperation. "I didn't do my job well enough. I should've been able to convince him to meet where we planned."

Brent placed his hand on Leah's shoulder. "No, you shouldn't. This maniac has been one step ahead of us for weeks. So why should this situation be different? He's too smart to let you have the upper hand. *He* knows if we pick the location, there would be a reasonable chance we're waiting for him."

Steve looked at Brent, "You realize that if *He* doesn't give her the location until five minutes before the meeting, there'll be no way to get my men in place to protect her. *He'll* be in place long before he calls her. If anyone but Leah walks in, it's over."

"Yes, I understand." Brent bent down to gaze directly into Leah's eyes. "Do you believe I can protect you and would never let anything happen to you? Because I'll be the only backup you have."

Leah returned Brent's stare with all the confidence she could muster. "You already hold my heart in your hands. Why would I ever be afraid to trust you with my life?"

Brent straightened and smiled. "You'll give me an inflated ego with comments like that?"

Amber clasped her forehead, "Please, his ego's big enough, don't give him more ammunition. Isn't that right, Steve?"

Steve laughed, nodding in agreement. "Ok. Enough. We need to prepare as much as possible with the little bit of information we have. We may not know the location until five minutes before the meeting, but I don't see why we can't have guys mingling undercover with the crowd. Leah, I need you and John to draw me a map outlining every corner, room, and angle inside and outside of that factory. We've work to do. Move people!"

An air of seriousness settled over the room, and a heavy feeling of the unknown enveloped each of them. Leah noticed one consistency through all of the planning. John and Martha looked confused and terrified while their minds visibly churned to produce possible suspects. The adored couple struggled to imagine how anyone could enjoy being so cruel.

Martha's "why" questions bombarded John. Why them? Why stop the merger? Why take Evan? Why Watts

Enterprises and Holcomb Industries? Leah attempted to comfort them as best she could.

"Hey, you two, everything's going to work out. Brent's very good at what he does and believes in Steve and Cooper. All you have to do is mingle with the crowd, thank them for coming, and smile. A piece of cake, right?" Leah patted their hands and smiled.

John looked at Leah. "We can't comprehend why this is happening, but you can count on us to do our part. The only thing that matters is everyone's safety." John reached for Martha hugging her tight.

The following day John, Martha, Charlie, and Leah made their way to the airport to board a plane bound for Bridgeport. Brent, Amber, Steve, and Cooper would travel on a later flight. They couldn't take the risk of anyone recognizing a connection between the two groups.

Brent and Amber entered the airport flanking Leah, one on her left and one her right side. Brent's sense of confidence comforted Leah. Unfortunately, she couldn't help but notice how in tune women in the airport were to his self-assurance and southern charm. Some women paused, staring, attempting to catch his eye. She knew his job placed him in the path of beautiful women who always wanted his attention. But Leah noted it was something she'd need to deal with. She was well aware of Brent's appeal before they began this journey. Women wouldn't stop looking because she had professed her undying love for him. As usual, Brent could read her emotions. Reaching down to clasp her hand in reassurance, he gave her a wink as they continued.

Leah smiled when one female, in particular, couldn't

take her eyes off Brent. Punching him with her elbow, Leah couldn't help herself, "You have an admirer." Brent noted the all-too-familiar look in the woman's eyes, even from a few feet away.

"Well, let's just show her who holds my interest." Brent eased Leah back against a chair, kissing her lovingly for what seemed an eternity. Ending their kiss softly, Brent twisted to stare at the woman, who turned and walked abruptly to the other side of the terminal. "You never have to worry about other women, Leah. They can look all they like, but they'll never have my heart."

Amber strolled over to the couple, shaking her head. "You two are sickening. You'll be together again tonight." Snatching Leah from Brent's grasp, she squeezed her tightly, whispering in her ear, "Please be careful."

Brent escorted Leah to her terminal, giving her directions as they walked. "If anything happens before we arrive, go straight to the police. Promise me you won't wait. I'll be in Bridgeport by seven tonight."

"I promise I will. Nothing is going to happen. Tomorrow will be our day of reckoning. We'll make sure of it. I love you, Brent Scott."

"I love you too. At least Charlie is with you to help keep John and Martha calm. See you soon." He kissed her again and sent her on her way. Sighing, Brent returned to join Amber, Steve, and Cooper.

CHAPTER THIRTY-SEVEN

As dawn arrived, Evan continued to play the seemingly helpless captive who would comply with any instructions to ensure Leah's safety. After his conversation with her, he knew using the sniper garble was a bluff by his captor. Leah said "they" had a plan, which meant Brent and others were there with her. That little piece of information altered his mindset regarding escape. Evan's time with this cocky little weasel would soon be drawing to an end. More determined than ever to seize any opportunity that presented itself, Evan vowed, *He* would get what *He* deserved. Unsure of Leah's plan, Evan readied himself to make his move. There would be a small increment in time that would offer just the right opening.

He strolled in without a care in the world. "Rise and Shine. The day has finally arrived. We'll be moving out of here very shortly. The festivities will begin in a few hours, which requires us to be in place before people arrive. How does it feel to find out that someone else holds your life in their hands? From my experience, I can say it's a pretty shitty vibe." Evan smiled back at him.

"Oh, so we're still going with the tough-guy attitude. Let's hope Leah has the power you and I think she does." *He* began wiping down any item that may hold any tangible evidence.

Evan monitored the man's motions as *He* meticulously cleaned. "I'm afraid you're wasting your time. This place is a pigsty. No one would ever be able to find evidence in here." Evan prayed his captor was distracted and remained arrogant enough to leave some small clue of their time in the house. If things ended unpleasantly, Evan at least wanted some evidence left to trace his killer.

"You're probably right, Holcomb. There can only be two endings to this situation. One, you live, and I escape. Or two, you die, and I escape. Somehow, I think I like my odds much better than yours." Laughing, *He* turned and strode toward Evan. "Time to go. Don't cause me any trouble when I untie you from the chair. Remember, I still have your friend Leah, let's say 'under the gun.' You know this is comical if you think about it. Leah's aware that she holds your life in her hands. However, she has no clue that you embrace her essence in yours."

Untying Evan cautiously while holding the gun in his other hand, *He* prodded Evan to move out of the chair toward the car as *He* motioned toward the trunk. Evan complied with every request. Sure *he* only had a few more hours.

CHAPTER THIRTY-EIGHT

Everyone arrived in Bridgeport safely. Leah and Charlie made sure John and Martha were comfortable and secure in their home. Charlie then headed for the newspaper office while Leah drove to her apartment to spend the night alone, knowing sleep would evade her until Brent arrived in Bridgeport. The plan involved Brent's group staying in a hotel. Any interaction with Brent might alert their suspect if they were being watched. Leah admitted to herself that she missed Brent. Marriage had never occurred to her before this moment. Now it seemed possible. The ringing phone startled her. Angry at first about being pulled away from her thoughts, Brent's husky voice on the opposite end offered a warm "Good Morning."

She sighed in relief, whispering, "Good Morning."

"If you answer the phone in that sweet voice for just anyone, we must stop it immediately. I want that tone reserved exclusively for me." Brent chuckled.

Leah giggled in response, "Yes, Sir. You have it." She answered the phone the same as always. It must be true love if Brent thought her coffee-deprived body issued a flirty summons. She giggled again.

"Seriously, Leah, are you ready for today? You know I'll be close by at all times. *He* is aware of what I look like, so it shouldn't be a surprise that I'm there. If luck remains on our side, my presence won't alert him to anything out of the ordinary. After all, as far as the media, employees, and community know, this will be the official ribbon cutting. Holcomb Industries and Watts Enterprises will have their key personnel in attendance. My gut tells me we'll need to keep a close eye on John and Martha. They seem rather shaken, and it is imperative they play their part flawlessly."

"I have faith in them. They'll be fine. Charlie will keep an eye on them if needed. Brent, promise me one thing." Leah whispered.

"That sounds like a burdened request. You know I'd do anything for you."

"Promise me if things go bad, you'll get out. Please don't risk your life for Evan or me. Evan wouldn't want it that way, and neither do I. I love you too much to see you hurt."

"That works both ways, Leah Reynolds. Nothing will happen to you, I promise. The important thing right now is to stay focused. You'll be back in my arms by the end of the day. As for Evan, I don't care whose arms he will be in as long as they are not yours!" Brent laughed.

"Funny, Mr. Big Shot. I'm trying to be serious, and you're joking around." Leah appreciated Brent's attempt to reduce her stress and loved him for it. But no amount of humor could lessen the fear she felt.

"Everything will go as scheduled. You know what to do when you get the call. I've reviewed the maps of the factory over and over. I'll be right behind you once you start moving. If you need reassurance throughout the day, look over your shoulder. Remember, I love you. I'll find you at the factory in just a little while."

Leah hung up the phone and carried on with her usual morning routine. Coffee, shower, hair, makeup, then clothes. In a few short hours, she'd be heading to the factory for what she hoped would be their final interaction with this madman. By day's end, *He* would be in police custody, Evan free, the merger concluded, and she and Brent alone together. Whewww. Leah acknowledged it was a robust list to accomplish, but she remained determined. This nightmare would end today, no matter what the cost.

CHAPTER THIRTY-NINE

The next two hours passed at lightning speed for them all. The family-oriented festivities attracted hundreds of people representing both companies, Bridgeport, and the surrounding communities. The promise of new commerce in the area boosted everyone's morale. People were optimistic again about Bridgeport's future, and it warmed Leah's heart to think she was responsible for even a tiny part of that optimism. They were touching so many lives in a good way. Ultimately, all she wanted to do was help people help themselves.

She scanned the crowd for familiar faces, instantly spotting Steve and several undercover officers. Steve's eyes locked with hers for a brief moment before he continued his conversation with the men. The other vision now before her produced a chuckle from deep within her gut. Carol and Cooper were engrossed in a very animated conversation. Their flirtatious mannerisms with each other helped take their minds off of the task at hand. Cooper and Carol both smiled at Leah as she passed. Rather than interrupt their fun, Leah gave Carol a quick wink and moved on.

Across the parking lot, she could see Charlie playing the journalist. Conducting interviews and taking photos. No surprise to Leah, Rhonda was sitting in the "dunking booth." She insisted the festivities include the game as old-fashioned as it was. Rhonda continuously searched for ways to meet eligible bachelors and what better way to get noticed than in a swimsuit! Kimberly, Suzanne, and Amber, all clad in checkered aprons, offered a quick wave before returning to their task of serving concessions. Leah smiled brightly. How fortunate she was to have made such wonderful friends during such an odd time. All the evil around them couldn't destroy the bonds she formed with these powerful women. Leah knew the "sisters seven" would support each other no matter the situation. It was that reassurance and the comforting feeling of being watched that gave Leah the confidence to proceed. Leah wasn't surprised to spot Brent chatting with another officer several booths behind her. Their ability to read the other one's thoughts almost frightened her. Brent never looked in her direction, but she knew what he was thinking.

God, I'm the luckiest woman in the world.

A sudden tap on her shoulder made Leah flinch. Apprehension clenched her gut until she turned to encounter Bridgeport's sweetest couple nervously smiling at her. "You're a sight for sore eyes. We've been looking everywhere for you. John and I were afraid you hadn't arrived. We want you to rest assured that you don't have to worry about us. We'll do our part." Martha spoke casually, trying to hide her fear.

"Oh, you two will be spectacular. I have no doubt. Just mingle and smile. Let the others do the hard stuff. All of this will be over soon. Stay with the crowd no matter what you hear or witness. You promise?" Both nodded in unison, gave her a big hug, and moved on to take in the sights.

CHAPTER FORTY

Evan and his captor arrived early in the morning, seeking refuge before the crowds and vendors gathered. Conversation between the two remained nonexistent as *He* forced Evan from the vehicle. Evan's opening for an escape eluded him due to his kidnapper's astute concentration and awareness of the task before them. Evan gave the devil his dues. Planning and execution were his captor's forte and why *He* was still on the loose. Each previous act had been meticulously thought out and initiated - today would be no exception. *He* was somehow aware that the factory would be completely shut down for a few hours allowing the employees to enjoy the festivities. There would be no risk of interruption inside the building during the meeting. After forcing an opening at the rear of the building, *He* quickly ushered Evan into one of the renovated equipment rooms. The room left minimal hiding places for any unwanted guests. There were only two ways in; one leading into the closed factory and the one they utilized.

Once inside, Evan felt a swift push shoving him to the factory floor, hands still bound behind him. *He* began circling the room, pacing from side to side. Evan studied the man, calculating all possible scenarios in his mind.

"Well, Holcomb, I selected the perfect location. There's only one way into the room openly accessible, the entrance we used. I'm familiar enough with this place to know the other would require a master key used at the door in the front of the factory. Since the factory's closed and locked, nobody will disturb us. Your beloved Leah will make her way to you through there." *He* nodded toward the opening created by their entry. *He* grabbed Evan's arm spinning his back toward the inoperable door.

"Your hour of destiny is rapidly approaching, Mr. Holcomb. It's time to discover if your girl can make good on her promise. I can't say it won't be interesting. I might even decide to have a little fun with her before letting her leave. She's rather hot."

Evan was fully aware *He* was toying with his emotions to enact a fit of rage. *He* fed off the feelings of those he terrorized. Working inconspicuously to untie his hands, Evan questioned his ability in hopes of provoking his arrogance, allowing him more time to free his hands.

Evan responded calmly, "I'm relatively sure that will not happen. I think she can take care of herself. After all, you tried your hand with her before, remember, and you were the loser. I don't think I'd try it again if I were you. She might embarrass you." Evan saw his face enflame with anger.

"I was in a room full of people. You forget who's tied up here. You didn't fare so well a few nights ago." Contempt spewed from his lips for being questioned.

"As I recall, you attacked me from behind and threatened Leah's safety. I'd never risk her life in place of my own. So why don't we have a go right now, man to man?" Evan awaited an answer.

"I bet you'd love to get your hands on me. I'm not stupid. I'm well aware that you have the ability to overtake me if you weren't tied up. Calm down, Holcomb. No need to start a testosterone war now. I'm too close to my end goal. Excuse me. I have a beautiful lady expecting my call." Snickering, *He* dialed Leah's number while taking one last look around the room.

The moment she dreaded arrived earlier than expected. Leah let the phone ring one time before answering with a quiet, "Hello." In a quick ten-second conversation, her instructions were clear. *He'd* selected one of the newly renovated rooms for the exchange. It would take her the entire five minutes *He* allotted to get there from her current location. She quickly glanced around for a familiar face but found no one in sight to alert. Her instincts screamed that Brent was close. However, Steve and the others would never know she had received the call. Leah knew she needed to handle this alone. Any further delays could mean disaster for everyone, especially Evan. She hoped someone would notice her walking away.

Leah walked briskly through the crowds, deftly weaving in and out of the droves of people laughing and having fun. Everyone remained blissfully unaware of the danger happening around them. Leah quelled the fear in her stomach, moving on to her appointment. Exiting the festivities, she made her way to the back of the factory, where she saw a door that stood slightly ajar. As she approached, she discovered the broken latch. Carefully opening the door, she cautiously stepped into what could be the last day of her life.

"Hello. I'm coming in alone."

As Leah's eyes adjusted to the dim light encompassing the room, the image before her forced a gasp from her lips. Evan and his abductor waited at the far end of the room, their backs parallel to the empty hallway leading back into the factory. Evan was seated, his face set in a grim stare, his hands bound behind his back. Leah was well aware she had to stall as long as possible and pray that Brent had followed her. Relieved to see no visible signs of injury on Evan, she turned to the sound of their aggressor's voice.

"Well, Ms. Reynolds, we meet face to face. I certainly hope you were able to hold up

your end of the bargain. Not only does loverboy's life depend on it, but so does yours. I figured you would come alone. You are too much of a 'by the rules' girl to play it differently. Now tell me, how are you going to fulfill your promise?" Arrogance oozed from his pores. His voice. His stance. *He* honestly thought he had the upper hand on everything.

Defiant, Leah demanded, "First things first. Evan, are you okay? I want him to stand and let me confirm that he's unharmed. If you've hurt him, the deal is off." A flash from down the hallway caught Leah's attention. Determined to remain focused, she concentrated on her words, drawing their eyes in her direction.

"I seriously doubt that you're the one here making the decisions, but I'll indulge your request for argument's sake." *He* moved closer to Evan's side, jerking him up from the floor.

Rising from the ground, Evan called out to Leah.

"I'm okay, Leah. I'm only waiting for the right time to show this maniac who's boss."

Leah smiled. Yep, Evan was fine. Leah opened her mouth to speak when, out of nowhere, John Watts appeared behind the two men.

What in the world was he doing here? Why hadn't Charlie kept an eye on him? Where was Brent? These questions, and many more, ran rampant through her mind in a matter of seconds.

He immediately sensed something was off. Turning around quickly, *He* saw John running toward him.

He yelled, "Stop. Or you'll die too!"

John turned ghastly white as his feet froze in place on the concrete floor. His eyes bulged in astonishment at the man before him.

Leah heard John whisper one word. "Cory?" John remained frozen in disbelief, never taking his eyes from the man's face. "It can't be you."

"Well, well. Now you recognize me. Isn't that a joke!" *He* knew John Watts.

Evan desperately worked the knot which bound his hands so tightly. Suddenly his hands broke free of the restraints, but he dared not make a move that may now endanger John's life also. Remaining still, Evan looked over at Leah, who slowly moved toward him. Her eyes stayed trained on the man John now called Cory.

John slowly bridged the gap between their captor and himself, walking gradually closer, anguish in his voice as he spoke. "They told us you were dead, that you both were dead. Your mother and I mourned your deaths every day of our lives for years. We blamed ourselves for not being there. Why would you do this? Why wouldn't you just come home? Where's your brother? Did he survive too?"

Fury escalated the madman's reply to a shout, "Oh, now you have questions. Why didn't you come and look for us? Wait, I can answer that. You were too busy making your precious factory a better place for your employees. They were all that ever mattered to you. You were never home to take care of us. I was always the one trying to take care of Josh. Mother wanted to be with us, but you always pulled her away to go to some charity event or a business retreat and left us with the nanny. Your focus was always on making more money to better the community. It was never about how much we needed you. Where were you when the floods hit? At the factory, making sure things were taken care of there. What about taking care of us?" *He* paced back and forth throughout his tirade, swinging the gun by his side.

"Son, that's not true. I worked all those long hours to make the company a better place for everyone, and that included you and your brother. I wanted to leave you with something you could be proud of and run as your own one day. A legacy that would not only provide for you, your brother, and your families but one based on helping community members better themselves."

"Yeah, that didn't work out too well, did it? I guess you could say Josh is the lucky one. He has no concept of his previous life before the accident." Spewing his bitter responses to John's questions, *He* completely forgot about his captive.

Leah inched as close to Evan as she dared, afraid any sudden movement might provoke Cory into using his weapon. Still, like a mouse, Leah listened intently as the dialogue between father and son played out.

Cory's anxious pacing had propelled him into the center of the equipment room and away from the safety of the outer walls. Flanked to his right by Leah and Evan, Cory now faced John, who stood only feet away from his son. John's large frame filled Cory's line of vision, obstructing his view into the dark factory.

John's grief turned to anguish. "But the floods swept you and Josh away. The authorities told us your bodies were unrecoverable. How could we have ever dreamed you were still alive?" Tears flowed from John's eyes, sliding down his cheeks.

"Maybe I should enlighten you with the true story of what happened since you didn't care enough to find out. I hurried Josh into the car and jumped into the driver's seat. As we eased forward to cross the road, a barrage of water came out of nowhere, sweeping the car into the swift currents. The water rose so quickly that we had to climb out the windows onto the roof, but it kept rising. We prayed someone would see us and help. But, no one came." *He* rubbed his eyes. Pain and sorrow overflowed through his words.

"Exhausted, we fell into the surging water, getting carried away by the current. I tried to hold on to Josh but wasn't strong enough. His hand slipped from mine. I lost sight of him; he was gone! God only knows how far the swirling water took us. I remember waking up in a hospital somewhere near Baton Rouge. Josh was missing. No one could answer my questions. All I heard were statements like, 'we have no record of a Josh Watts' and 'we can't find a body matching that description.' The anger I felt toward you and my mother was incomprehensible. Josh was gone, and I knew you weren't looking for me. I made a vow right then that I'd heal and make you pay for what you had done."

Tears poured down John's cheeks. "But why didn't someone tell us you were alive? We would have come to you if someone had notified us."

"There were no signs that you were looking for me.

There wasn't a single story in the news regarding your attempts to locate either of us. You just took it for granted that we were gone. Our deaths allowed you to live your life in your precious factory with no distractions. Hatred for you both consumed me. Unwilling to let your betrayal go, I gave the authorities false information. They only had bits and pieces of a story involving a poor guy washed away in the floodwaters with no family or living relatives. In the aftermath of the storms, officials never questioned my story. Why would they? There was too much chaos and confusion for the authorities to handle. Too many other people with families needed help. So, Father, all this brings us to our current situation. I would never be able to implement my plan to destroy your company and you at the same time if I'd given the authorities my real name."

Stunned by the story, John mumbled, "What happened to your brother? Where's Josh? Is he dead?"

The sinister laugh brought back the diabolical man Leah and Evan had come to know. "Why would you care now? You never cared before, but if you must know, as I said earlier, Josh is the lucky one. He was in the water, pounded by floating debris much longer than I was. He suffered severe injuries to his face, internal organs, and head. The head wound was so severe it wiped out all of his memories. To this day, he can't remember anything from the past. I decided to leave it that way. Why tell him the truth about our lives with parents who never loved us? He's lucky he doesn't remember."

He locked eyes with John. "Do you want to hear the real irony of the situation? Josh went on to college, obtained his degree, and is currently a prominent staff member for none other than Evan Holcomb at Holcomb Industries." *He* bellowed evil chuckles.

"Isn't it the damndest thing? Josh is living a whole new life as Troy Marshall."

Leah gasped. The eyes. That's why Troy Marshall continued to cloud their thoughts this whole time. It was the only feature recognizable on both men that remotely connected them.

"How do you like that, Holcomb? You've worked with a member of the Watts family for years and didn't even know it. Guess you were lucky he was the good child." Cory sneered.

Leah tried to speak, but John's tearful plea pierced the silence.

"Cory, please don't do this. We can straighten all this out. Please know that your mother and I have always loved you. It was all a terrible mix-up that we can now correct. You can turn yourself in and take responsibility for the crimes you've already committed. I promise we will be waiting to welcome you with open arms."

"Welcome me? Why in the world would I ever want you to welcome me home? That bridge burned a long time ago. I'd rather die than face punishment for what I have done. No, I'm afraid mother will be mourning another loss in the family. The only person making it out of this room alive is Leah, and that's because I need her to address the media. The merger will not happen, and if she plays her cards right, I may keep her around for my entertainment."

He leveled the gun, pointing it in Evan's direction. Leah realized *He* planned to immobilize the more significant threat in the room first. The trigger's clicking sound sent John lunging forward, tackling Cory. The shuffle jarred Cory's aim, propelling the misfired shot into Evan's right shoulder. Jerking in response, Evan shoved Leah to the ground and covered her with his body.

Recovering quickly, Cory kicked John in the stomach,

sending him sailing onto the floor. Then, jumping to his feet, Cory pointed the gun at his father's chest. "This will be even better than just destroying the factory. I'll also get my revenge against you, Dad."

Leah yelled, "Cory, stop. You do not want to do this. Don't hurt your father."

Leah held her breath, only to watch the same sick expression of madness from their previous meetings distort his features. The years of anger and hurt had destroyed his mind and denied him the ability to reason. She knew he wouldn't hesitate to kill John. Someone had to do something. She pushed Evan from atop her and lunged toward Cory, providing just enough of a distraction for someone to aim and fire. The bullet hit Cory in his midsection. Crippled, *He* clutched his gut and fell to the ground. Leah screamed, frozen in place. Grimacing in pain, Cory pointed the gun at Leah, his aim shaky from the excruciating pain ripping through his body. Determined to hurt them all, *He* intended to kill Leah.

Brent's entry into the equipment room went undetected thanks to Leah's foresight to leave the door ajar. His position behind the giant metal turnstiles offered the sharpest view of the chaos occurring in the room. Brent's former military experience kicked in, placing his senses on high alert. He'd been in this position before, and it never ended well. Brent, now sure the man now called "Cory" would never settle for an amicable solution, upped his game. With his gun drawn, ready for the unknown, Brent inched closer, angling for a clean shot at the madman.

Within mere seconds, Cory's hostile posturing and the sound of a gunshot triggered Brent's return fire. The bullet sailed through the air striking Cory in the abdomen. Unwilling to relent, Cory trained his gun on Leah, sending Brent's instincts into overdrive. Brent offered one final warning before he fired a second shot.

"Don't do it. Put the gun down. We can resolve this another way." Brent's demand fell on deaf ears. The mentally unstable man's determination to have his way grew in ferocity.

He smirked at Brent and Evan, leveling the gun barrel at Leah's chest. Before *He* could pull the trigger again, Brent's deadly shot found its mark, and Cory's lifeless body lay crumpled on the factory floor. John crawled to his son, hysterical with grief, and cradled him in his arms for the last time.

Leah looked first at Evan for assurance that he was okay. Then, the nod of his head sent her running full speed into Brent's open arms. Leah rained kisses all over his face, neck, and head, with her final kiss landing on target.

Leah lifted her lips from his for a brief moment. "I thought I would never taste the sweetness of those lips again," she declared.

In response to Leah's loving declaration, Brent returned her kiss, washed with relief. They'd all come too close to losing something precious today. Unfortunately for John, he mourned the loss of his oldest son once again. Cory's death induced a second painful grieving process.

Leah released Brent and walked to John's crouched form.

"John, we had no idea who was threatening our lives or the company. If we'd only discovered his true identity sooner, maybe you could have talked to Cory and shown him how much you loved him." Leah gently placed her hand on John's shoulder, her agony for her boss engraved on her face.

"I wish I could have, Leah, but I think his mind formulated the story he wanted to believe. It was a story that evoked all the anger and bitterness from earlier in his life. An untrue story, but to him, it was the real story. He instigated the sick events that snowballed into what we just experienced. I'm only glad Martha wasn't here to witness it."

"What will you tell Martha?" Leah knew what John's response would be.

"The truth. I'll tell Martha the truth. The media must never learn of Cory's true identity or the identity of Troy Marshall, for that matter. As for Martha and me, we will once again grieve the loss of our oldest son, but this time it will be in private."

Witnessing the heartbreaking conversation between John and Leah, Brent made his way over to Evan. Still seated on the floor, Evan reached for Brent's extended hand. "Let's go find someone to bandage that shoulder." Evan stood, shaking his head in disbelief that Troy Marshall was John's son and his eldest son was their terrorist. He turned to Brent.

"I guess we should. It's not that bad. Brent, you and John probably saved my life. Don't think I'll forget that anytime soon. I owe you one."

Brent smiled. "Don't think I'll ever forget how you sacrificed yourself for Leah. I'd say that makes us even. I understand now why we were all drawn to Troy Marshall as a suspect. It's uncanny. How were we so close to the solution but yet so far away? I agree with Cory in one respect; Troy's lucky that he too was not a pawn in his brother's gruesome plot for revenge."

"Brent, I've worked with Troy Marshall for several years. But unfortunately, I never made the connection between the two except for the similarity of their eyes." Evan's words verbalized the punishment he now felt for not making the connection sooner.

Brent placed his hand on Evan's other shoulder. "There was no way for us to know. We were all around

Troy Marshall at one point or another. No one picked up on the similarities, even John. So don't be too hard on yourself."

Steve Alexander and Cooper ran into the room only to find the whole nightmare was over. While Steve called for his officers and medical personnel, they surveyed their surroundings. The men walked toward Brent shaking their heads. "I should've known you would have things under control. What happened? Did *He* give you any clues regarding his identity or why *He* was so intent on stopping the merger?" Steve awaited Brent's reply.

Glancing at each other, Brent and Evan sighed. Brent rubbed his brow. "No indication whatsoever. *He* was some maniac fed up with technology and determined to wreak havoc in the corporate world. We tried to resolve the issue, but *He* wasn't having any part of a peaceful solution. Leah and Evan's lives were in immediate danger, so I made my choice."

Evan interjected, "Brent's right. I owe my life to his quick thinking. Now, if you don't mind, I think I'll take care of this small issue now." Pointing to his arm, Evan headed toward the medical team as Amber appeared in the doorway. Evan saw the concern for his welfare and the beauty of her face as if for the first time. Smiling, he ushered her over to escort him to the ambulance.

The disastrous results of the horrendous nightmare that began months ago laid before them at the rear of the factory. Leah struggled to believe the last hour was real and not a dream as detectives encouraged the group to return to the festivities. Crowds of people oblivious to the previous hour's events were awaiting the ribbon cutting.

Evan concealed his injury for a speech filled with introductions and promises of great things to come for Bridgeport. John and Leah stood by his side in support of their commitment to returning prosperity to their beloved small town.

Brent watched from the sidelines, grateful for the safety of everyone involved. Charlie continued taking photos and making notes for her big headline in tomorrow's paper. Suzanne and Kimberly chatted with Amber making plans for a girl get-together before their flight departed tomorrow morning. Rhonda and Carol, oblivious to what was happening around them, remained engrossed in conversations with Steve Alexander and Cooper.

Lining up to cut the ribbon at the factory door, Leah, Evan, and John looked at each other with a smile and a sense of promise. Scanning the crowd in search of Brent, Leah found him staring in her direction like the cat that swallowed the canary. His smile and sparkling eyes made her feel secure and loved.

Leah couldn't recall why she had tripped entering the airplane that day; she was just eternally grateful that she did. In that fateful misstep, her life had traveled down a path that yielded true love and a group of dear friends now known as "The Sisters Seven."

EPILOGUE

The ear-piercing noise level inside the house forced Brent and Evan to excuse themselves from the room. The two had become the token males of the group during their trip. Evan's promise of a Caribbean vacation agreed with everyone by all appearances. However, seven women in one room combined with red wine turned out to be a little more than the men could bear at the moment. Their desperate attempt to escape the thunderous giggles and laughter urged the men onto the peaceful lanai.

"Tell me again why you didn't at least invite Steve and Cooper?" Brent watched Evan for some legitimate response. Forlorn, Evan chugged the brown liquid in his glass.

"For the life of me, I don't know. It was only supposed to be the four of us. Then Amber called me and wanted to invite Charlie. After that, my sister thought it would be good to invite Suzanne and Kimberly to thank them for their kindness during the gala. The next thing I hear, Leah's talking about how they can't leave Rhonda and Carol behind." Brushing the hair from his brow, Evan turned to Brent.

"You've seen the two of them; how was I supposed to tell Amber and Leah no? And don't give me that look, Brent. They've both worked you over a time or two."

Brent began to laugh. "You're right about that one, my friend. It's kind of hard to tell them no. Listen to them.

I'm not sure I can take that for two weeks. You have plenty of room in this tropical paradise you own. Can't we at least call Steve and Cooper and find out if they can leave Charlotte for a few days? If we don't call in some male backup, I'm afraid our plans for a quiet getaway will turn into a 'girls gone wild' trip. I'll never have time alone with Leah, and you, Romeo, will not progress in getting to know my sister better. Who, by the way, has a huge crush on you."

"I second your motion. Make the call now; I don't care what time it is in the states." Evan's mind lingered on the words Brent shared regarding Amber and smiled.

Before Brent could make his way to the phone, Leah strolled into the room, fell into his lap, and planted a big kiss on his right cheek. Never growing tired of her infectious smile, he pressed his luck,

"So, all you've got for me is a kiss on the cheek?" Grinning, Brent poked at the dragon. Never willing to back down from a challenge, Leah kissed him with such ferocity and passion Brent reeled backward into the chair. Leah's eyes twinkled with success. Brent looked at her, then at Evan, and blinked.

Evan held in a chuckle, uttering politely, "Well, I guess there's no question as to who is boss in this relationship." Both men started to laugh when Leah stood and turned with a wink, "Yes, and don't either of you forget it. Mr. Scott, we'll finish that later." Leaving behind a tease as she sashayed out of the room.

Brent eased back into his chair, "Sometimes you just have to let them think they're in charge."

"Funny, and if you think I'm buying that one, you're crazy," Evan replied.

Both men burst into laughter, stretched back in their oversized rattan loungers, and gazed at the serene waters, content for a moment of peace from the hordes of estrogen among them.

Leah waltzed back into the glass-enclosed billiard room, all smiles. In complete unison, the “Sisters Seven” gazed in her direction and declared, “No doubt where you have been!” The truth of their statement induced hysterical laughter from everyone but Charlie. She’d moved toward the windows and stared out at the crystal waters. The image in the distance caused Charlie to beckon the ladies' presence on the balcony.

“Hey, everyone, come here.”

The room’s interior filled with mumbles questioning why they needed to leave their comfy surroundings to look at water. Nevertheless, the women grabbed their wine and headed toward the windows.

Rhonda, always first to speak, shouted, “There better be a good-looking man walking along the beach. I was way too comfy to move.”

“What is it, Charlie?” Amber strained to see if there was something out of the ordinary.

“I think someone’s trying to catch our attention. Do any of you see that light flashing across the bay?” Charlie raised a finger and pointed in the vicinity of the light beams angled in their direction.

“Catch our attention? Why would anyone want to get our attention?” Carol anxiously spouted. “We’re in the middle of the Caribbean. No one here knows us.”

Leah detected the hint of excitement in Carol’s voice. But, truthfully, they all felt a sense of fear. The Caribbean vacation was a present from Evan for them all to relax and forget the nightmare they’d experienced in Bridgeport.

“I’m sure it’s just a coincidence. Let’s venture back to fun, girls. We have an excursion planned for tomorrow, remember." Leah's attempts to calm the group fell on welcome ears. The women agreed, but Leah couldn't overlook Charlie's cautious expression.

As "the sisters" headed back to their chairs, Charlie grabbed Leah's arm. "Leah, those beams aren't just random flashes of light. They're signals meant for someone on this side of the island. And since we're the only ones presently inhabiting a house on this end, I can only assume the signal's intended for us."

"Why would someone send a signal to us, Charlie? We don't know anyone here." Leah whispered.

"I'm not sure. But, if I'm correct, that's not the kind of message I want."

"What message? Charlie, don't tell me you can interrupt a bunch of inconsistent beams of light." Leah's quizzical gaze forced Charlie to explain.

"I can, and I have. The flashes are not random. They appear sequential, like a series of codes used by the military called Morse Code, and I don't like what it says." Charlie strained her eyes, hoping to catch something identifiable in the vicinity of the rays.

"Should I even ask what it means?" Leah questioned, biting her lower lip.

"Probably not. It says GO HOME." Charlie whispered.

The women, wrought with confusion, stood gaping at the repeated flashes from the island's peninsula. In reality, they both knew those flashes also translated into another phrase, "here we go again."

Terri Wilson was born in Georgia, a few miles from the infamous Augusta National golf course, home of the Masters. The mother of two resides with her husband, Randy, in the quaint equestrian town of Aiken, South Carolina. She considers her faith, family, and friends to be her cornerstone. Her debut novel, *Finding A Stranger,* was penned from her love of romantic suspense and the encouragement of lifelong friends.

Terri is an avid fan of everything related to the NHL, excluding the cold. She survives the mild southern winters watching her two favorite teams pass the puck, often accompanied by her beloved "grand-dogs" Henley, Elee, and Azalea.

Made in the USA
Columbia, SC
13 February 2024

31404066R00161